Ly.

A Midnight Chat

Through half-closed eyelids, Florian saw Melior steal from their bedroom.

He lay still for a moment, then rose and followed her. Melior went out through the courtyard and disappeared into the Chapel. Florian went after her, quite silently.

Melior knelt in the alcove where his earlier wives were buried. She was praying, no doubt, for the intercession of her meddlesome patron saint . . .

Of a sudden the place was flooded with a wan throbbing bluish luminousness. The effigies upon the tombs of Florian's wives were changed; and the recumbent marble figures yawned and stretched themselves, then sat erect and looked compassionately at Melior.

"Beware, poor lovely child," said the likeness of Aurélie, "for it is apparent that Florian intends to murder you also."

"I was beginning to think he had some such notion," Melior replied thoughtfully.

THE SAGA OF POICTESME
By JAMES BRANCH CABELL

The
High
Place

James Branch Cabell

Illustrations by Frank C. Papé

A Del Rey Book

BALLANTINE BOOKS • NEW YORK

A Del Rey Book
Published by Ballantine Books

ISBN 0-345-28284-1

Ballantine Books edition printed from the *Storisende Edition*.

Manufactured in the United States of America

First U.S. Edition: February 1970
Second Printing: August 1979

Cover art by Howard Koslow

To

Robert Gamble Cabell III

THIS BOOK, WHERE SO MUCH MORE IS DUE

"Build an high place for Chemosh, the abomination of Moab, and for horned Ashtoreth, the abomination of Zidon, and for Moloch, the abomination of the children of Ammon."

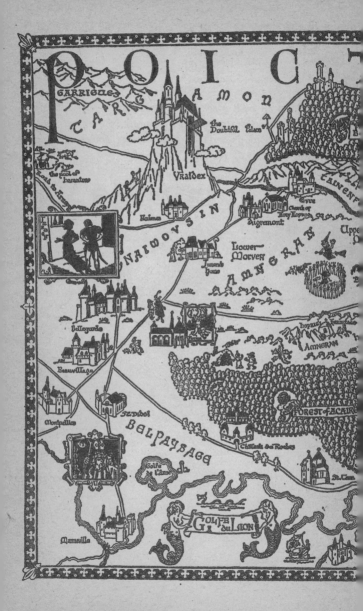

ESME

UPPER ARDRA

YAL ARDRAY

Bazauda

Zait

Varnerez

PIEDMONTS

Perdigon

MUNDUS VULT DECIPI

LOWER ARDRA

Road to Zait

CORE of the Rocks

Lisuarte

Queen Freydis

STORISENDE

Darkling

Road to Provence via Porois

Rance

Sorioroz

DUARDENOIS

Vraie sur Mer

Gole's MEYESMORTES

Peter Koch - 29

The
High Place

Author's Note

IN "The Line of Love" the Biography has followed the life of Manuel through ten generations, down to its introduction into the Musgrave family. We pass now to the sixteenth generation of that life, in a somewhat different line. For the Biography now turns again to the gallant race of Puysange.

Raoul de Puysange, as you may recall, removed permanently into England in 1485: but his younger brother, Aristide, remained in France, where he appears in no way particularly to have distinguished himself. It was the son of this Aristide, the Marshal Henri-Jean de Puysange (1493–1555), who rose to some eminence under François the First, and who started the cadet branch of Puysange upon its ascent to power in France,—an ascent so curiously balanced by the decadence, under the name of Pierson, of the older branch in England.

My immediate concern, however, is not with these historical matters. Instead, I have aimed, in "The High Place," to approach a bit more intimately the gallant attitude toward human life. That is the attitude which John Charteris has outlined for you: it is the attitude which Jurgen has tested, very provisionally, and upon the whole without committing himself to any verdict. It is, in "The High Place," the attitude which this second Florian de Puysange attempted: and it is the attitude in which this Florian failed to achieve success. I mean, of course, the first time: for eventually his history had the most happy of endings, in—as it were—an epigeal way.

MEANWHILE I find, in a newspaper symposium printed in the early spring of 1924, wherein various authors explained why each had written his or her most recently published book, a paragraph under my own name:—

"'The High Place' was written to supply in my Biography of Manuel's life, the link uniting 'The Line of Love' with 'Gallantry.' I have therein endeavored, as a needed part of the complete Biography, to illustrate the alternative of Jurgen's choice in the delicate matter of lifting or of leaving untouched the barriers between the material and the ideal. This has been, perhaps naturally, interpreted as an announcing that few wives wear well. I, married, question this construing with great emphasis and discretion. . . . And I must likewise, in passing, modestly disclaim all credit, over-generously accorded me by the illiterate, for endowing the book's milieu and social customs with my private funds of perversity: for that these constituents, also, are plagiarized, anybody can discover who cares to dip into the mildest of the Regency memoirs,—say, of the Duc de Richelieu or even of Saint-Simon."

I could better the wording of that. . . . Still, that really is, in itself, a sufficient preface, although this explanation, too, requires a bit of explaining in a world wherein perceptive intelligence is rare. . . . It was Florian's fault, then, that he attempted to introduce beauty and holiness into his daily living. It was his error that, when he reached the bedside of the sleeping princess, precisely as Jurgen once stood at the bedside of Queen Helen, Florian did not emulate the clinic restraint of his gallant ancestor. Jurgen, you may remember, half drew the violet coverlet and then replaced it, and so went away forever, blessed with memories, and with no illusion exposed to any possibility of being marred. But Florian raised the coverlet, and awakened the sleeper, with results which this book commemorates.

Yet later, as you may remember also, Jurgen entered the Heaven of his grandmother, and came face to face with holiness. His conduct in Heaven is upon record: and the fact too is upon record that Heaven was the second of the places visited by Jurgen from which he went away very hastily,—once more, I must repeat, blessed with his memories, and with no illusion exposed to any possibility of being marred. But Florian had the ill luck to fetch home with him that holiness which hitherto he had, from an appropriate distance, respectfully and lovingly admired.

It has, thus, naturally occurred to a great many persons that Florian's history is but an enfeebled copy of Jurgen's history, because each is in every respect the exact opposite of the other. Indeed I always find my circumstances regrettable whensoever the scheme of the Biography involves a return to the same situation, so as to weigh the result, at this crux, of a different choice by my protagonist—who remains, throughout the Biography, the life of Manuel,—because to so many persons a different solving of the same problem appears, for some obscure reason, to be mere repetition. I regret this; I reflect that "Dombey and Son" and Mr. Hergesheimer's "Cytherea" differ from each other as markedly as they do from the Iliad, even though all three of them deal with the elopement of a married woman. But upon the whole I have preferred to work out the Biography rather than the mental quirks of its potential readers.

A word more: I have said, it was Florian's fault that he attempted to introduce beauty and holiness into his

daily living. I have written to small purpose if that statement appears to asperse beauty and holiness. They are
fine and, in some sense, they are useful qualities when
one pursues either the chivalrous or the poetic attitude: but with the gallant attitude they simply and
starkly do not blend. It was Florian's fault that he attempted to combine the incompatible. The really gallant person accepts the plane of daily life and makes
the best of it: his choice, upon the whole, is wisdom:
but, as any dictionary or as any portrait of the judi-
ciary of the Supreme Court of the United States will
assure you, wisdom is different from beauty and more
than often it is at odds with holiness. For wisdom is an
earthly quality: I suspect that its appropriate symbol is
less the owl than the ostrich, who attempts no flights
above earth, who shuts out whatsoever is dreadful by
veiling his gaze with earth, and who permits nothing
upon earth to upset his digestion. It is gratifying to
note that Florian, too, discovered this incongruity in
the end; and that, with his over-ambitious errors can-
celed, he lived gallantly all the pleasant way to the
graveyard amid the well-merited respect of his fellows.

I RETURN to my previously quoted text: already it
seems droll that in 1923 "The High Place" was regarded as indecent in that it touches upon sexual eccentricities which were modish during the Orléans Regency. Me that surprised in 1923, when, as my text
points out, the memoirs of Richelieu and Saint-Simon
were in general circulation; and when for that matter
the letters of Madame Charlotte Elizabeth, the Regent's mother, were enjoying in translation a mild ce-
lebrity. I record here her candid summing up, as ad-
dressed to the Duchess of Hanover:—"All the young
fellows and many of the older ones are so steeped in
this vice that they talk of nothing else. Any other form

of gallantry is ridiculed; and it is only the common men who make love to women."

THE writing of "The High Place" was begun in July 1922, during the first visit that I paid to Mountain Lake, in Virginia: and the book reveals, they tell me, sufficing marks of the mountain scenery where-among this story was begun. It is certain that, when the book was planned, at Dumbarton, in the early spring of 1922, the castle of Brunbelois, after the accredited custom of other enchanted castles, stood in the low heart of an ancient forest, upon no elevation at all. But when I began to write out the tale, under its first title of "The Place That Ought Not to Be," it chanced that I too was surrounded by forests, of quite respectable antiquity, falling away beneath me as far as the eye could reach: and it presently occurred to me that, through a little editing of altitudes, I would to all intents be sitting upon the castle porch in the while that I described Brunbelois, without ever having to leave my writing table. Sheer laziness thus prompted me to lift the castle a mile or two, to my own physical level: and through the ever insidious counsels of indolence "The Place That Ought Not to Be" had become within ten minutes "The High Place."

So was beauty provided with its secret habitation: and for the corresponding high place of holiness I drew upon my memories of the now deserted and fallen Rockbridge Alum Springs, to which, if it at all matters, the curious may discover that Upper Morven bears a remarkable resemblance. And while I was about this scene shifting, I lifted from the ruined Alum lawns the boulder beside which Florian builds his little fire.

Thereafter, once the stage was set, the tale flowed on with unusual celerity. This was caused, I think, by the fact that "The High Place" is unique among my writings in possessing a distinct and tolerably symmetrical plot, which, when once set agoing, ran onward of its own momentum to its one logical close. . . . I was at this time naïvely proud of my plot: and I honored it to the extent of not anywhere indulging in the loved pursuit of inserting more or less extraneous matter which happened at that moment to occur to and please my fancy. All, I insisted, must bear directly upon the story. . . . Well, and thus I wasted a great deal of pains and some self-denial, because I do not think that to this date anybody has ever noticed that "The High Place" possesses a plot.

In any case, the tale was finished in June 1923. It was published the following November, in a first edition of 1,000 copies illustrated by Frank C. Papé. The book was reissued, during the same month, in the unillustrated Kalki edition.

And it sold fairly well, in the teeth of the most unanimously abusive press accorded to any of my books. An even half of the reviews, of course, complained that this was merely "Jurgen" all over again; the remainder regretted that this was by no means another "Jurgen." But upon the loftier grounds of morality their agreement was general. "The High Place" did not prove, perhaps, quite so individually irritating as "The Cords of Vanity,"—a volume which, for no reason ever known to me, has in each of its several editions revealed in nine out of ten of its reviewers some manifest sense of unprovoked and strong personal injury. But "The High Place" excelled even "The Cords of Vanity" as an awakener of moral reprehension.

And it really does seem rather quaint nowadays. . . . The earliest of all reviews, I find was in the New York Times. I record the judicious verdict of Mr. Lloyd Morris: "This book is definitely distasteful in its explicit—and gratuitous—suggestion of sexual aberration and sexual perversion." That in itself was mild enough, and of course would never have been written if Mr. Morris had happened to know anything about the Regency period. But the linotypes of half a continent were echoing his sentiments within the week. Then—just as had been the case with that other once salacious volume, "The Eagle's Shadow,"—then earnest-minded and unliterary persons began to write to their favorite papers to stigmatise this book also as a regrettable instance of what modern literature was coming to. Brentano's Book Chat also printed many letters concerning "The High Place," from standpoints so far diverse (geographically) that I find Mr. R. G. Kirk of Santa Monica, California, lamenting my "stinking filth and vileness" side by side with Mr. E. E. Robinson's petition—as despatched heavenward, via the columns of Book Chat, from Pensacola, Florida, —"never to be besmirched with the fancies of a distorted brain such as Cabell's." The New York Tribune helpfully suggested, in an editorial, that the then world-famous Leopold-Loeb murder had been prompted by a reading of "The High Place." I personally was favored with much unsolicited correspondence which candidly defied me and the over-prudish Postal Regulations also. And I find that even the very lateliest dated of the hundred or so reviews now in my scrapbook—by H. W. A. in the Akron Press,—is regrettably a piece with the others: " 'The High Place' is an utterly impossible, sacrilegious, immoral and obscene work that could not be too strongly condemned."

—Upon which note I close, in deep and honest sadness; for it really is dejecting, to observe how soon, how strangely soon—in what humiliating trice and jiffy and twinkling of Time's eye,—the very loftiest rhetoric which is envenomed by moral indignation goes out of date. . . . Milton shrieks in his only too well justified wrath at Salmasius; the finest sensibilities of John Wilson Croker are nauseated by a Cockney Keats; Demosthenes lays bare the unbearable iniquities of King Philip; and Isaiah regards without any approval the civic morals of Babylon:—and it all seems tremendously important, at the time. But presently the small sour voices are stilled. Cold type alone records their ardors, in a shrivelled parody. And they are quite forgotten save for a few sporadic persons who wonder now and then what, after all, the rumpus was about precisely.

JAMES BRANCH CABELL

Richmond-in-Virginia
March 1928

Contents

Part One

The End
of Long Wanting

"Lever un tel obstacle est à moy peu de chose. Le Ciel défend, de vray, certains contentemens; Mais on trouve avec luy des accommodemens."

I
The Child Errant

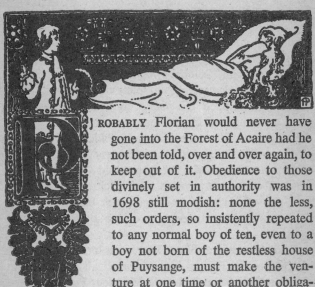

PROBABLY Florian would never have gone into the Forest of Acaire had he not been told, over and over again, to keep out of it. Obedience to those divinely set in authority was in 1698 still modish: none the less, such orders, so insistently repeated to any normal boy of ten, even to a boy not born of the restless house of Puysange, must make the venture at one time or another obligatory.

Moreover, this October afternoon was of the sun-steeped lazy sort which shows the world as over-satisfied with the done year's achievements, of the sort which, when you think about it so long, arouses a dim dissent from such unambitious aims. It was not that the young Prince de Lisuarte—to give Florian his proper title,—was in any one especial point dissatisfied with the familiar Poictesme immediately about him: he liked the place well enough. It was only that he preferred another place,

which probably existed somewhere, and which was not
familiar or even known to him. It was only that you
might—here one approximates to Florian's vague
thinking, as he lay yawning under the little tree from
the East,—that you might find more excitement in
some place which strove toward larger upshots than
the ripening of grains and fruits, in a world which did
not every autumn go to sleep as if the providing of
foodstuffs and the fodder for people's cattle were
enough.

To-day, with October's temperate sunlight everywhere, the sleek country of Poictesme was inexpressibly asleep, wrapped in a mellowing haze. The thronged
trees of Acaire, as Florian now saw them just beyond
that low red wall, seemed to have golden powder scattered over them, a powder which they stayed too motionless to shake off. Yet, logic told him, these still
trees most certainly veiled wild excitements of some
sort, for otherwise people would not be at you, over
and over again, with exhortations to keep out of that
forest.

Nobody was watching. There was nothing in especial to do, for Florian had now read all the stories in
this curious new book, by old Monsieur Perrault of the
Academy, which Florian's father had last month
fetched back from Paris: and, besides, nobody at Storisende had, for as much as a week, absolutely told
Florian not to leave the gardens. So he adventured:
and with the achievement of the adventure came a
strengthening of Florian's growing conviction that his
elders were in their notions, as a rule, illogical.

For in Acaire, even when you went as far as Brunbelois, the boy found nothing hurtful. It was true that,
had he not at the beginning of his wandering met with
the small bright-haired woman who guided him thereafter, he might have made mistakes: and mistakes, as
Mélusine acknowledged, might have turned out awk-

wardly in approaching the high place, since monsters have to be handled in just the right way. She explained to Florian, on that warm long October afternoon, that sympathy is the main requisite, because the main trouble with such monsters as the bleps and the strycophanês and the calcar (she meant only the gray one, of course) is that each is unique, and in consequence lonely.

The hatred men feel for every ravening monster that wears fangs and scales, she pointed out, is due to its apparel being not quite the sort of thing to which men are accustomed: whereas people were wholly used to having soldiers and prelates and statesmen ramping about in droves, and so viewed these without any particular wonder or disapproval. All that was needed, therefore, was to extend to the bleps and the strycophanês a little of the confidence and admiration which men everywhere else accorded to the destroyers of mankind; and then you would soon see that these glittering creatures—as well as the tawny eale, and the leucrocotta, with its golden mane and whiskers, and the opal-colored tarandus,—were a great deal nicer to look at than the most courted and run-after people, and much less apt to destroy anybody outside of their meal hours.

In any event, it was Mélusine who had laid an enchantment upon the high place in the midst of the wood, and who had set the catoblepas here and the mantichora yonder to prevent the lifting of her spell, so that Florian could not possibly have found a better guide than Mélusine. She was kindly, you saw, but not very happy: and, from the first, Florian liked and, in some sort, pitied her. So he rode with her confidingly, upon the back of the queerest steed that any boy of ten had ever been privileged to look at, not to speak of riding on it: and the two talked lazily and friendlily as they went up and up, and always upward, along the windings of the green way which, very long ago, had been a public thoroughfare for the Peohtes.

As they rode thus, the body of this sweet-smelling Mélusine was warm and soft against the boy's body, for Mélusine was not imprisoned in hard-feeling clothes such as were worn by your governesses and aunts. The monsters stationed along the way drew back as Mélusine passed; and some purred ingratiatingly, like gigantic kettles, and others made obeisances: and you met no other living creatures except three sheep that lay in the roadway asleep and very dingy with the dust of several hundred years. No self-respecting monster would have touched them. Thus Florian and Mélusine came through the forest without any hindrance or trouble, to the cleft in the mountain tops where the castle stood beside a lake: and Florian liked the stillness of all things in this high place, where the waters of the lake were without a ripple, and the tall grass and so many mist-white flowers were motionless.

He liked it even more when Méslusine led him through such rooms in the castle as took his fancy. He was glad that Mélusine did not mind when Florian confessed—in the room hung everywhere with curtains upon which people hunted a tremendous boar, and stuck spears through one another, and burst forth into peculiarly solid-looking yellow flames,—that the princess who lay asleep there seemed to him even more lovely than was Mélusine. They were very much alike, though, the boy said: and Mélusine told him that was not unnatural, since Melior was her sister. And then, when Florian asked questions, Mélusine told him also of the old unhappiness that had been in this place, and of the reasons which had led her to put an enduring peacefulness upon her parents and her sister and all the other persons who slept here enchanted.

Florian had before to-day heard century-old tales about Mélusine's father, Jelmas the Deep-Minded. So it was very nice actually to see him here in bed, with his scarlet and ermine robes neatly folded on the armchair, and his crown, with a long feather in it, hung on a peg in the wall, just as the King had left everything when he went to sleep several hundred years ago. The child found it all extremely interesting, quite like a fairy tale such as those which he had lately been reading in the book by old Monsieur Perrault of the Academy.

But what Florian always remembered most clearly, afterward, was the face of the sleeping princess, Melior, as he saw it above the coverlet of violet-colored wool; and she seemed to him so lovely that Florian was never wholly willing, afterward, to admit she was but part of a dream which had come to him in his own sleeping, on that quiet haze-wrapped afternoon, in the gardens of his home. Certainly his father had found him asleep, by the bench under the little tree from the East, and it was true Florian could not recollect how he had got back to Storisende: but it was true, also, that he remembered Brunbelois, and his journeying to the high place, and the people seen there, and, above all, the Princess Melior, with a clarity not like his memories of other dreams. Nor did the memory of her loveliness quite depart as Florian became older; and neither manhood nor marriage put out of Florian's mind the beauty which he in childhood had, although but briefly, seen.

II

Sayings About Puysange

HEN Florian awakened he was lying upon the ground, with the fairy tales of Monsieur Perrault serving for Florian's pillow, in the gardens of Storisende, just by the little tree raised from the slip which his great-uncle, the Admiral, had brought from the other side of the world. Nobody knew the right name of this tree: it was called simply the tree from the East. Caterpillars had invaded it that autumn, and had eaten every leaf from the boughs, and then had gone away: but after their going the little tree had optimistically put forth again, in the mild October weather, so that the end of each bare branch was now tipped with a small futile budding of green.

It was upon the bench beneath this tree that Florian's father was sitting. Monsieur de Puysange had laid aside his plumed three-cornered hat, and as he sat there, all a subdued magnificence of dark blue and gold, he was looking down smilingly at the young lazybones whom the Duke's foot was gently prodding into wakefulness. The Duke was wearing blue stockings with gold clocks, as Florian was to remember. . . .

Not until manhood did Florian appreciate his father, and come properly to admire the exactness with which the third Duke of Puysange had kept touch with his times. Under the Sun King's first mistress Gaston de Puysange had cultivated sentiment, under the second, warfare, and under the third, religion: he had thus stayed always in the sunshine. It was Florian's lot to know his father only during the last period, so the boy's youth as spent dividedly at the Duke's two châteaux, at Storisende and at Bellegarde, lacked for no edifying influence. The long summer days at Storisende were diversified with all appropriate religious instruction. In winter that atmosphere of Versailles itself —where the long day of Louis Quatorze seemed now to be ending in a twilight of stately serenity through which the old King went deathward, handsomely sustained by his consciousness of a well-spent life and by the reverent homage of all his bastards,—was not an atmosphere more pious than that which young Florian breathed in the sedate environment of Bellegarde.

Let none, however, suppose that Monsieur de Puysange affected superhuman austerities. Rather, he exercised tact. If he did not keep all fast days, he never failed to secure the proper dispensations, nor to see that his dependants fasted scrupulously: and if he sometimes, even now, was drawn into argument, Monsieur de Puysange was not ever known after any lethal duel to omit the ordering of a mass, at the local Church of Holy Hoprig, for his adversary's soul. "There are amenities," he would declare, "imperative among well-bred Christians."

Then too, when left a widower at the birth of his second legitimate son, the Duke did not so far yield to the temptings of the flesh as to take another wife; for he confessed to scruples if marriage, which the Scriptures assert to be unknown in heaven, could anywhere be a quite laudable estate: but he saw to it that his boys were tended by a succession of good-looking and amiable governesses. His priests also were kept sleek, and his confessor unshocked, by the Duke's tireless generosity to the Church; and were all of unquestioned piety, which they did not carry to excess. In fine, with youth and sentiment, and the discomforts of warfare also, put well behind him, the good gentleman had elected to live discreetly, among reputable but sympathetic companions. . . .

When Florian told his father now about Florian's delightful adventure in Acaire, the Duke smiled: and he said that, in this dream begotten by Florian's late reading of the fairy tales of Monsieur Perrault, Florian had been peculiarly privileged.

"For Madame Mélusine is not often encountered nowadays, my son. She was once well known in this part of Poictesme. But it was a long while ago she quarreled with her father, the wise King Helmas, in the land of the Peohtes, and imprisoned him, with all his court, upon the high place in Acaire. Yet Mélusine, let me tell you, was properly punished for her unfilial conduct; since upon every Sunday after that, her legs were turned to fishes' tails, and they stayed thus until Monday. This put the poor lady to great inconvenience: and when she eventually married, it led to a rather famous misunderstanding with her husband. And so he died unhappily; but she did not die, because she was of the Léshy, born of a people who are not immortal but are more than human—"

"Of course I know she did not die, monsieur my father. Why, it was only this afternoon I talked with her. I liked her very much. But she is not so pretty as Melior."

It seemed to Florian that the dark curls of his father's superb peruke now framed a smiling which was almost sad. "Perhaps there will never be in your eyes anybody so pretty as Melior. I am sure that you have dreamed all this, jumbling together in your dreaming old Monsieur Perrault's fine story of the sleeping princess—La Belle au Bois Dormant,—with our far older legends of Poictesme—"

"I do not think that it was just a dream, monsieur my father—"

"But I, unluckily, am sure it was, my son. And I suspect, too, that it is the dream which comes in vary-

ing forms to us of Puysange, the dream which we do
not ever quite put out of mind. We stay, to the last,
romantics. . . . So Melior, it may be, will remain to you
always that unattainable beauty toward which we of
Puysange must always yearn,—just as your patron St.
Hoprig will always afford to you, in his glorious life
and deeds, an example which you will admire and, I
trust, emulate. I admit that such emulation," the Duke
added, more drily, "has not always been inescapable
by us of Puysange."

"I cannot hope to be so good as was Monseigneur
St. Hoprig," Florian replied, "but I shall endeavor to
merit his approval."

"Indeed, you should have dreamed of the blessed
Hoprig also, while you were about it, Florian. For he
was a close friend of your Melior's father, you may remember, and performed many miracles at the court of
King Helmas in the land of the Peohtes."

"That is true," said Florian. "Oxen brought him
there in a stone trough: and I am sure that Monseigneur St. Hoprig must have loved Melior very much."

And he did not say any more about what his father
seemed bent upon regarding as Florian's dream. At ten
a boy has learned to humor the notions of his elders.
Florian slipped down from the bench, and tucked his
book under his arm, and agreed with his father that it
was near time for supper.

None the less, though, as the boy stood waiting for
that magnificent father of his to arise from the bench,
Florian reflected how queer it was that, before the falling to the Nis magic, this beautiful Melior must have
known and talked with Florian's heavenly patron, St.
Hoprig of Gol. It was to Holy Hoprig that Florian's
mother had commended the boy with her last breath,
and it was to Holy Hoprig that Florian's father had
taught the boy to pray in all time of doubt or pecca-
dillo, because this saint was always to be the boy's pro-

tector and advocate. And this made heaven seem very
near and real, the knowledge that always in celestial
courts this bright friend was watching, and, Florian
hoped, was upon occasion tactfully suggesting to the
good God that one must not be too severe with growing boys. Melior—Florian thought now,—was re-
motely and half timidly to be worshiped: but Hoprig,
the untiring friend and intercessor,—a being even
more kindly and splendid than was your superb father,
—you loved. . . .

Florian had by heart all the legends about Holy Hoprig. Particularly did Florian rejoice in the tale of the
Saint's birth, in such untoward circumstances as caused
the baby to be placed in a barrel, and cast into the sea,
to be carried whither wind and tide directed. Florian
knew that for ten years the barrel floated, tossing up
and down in all parts of the ocean, while regularly an
angel passed the necessary food to young Hoprig
through the bunghole. Finally, at Heaven's chosen
time, the barrel rolled ashore near Manneville, on the
low sands of Fomar Beach. A fisherman, thinking that
he had found a cask of wine, was about to tap it with a
gimlet; then from within, for the first time, St. Hoprig
speaks to man: "Do not injure the cask. Go at once to
the abbot of the monastery to which this land belongs,
and bid him come to baptize me."

It seemed to Florian that was a glorious start in life
for a boy of ten, a boy of just the same age as Florian.
All the later miracles and prodigies appeared, in comparison with that soul-contenting moment, to be compact of paler splendors. Nobody, though, could hear
unenviously of the long voyage to the Red Islands and
the realm of Hlif, and to Pohjola, and even to the
gold-paved Strembölgings, where every woman contains a serpent so placed as to discourage love-making,
—of that pre-eminently delightful voyage made by St.
Hoprig and St. Hork in the stone trough, which, after

its landing upon the coasts of Poictesme, at midwinter, during a miraculous shower of apple blossoms, white oxen drew through the country hillward, with the two saints by turns preaching and converting people all the way to Perdigon. For that, as Florian well remembered, was the imposing fashion in which Holy Hoprig had traveled northward, even to the court of Melior's father,—and had wrought miracles there also, to the discomfiture of the abominable Horrig. But more important, now, was the reflection that St. Hoprig had in this manner come to Melior and to the unimaginable beauty which, in the high place, a coverlet of violet stuff just half concealed. . . .

Certainly Monseigneur St. Hoprig must have loved Melior very much, and these two must have been very marvelous when they went about a more heroic and more splendid world than Florian could hope ever to inhabit. It was of their beauty and holiness that the boy thought, with a dumb yearning to be not in all unworthy of these bright, dear beings. That was the longing—to be worthy,—which possessed Florian as he stood waiting for his father to rise from the bench beneath the little tree from the East. There, the Duke also seemed to meditate, about something rather pleasant.

"You said just now, monsieur my father," Florian stated, a trifle worried, "that we of Puysange have not always imitated the good examples of St. Hoprig. Have we been very bad?"

Monsieur de Puysange had put on his plumed hat, but he stayed seated. He appeared now, as grown people so often do, amused for no logical or conceivable reason: though, indeed, the Duke seemed to find most living creatures involuntarily amusing.

He said: "We have displayed some hereditary foibles. For it is the boast of the house of Puysange that we trace in the direct male line from Poictesme's old Jurgen. That ancient wanderer, says our legend, somehow strayed into the bedchamber of Madame Félise de Puysange and the result of his errancy was the vicomte who flourished under the last Capets."

Young Florian, in accord with the quaint custom of the day, had been reared without misinformation as to how or whence children came into the world. So he said only, if a little proudly,—

"Yes,—he was another Florian, like me."

"There were queer tales about this first Florian, also, who is reputed to have vanished the moment he was married, and to have reappeared here, at Storisende, some thirty years later, with his youth unimpaired. He declared himself to have slept out the intervening while,—an excuse for remissness in his marital duties which skeptics have considered both hackneyed and improbable."

"Well," Florian largely considered, "but then there is Sir Ogier still asleep in Avalon until France has need of him; and John the Divine is still sleeping at Ephesus until it is time to bear his witness against Antichrist; and there is Merlin in Brocæliande, and there is St. Joseph of Arimathæa in the white city of Sarras—and really, monsieur my father, there is Melior, and all the rest of King Helmas' people up at Brunbelois."

"Are you still dreaming of your Melior, tenacious child! Certainly you are logical, you cite good precedents for your namesake, and to adhere to logic and precedent is always safe. I hope you will remember that."

"I shall remember that, monsieur my father."

"Certainly, too, this story of persons who sleep for a miraculous while is common to all parts of the world. This Florian de Puysange, in any event, married a granddaughter of the great Dom Manuel; so that we descend from the two most famous of the heroes of Poictesme: but, I fancy, it is from Jurgen that our family has inherited our major traits."

"Anyhow, we have risen from just being vicomtes—"

Florian's father had leaned back, he had put off his provisional plan of going in to supper. You could not say that the good gentleman exactly took pride in his ancestry: rather, he found his lineage worthy of him, and therefore he benevolently approved of it.

So he said now, complacently enough: "Yes, our house has prospered. Steadily our fortunes have been erected, and in dignity too we have been erected. Luck seems to favor us, however, most heartily when a woman rules France, and it is to exalted ladies that we owe most of our erections. Thus Queen Isabeau the Bavarian notably advanced the Puysange of her time, very much as Anne of Beaujeu and Catherine de Medici did afterward. Many persons have noted the coincidence. Indeed, it was only sixty years ago that Marion Delorme spoke privately to the Great Cardinal, with such eloquence that the Puysange of the day —another Florian, and a notably religious person,— had presently been made a duke, with an appropriate estate in the south—"

"I know," said Florian, not a bit humble about his erudition. "His uncle was burnt up for being a werewolf. That is how we came to be here in Poictesme. Mademoiselle Delorme was a very kind lady, was she not, Monsieur my Father?"

"She was so famed, my son, for all manner of generosity that when my grandfather remodeled Bellegarde, and erected the Hugonet wing of the present château, he sealed up in the cornerstone, just as people sometimes place there the relics of a saint, both of Madmoiselle Delorme's garters. Probably there was some salutary story connected with his acquiring of them; for my pious grandfather cared nothing for such vanities as jeweled garters, his mind being wholly set upon higher things."

"I wish we knew that story," said Florian.

"But nobody does. My grandfather was discreet. So he thrived. And his son, who was my honored father, also thrived under the regency of Anne of Austria. He thrived, rather unaccountably, in the teeth of Mazarin's open dislike. There was some story—I do not know what,—about a nightcap found under the Queen's pillow, and considered by his Eminence to need some explaining. My honored father was never good at explaining things. But he was discreet, and he thrived. And I too, my son, was lucky in Madame de Montespan's time."

Now Madame de Montespan's time antedated Florian's thinking: but about the King's last mistress,—and morganatic wife, some said,—Florian was better informed.

"Madame de Maintenon also is very fond of you, monsieur my father, is she not?"

The Duke slightly waved his hand, as one who disclaims unmerited tribute. "It was my privilege to know that incomparable lady during her first husband's life. He was a penniless cripple who had lost the use of all his members, and in that time of many wants I was so lucky as to comfort Madame Scarron now and then. Madame de Maintenon remembers these alleviations of her unfortunate youth, and notes with approval that I have forgotten them utterly. So Madame is very kind. In short,—or, rather, to sum up the tale,—the lords of Puysange are rumored, by superstitious persons, to have a talisman which enables them to go farther than most men in their dealings with ladies."

"You mean, like a magic lamp or a wishing cap?" said Florian, "or like a wizard's wand?"

"Yes, something in that shape," the Duke answered, "and they tell how through its proper employment, always under the great law of living, our house has got much pleasure and prosperity. And it is certain the Collyn aids us at need—"

"What is the Collyn?"

"Nothing suitable for a boy of ten to know about. When you are a man I shall have to tell you, Florian, about that legacy which our incinerated old kinsman, of whom you were just now speaking, has bequeathed to the family. That will be soon enough."

"And what, monsieur my father, is this great law of living?"

The Duke looked for a while at his son rather queerly. "Thou shalt not offend," the Duke replied, "against the notions of thy neighbor."

With that he was silent: and, rising at last from the bench, he walked across the lawn, and ascended the broad curving marble stairway which led to the south terrace of Storisende. And Florian, following, was for an instant quiet, and a little puzzled.

"Yes, but, monsieur my father, I do not see—"

The Duke turned, an opulent figure in dark blue and gold. He was standing by one of the tall vases elaborately carved with garlands, the vases that in summer overflowed with bright red and yellow flowers: these vases were now empty, and the gardeners had replaced the carved lids.

"Youth never sees the reason of that law, my son. I am wholly unprepared to say whether or not this is a lucky circumstance." The Duke again paused, looking thoughtfully across the terrace, toward the battlemented walls and the four towers of the southern façade. His gazing seemed to go well beyond the fountain and the radiating low hedges and graveled walk ways of the terrace, to go beyond, for that matter, the darkening castle. Twilight was rising: you saw a light in one window. "At all events, we are home again, young dreamer. I too was once a dreamer . . . And there is Little Brother waiting for us."

III

Widowers Seek Consolation

ITTLE BROTHER was indeed waiting for them, at the arched doorway, impatient of his governess' restraint. At sight of them he began telling, coincidently, of how hungry he was, and of how he had helped old Margot to milk a cow that afternoon, and of how a courier was waiting for Monsieur my Father in great long boots, up to here. The trifold tale was confusing, for at eight little Raoul could not yet speak plainly. His sleeve was torn, and he had a marvelously dirty face.

Behind him stood pallid pretty Mademoiselle Berthe, the governess who a trifle later, during the next winter, killed herself. She had already begun bewailing her condition to the Duke, even while she obstinately would have none of the various husbands whom her kindly patron recommended, from among his dependants, as ready to make that condition respectable. There seemed no pleasing the girl; and Florian could see that his father, for all his uniform benevolence, regarded her nowadays as a nuisance.

But the Duke nevertheless gazed down, at the pale frightened-looking creature, with that serene and condescending smile which he accorded almost everybody. "Mademoiselle, children are a grave responsibility. I have just found Florian asleep in the mud yonder, whereas you have evidently just plucked this other small pest from the pigsty. It is lucky, is it not, that we have no more brats to contend with, mademoiselle, for the present?"

Florian wondered, long afterward, how Mademoiselle Berthe had looked, and what she answered. He could not recollect. But he did remember that at this instant Little Brother ran from her and hugged first one of his father's superb legs and then Florian. Little Brother was warm and tough-feeling and astonishingly strong, and he smelled of clean earth.

Florian loved him very much, and indeed the affection between the two brothers endured until the end of their intercourse. Florian was always consciously the elder and wiser, and felt himself the stronger long after Raoul had become taller than Florian. Even after Raoul was well on in his thirties, and both the boys had boys of their own, Florian still thought of the Chevalier de Puysange as a little brother with a smudged face and a smell of clean earth, whom you loved and patronized, and from whom you had one secret only. For of course you never told Raoul about Melior.

You spoke to nobody about Melior. You found it wiser and more delicious to retain all knowledge of her loveliness for your entirely private consideration, and, thus, not to be bothered with people's illogical notion that Melior was only a dream.

For the memory of the Princess Melior's loveliness did not depart as Florian became older, and neither manhood nor marriage could put quite out of his mind that beauty which he in childhood had, howsoever briefly, seen. Other women came and in due season went. His wives indeed seemed to die with a sort of uniform prematureness in which the considerate found something of fatality: nor did the social conventions of the day permit a Puysange to shirk amusing himself with yet other women. And Florian amused himself so liberally, once his father was dead, and the former

Prince de Lisuarte had succeeded to the major title and to his part of the estates, that they of Bellegarde were grieved when it was known that the fourth Duke of Puysange now planned to marry for the fifth time.

For all agreed that, at Florian's château of Bellegarde, affairs had sped very pleasantly since the death of his last wife, and the packing off of his son to Storisende. Storisende, by the old Duke's will, had fallen to Raoul. Affairs had sped so pleasantly, they said at Bellegarde, that it seemed a deplorable risk for monseigneur to be marrying a woman who might, conceivably, be forthwith trying to reclaim him from all fashionable customs. Besides, he was upon this occasion marrying a daughter of the house of Nérac, just as his brother the Chevalier had done. And this was a ruiningly virtuous family, a positively dowdy family who hardly seemed to comprehend—they said at Bellegarde,—that we were now living in the modern world 1723, and that fashions had altered since the old King's death.

"For how long, little monster, will this new toy amuse you!" asked Mademoiselle Cécile.

It appears unfair here to record that at nine o'clock in the morning they were not yet up and about the day's duties, without recording also, in palliation of such seeming laziness, that there was no especial need to hurry, for all of mademoiselle's trunks had been packed overnight, and she was not to leave Bellegarde until noon.

"Parbleu, one never knows," Florian replied, as he lay smiling lazily at the smiling cupids who held up the bed-canopies. "It is a very beautiful feature of my character that at thirty-five I am still the optimist. When I marry I always believe the ceremony to begin a new and permanent era."

"Oh, very naturally, since everywhere that frame of mind is considered appropriate to a bridegroom." The girl turned her sleek brown head a little, resting it more comfortably upon the pillow, and she regarded Florian with appraising eyes. "My friend, in this, as in much else, I find your subserviency to convention almost excessive. It becomes a notorious mania with you to do nothing whatever without the backing of logic and good precedent—"

"My father, mademoiselle, impressed upon me a great while ago the philosophy of these virtues."

"Yes, all that is very fine. Yet I at times suspect your logic and your precedents to be in reality patched-up excuses for following the moment's whim: or else I seem to see you adjusting them, like colored spectacles, to improve in your eyes the appearance of that which you have in hand."

"Now you misjudge me, mademoiselle, with the ruthlessness of intimate personal acquaintance—"

"But indeed, indeed, those precedents which you educe are often rather far-fetched. You are much too ready to refer us to the customs of the Visigoths, or to cite the table-talk of Aristotle, or to appeal to the rulings of Quintilian. It sounds well: I concede that. Yet these, and the similar sonorous pedantries with which you are so glib to justify your pranks, do not, my friend, seem always wholly relevant—"

"My race descends from a most notable scholar, mademoiselle, and it well may be the great Jurgen has bequeathed to me some flavor of his unique erudition. For that I certainly need not apologize—"

"No, you should rather apologize because that ancient hero appears also to have bequeathed to you a sad tendency to self-indulgence in matrimony. Now to get married has always seemed to me an indelicate advertising of one's intentions: and I assuredly cannot condone in anybody a selfish habit which to-day leads to my being turned out of doors—"

."A pest! you talk as if I too did not sincerely regret

those social conventions which make necessary your departure—"

"Yet it is you who evoke those silly conventions by marrying again."

"—But in a grave matter like matrimony one must not be obstinate and illiberal. Raoul assures me, you conceive, that his little sister-in-law is a delightful creature. He thinks that as a co-heiress of Nérac, without any meddlesome male relatives, she is the person logically suited to be my wife. And I like to indulge the dear fellow's wishes."

"Behold a fine sample of your indulgence of others, by marrying a great fortune! After all, though," Cécile reflected, philosophically, "I would not change shoes with her. For it is not wholesome, my friend, to be your wife. But it has been eminently pleasant to be your playfellow."

Florian smiled. And Florian somewhat altered his position.

"Bels dous amicx," said Florian, softly, *"fassam un joc novel—!"*

"I must ask for some explanation of, at least," Cécile stated, with that light, half-muffled laugh which Florian found adorable, "your words."

"I was about to sing, mademoiselle, a very ancient aubade. I was beginning a morning-song such as each lover in the days of troubadours was accustomed, here in Poictesme, to sing to his mistress at arising."

"So that, now you are, as I can perceive, arising, you plan to honor the old custom? That is well enough for you, who are a Duke of Puysange, and who have so much respect for precedent and logic. But I am not logical, I am, as you in your turn can well see, a woman. Moreover, I am modern in all, I abhor antiquity. I find it particularly misplaced in a bedroom."

"And therefore, mademoiselle—? "

"And therefore, my friend, I must entreat you, whatever else you do, not to sing any of those old songs, which may, for anything I know, have some improper significance."

Florian humored this young lady's rather strict notions of propriety, and they for a while stopped talking. Then they parted with a friendly kiss, and they dressed each for traveling: and Mademoiselle Cécile rode south upon a tentative visit to Cardinal Borgia, whose proffered benefactions had thus far been phrased with magniloquence and vagueness. This fair girl had the religious temperament, and she delighted in submitting herself to her spiritual fathers, but she required some daily comforts also.

Florian next sent for the boy Gian Paolo, who had now for seven months been Florian's guest. "I am marrying," said Florian. "We must part, Gian Paolo."

"Do you think so?" the boy said. "Ah, but you would regret me!"

"Regretting would become a lost art if people did not sometimes do their duty. Now that I am about to take a wife, you comprehend, I shall for the while be more or less preëmpted by my bride. It is unlikely that I shall be able, at all events during the first ardors of the honeymoon, to entertain my friends with any adequacy. Let us be logical, dear Gian Paolo! I find no fault in you, beloved boy, I concede you to be fit friend for an emperor. It is merely that the advent of my new duchess now compels me to ensure the privacy of our honeymoon by parting, howsoever regretfully, with you also."

"Your decision does not surprise me, Florian, for they say you have parted with many persons who loved you, and who left you—"

"Yes?" said Florian.

"—Very suddenly—"

"Yes?" Florian said, again.

"—And yet without their departure surprising you at all, dear Florian."

"Oh, it is merely that in moments of extreme anguish I attempt to control my emotions, and to give them no undignified display," said Florian. "Doubtless, I was as surprised as anybody. Well, but this foolish gossip of this very censorious neighborhood does not concern us, Gian Paolo: and, now that you are about to go, I can assure you that all your needs"—here for an instant Florian hesitated,—"have been provided for."

"Indeed, I see that you have wine set ready. Is it"— and the boy smiled subtly, for he was confident of his power over Florian,—"is it my stirrup-cup, dear Florian?"

Florian now looked full upon him. "Yes," Florian said, rather sadly. Then they drank, but not of the same wine, to the new Duchess of Puysange. And the boy Gian Paolo died without pain.

"It is better so," said Florian. "Time would have spoiled your beauty. Time would have spoiled your joy in life, Gian Paolo, and would have shaken your fond belief that I was your slave in everything. Time lay in wait to travesty this velvet chin with a harsh beard, to waken harsh doubtings in the merry heart, and to abate your lovely perversities with harsh repentance. For time ruins all, but you escape him, dear Gian Paolo, unmarred."

Now Florian was smiling wistfully, for he found heartache in this thinking of the evanescence of beauty everywhere, and heartache too in thinking of the fate of that charming old lady, La Tophania, who had been so kind to him in Naples. For Florian could rarely make use of her recipes without recollecting how cruelly the mob had dealt with his venerable instructress: that was, he knew, a sentimental side to his nature, which he could never quite restrain. So he now thought sadly of this stately old-world gentle-woman, so impiously dragged from a convent and strangled, now four years ago, because of her charity toward those who were afflicted by the longevity of others. Yes, life was wasteful, sparing nobody, not even one who was so wise and amiable as La Tophania, nor so lovable as Gian Paolo. The thought was depressing; such wastefulness appeared illogical: and it seemed to Florian, too, that this putting of his household into fit order for the reception of his bride was not wholly a merry business.

Then Florian, stroking the dead hand which was as yet soft and warm, said gently: "And though I have slain you, dear Gian Paolo, rather than see you depart from me to become the friend of another, and perhaps to talk with him indiscreetly after having learned more about me than was wise, I have at worst not offended against convention, nor have I run counter to the fine precedents of the old time. Just so did the great Alexander deal with his Clitus, and Hadrian with his Antinous; nor did divine Apollo give any other parting gift to Hyacinthos, his most dear friend. Now the examples afforded us by ancient monarchs and by the heathen gods should not, perhaps, be followed blindly. Indeed, we should in logic remember always that all these were pagans, unsustained by the promptings of true faith, and therefore liable to err. Nevertheless do these old-world examples raise up a tenable precedent; they afford people of condition something to go by: and to have that is a firm comfort."

He kissed the dead lips fondly; and he bade his lackeys summon Father Joseph to bury Gian Paolo, with due ceremony, in the Chapel, next to Florian's wives.

"We obey. Yet, it will leave room for no more graves," one told him, "in the alcove wherein monseigneur's wives are interred."

"That is true. You are an admirable servant, Pierre, you think logically of all things. Do you bury the poor lad in the south transept."

Then Florian took wine and wafers into the secret chamber which nobody else cared to enter, and he made sure that everything there was in order. All these events happened on the feast day of St. Swithin of Winchester which falls upon the fifteenth of July: and on that same day Florian left Bellegarde, going to meet his new wife, and traveling alone, toward Storisende.

IV
Economics of an Old Race

LORIAN rode alone, spruce and staid in a traveling suit of bottle-green and silver, riding upon a tall white horse, riding toward Storisende, where his betrothed awaited him, and where the wedding supper was already in preparation. He went by the longer route, so that he might put up a prayer, for the success of his new venture into matrimony, at the church of Holy Hoprig. Nobody was better known nor more welcome at this venerable shrine than was Florian, for the Duke de Puysange had spared nothing to evince his respect for the fame and the favorable opinion of his patron saint. Whether in the shape of candles or a handsome window, or a new chapel or an acre or two of meadow land, Florian was always giving for the greater glory of that bright intercessor who in heaven, Florian assumed, was tactfully suggesting that such generosity should not be overlooked. So it was that Florian kept his accounts balanced, his future of a guaranteeable pleasantness, and his conscience clear.

Having prayed for the success of this new marriage and for the soul of Gian Paolo, and having confessed to all the last month's irregularities, Florian went eastward. He passed Amneran and a spur of the great forest, now that he went to ford the Duardenez. As he neared Acaire he thought, idly, and with small shrugs, of a boy's adventuring to the sleeping princess in the midst of these woods, and of the beauty which he had not ever forgotten utterly: and his heart was troubled with that worshipful and hopeless longing which any thinking about this Melior would always evoke in Florian, because he knew that his "dream," as people would call it, was a far more true and vital thing than Florian's daily living.

Then on a sudden he reined up his horse, and Florian waited there, looking down upon the dark woman who had come out of this not over-wholesome forest. Florian did not speak for some while, but he smiled, and he shook his head in a sort of humorous disapprobation.

This woman was his half-sister, whom Florian's father had begotten, with the coöperation of the bailiff of Ranec's daughter, some while before middle age and the coming into extreme fashion of continence had made such escapades criticizable. Marie-Claire Cazaio was thus of an age with Florian, being his senior by only three months. In their shared youth these two had not been strangers, for the old Duke had handsomely recognized his responsibility for this daughter, and had kept Marie-Claire about his household until the girl had outraged propriety by bearing an illegitimate child. After this the Duke had no choice except to turn her out of doors. She had since then taken up with companions whose repute was not even dubious: and her manner of living was esteemed intemperate by the most broad-minded persons in Poictesme, where sorcery was treated with all reasonable indulgence.

"My dear," said Florian, at last, still shaking his head, "I must tell you, howsoever little good it does, that there was another deputation of peasants and declamatory grocers at me, only last week, to have you seized and burned. You are too careless, Marie-Claire, about offending against the notions of your neighbors. You should persuade your unearthly lovers to curb their ardors until after dark. You should at least induce them not to pass over Amneran in such shapes as frighten your neighbors in the twilight, and so provoke their very natural desire to burn you at broad noon."

"These little peasants will not burn me yet," she answered. "My term is not yet run out—" You saw that Marie-Claire was thinking of quite other matters. She said, "So, they tell me, you are to marry again?"

She had lifted to him now that half-pensive, half-blind staring which he uneasily recognized. Florian had always under this woman's gaze the illogical feeling that, where he was, Marie-Claire saw some one else, or, to be exact, saw some one a slight distance behind him. . . . Her eyes could not be black. Florian knew that nobody's eyes were really black. But this woman's small eyes were very dark, they had such extraordinarily thick and rather short lashes upon both upper and lower lids, that these little eyes most certainly seemed blobs of infernal ink. There was, moreover, in his sister's eyes a discomfortable knowingness. Puysange looked at Puysange. . . .

He answered, quietly, "Yes, Mademoiselle de Nérac is now about to make me the happiest of men."

"Unhappy child! for she too is flesh and blood."

"And what does that anatomical truism signify when it is so cryptically uttered, Marie-Claire?"

"It means that you and I are not enamored of flesh and blood."

Florian did not reply to this in words. But he smiled at his half-sister, for he was really fond of her, even now, and they understood each other excellently.

So he stayed silent. By and by he said:

"You come out of a wood that is not often visited by abbots and cherubim, and you carry a sieve and shears. Who is yonder?"

Marie-Claire replied, "How should I know the real name of the adversary of all the gods of men?"

"Pardieu!" said Florian, "so it is company of such sinister grandeur that you entertain nowadays. You progress toward a truly notable damnation."

"We of our coven call him Janicot—"

"Yes, I know," said Florian, "and, certainly, his local name does not matter in the least." Florian smiled benevolently, and said, "Good luck to you, my dear!"

Then he rode on, into the pathway from which Marie-Claire had just emerged. He was interested, for it might well be rather amusing to overtake this whispered-about Janicot in the midst of his somber work: but, even so, the thoughts of Florian were not wholly given over to Janicot, or to Marie-Claire either. Instead, he was still thinking of the sleeping woman's face which he had not ever forgotten utterly: and this dark sullen sister of his—who had once been so pretty too, he recollected,—and all her injudicious traffic seemed, somehow, a bit futile.

No, he reflected, Marie-Claire was not pretty now. Her neck remained wonderful: it was still the only woman's neck familiar to Florian that really justified comparison with a swan's neck by its unusual length and roundness and flexibility. But her head was too small for that superb neck: she had taken on the dusky pallor of a Puysange: she was, in fine, thirty-five, and looked rather older. It showed you what irregular and sorcerous living might lead to. Florian at thirty-five looked—at most, he estimated,—twenty-eight. Yes: it was much more sensible to adhere to precedent, and to keep all one's accounts in order, through St. Hoprig's loving care, and to retain overhead a thrifty balance in one's favor.

V

Friendly Advice of Janicot

 HEN he had entered a little way into Acaire, Florian came to an open place, where seven trees had been hewn down. A brown horse was tethered here, and here seven lilies bloomed with a surprising splendor of white and gold. These stood waist-high about a sedate looking burgess, unostentatiously but very neatly dressed in some brown stuff, which was just the color of his skin. At his feet was a shrub covered with crimson flowers: no sun shone here, the sky was clouded and cast down a coppery glow.

Such was Janicot. Florian saluted him, quite civilly, but with appropriate reserve.

"Come," Janicot said, smiling, "And is this the rapturous countenance of a bridegroom? I am not pleased with you, Monsieur the Duke, I must have happy faces among my friends."

"So you also have heard of my approaching marriage! Well, I am content enough, and for me to marry the co-heiress of Nérac seems logical: but in logic, too, I cannot ignore that I ride toward a disappointing business. There is magic in the curiously clothed woman who is mistress of herself, the hour and you: but the prostrate, sweating and submissive meat in a tangle of bed-clothing—!" Florian shrugged.

"In fact," said Janicot, as if pensively, "I have observed you. You do not enter wholly into the pleasures suitable for men and women: you do not avoid these agreeabilities, but your sampling of them is without self-surrender, and there is something else which you hold more desirable."

"That is true." Florian for an instant meditated. Florian shrugged. Then Florian dismounted from his white horse, and tethered it. Here was the one being in whom you might confide logically. Florian told Janicot the story of how, in childhood, Florian had ascended to the high place, and had seen the Princess Melior, whom always since that time his heart had desired.

And Janicot heard him through, with some marks of interest. Janicot nodded.

"Yes, yes," said Janicot. "I do not frequent high places. But I have heard of this Melior, from men a long while dead, and they said that she was beautiful."

"Then they spoke foolishly," replied Florian, "because they spoke with pitiable inadequacy. Now I do not say that she is beautiful. I do not speak any praise whatever of Melior, because her worth is beyond all praising. I am silent as to the unforgotten beauty of Melior, lest I cry out against that which I love. When I was but a child her loveliness was revealed to me, and never since then have I been able to forget the beauty of which all dreams go envious. I jest with women who are lovable and nicely colored; they have soft voices, and their hearts are kind: but presently I yawn and say they are not as Melior."

"Ah, but in fact," said Janicot, "in fact, you do—without caring to commit yourself formally,—believe that this Melior is beautiful?"

Now Florian's plump face was altered, and his voice shook a little. He said:

"Her beauty is that beauty which women had in the world's youth, and whose components the old world forgets in this gray age. It may be that Queen Helen possessed such beauty, she for whom the long warring was. It may be that Cleopatra of Egypt, who had for her playmates emperors and a gleaming snake, and for her lovers all poets that have ever lived, or it may be that some other royal lady of the old time, in the world's youth, wore flesh that was the peer of Melior's flesh in loveliness. But such women, if there indeed was ever Melior's peer, are now vague echoes and blown dust. I cry the names that once were magic. I cry to Semiramis and to Erigonê and to Guenevere, and there is none to answer. Their beauty has gone down into the cold grave, it has nourished grasses, and cattle chew the cud which was their loveliness. Therefore I cry again, I cry the name of Melior: and though none answers, I know that I cry upon the unflawed and living beauty which my own eyes have seen."

Janicot sat on a tree stump, stroking his chin with thumb and forefinger. He was entirely brown, with white and gold about him, and the flowering at his neatly shod feet was more red than blood. He said:

"In that seeing, denied to all other living persons,— in that, at least, you have been blessed."

"In that," said Florian, bitterly, "I was accursed. Because of this beauty which I may not put out of mind, the tinsel prettiness of other women becomes grotesque and pitiable and hateful. I strive to make with them, and I lie lonely in their arms. I seek for a mate, and I find only meat and much talking. Then I regard the tedious stranger in whose arms I discover myself, and I wonder what I am doing in this place. I remember Melior, and I must rid myself of the fond foolish creature who is not as Melior."

"Ah, ah!" said Janicot then, "So that is how it is. I perceive you are romantic. The disorder is difficult to cure. Yet we must have you losing no more wives: there must be an end to the ill luck which follows your matrimonial adventures and causes hypercritical persons to whisper. Yes, since you are a romantic, since all other women upset your equanimity and lead you into bereavements which people, let me tell you, are festooning with ugly surmises, you certainly must have this Melior."

"No," Florian said, wistfully, "there is an etiquette in these matters. Even if I cared to dabble in sorcery, it would not be quite courteous for me to interfere with the magic which Madame Mélusine has laid upon the high place and her blood relations. It would be meddling in her family affairs, it would be an incivility without precedent, to her who was so kind to me in my childhood."

"You think too much about precedent, Monsieur the Duke. In any event, Mèlusine has half forgotten the matter. So much has happened to her, in the last four hundred years, that her mind has quite gone. She cares only to wail upon battlements and to pass through dusky corridors at twilight, predicting the deaths of her various descendants. You can see for yourself that these are not the recreations of a logical person. No, Florian, you are considerate, and it does you great credit, but you would not annoy Madame Mélusine by releasing Brunbelois."

Said Florian, gently: "My intimates, to be sure, address me as Florian. But our acquaintance, Monsieur Janicot, howsoever delightful, remains as yet of such brevity that, really whether you be human or divine—"

"Oh, but, Monsieur the Duke," replied the other, "but indeed I entreat your pardon for my inadvertence."

And Florian too bowed. "It is merely a social convention, of course. Yet it is necessary to respect the best precedents even in trifles. Well, now, and as to your suggestion, I confess you tempt me—"

"Only, you could not free Brunbelois unaided, nor could any living sorcerer. For Mélusine's was the Old Magic that is stronger than the thin thaumaturgy of these days. Yet I desire to have happy faces about me, so I will give you this Melior for a while."

"And at what price?"

"I who am the Prince of this world am not a merchant to buy and sell. I will release the castle, and you may have the girl as a free gift. I warn you, though, that, since she is of the Léshy, at the year's end she will vanish."

Florian shook his head, smilingly. He knew of course that marriage with one of the Léshy could not be permanent. But this fiend must believe him very simple indeed, if Janicot thought Florian so uninformed as not to know that whoever accepts a gift from hell is thereby condemned to burn eternally: and to perceive this amused Florian.

"Ah, Monsieur Janicot, but a Puysange cannot take alms from anybody. No, let us be logical! There must be a price set and paid, so that I may remain under no distasteful and incendiary debts."

Janicot hid excellently the disappointment he must have felt. "Suppose we say that she is yours until you have had a child by her? And that then she will vanish, and the child be given me, as my honorarium, by"— Janicot explained,—"the old ritual."

"Well," Florian replied, "I may logically take this to be a case of desperate necessity, since all my happiness depends upon it. Now in such cases Paracelsus admits the lawfulness of seeking aid from—if you will pardon the technical term, Monsieur Janicot,—from unclean spirits. He is supported in this, as I remember it, by Peter Ærodius, by Bartolus of Sassoferato, by Salecitus, and by other divines and schoolmen. So I have honorable precedents, I do not offend against convention. Yes, I accept the offer; and the child, whatever my paternal pangs, shall be given, as your honorarium, by the old ritual."

"Of course," said Janicot, reflectively, "if there should be no child—"

"Monsieur, I am Puysange. There will be a child."

"Why, then, it is settled. Now I think of it, you will need the sword Flamberge with which to perform this rite, since Melior is of the Léshy, and that sword alone of all swords may spill their blood—"

"But where is Flamberge nowadays?"

"There is one at home, in an earthen pot, who could inform you."

"Let us not speak of that," said Florian, hastily, "but do you tell me where is this sword."

"I have not any least notion, unless it be somewhere in Antan. Nor, since you stickle for etiquette, is it etiquette for me to aid you in finding this sword until you have made me a sacrifice."

"Why, but you offered Melior as a free gift!" said Florian, smiling to see how obvious were the traps this Janicot set for him. "Is a princess of smaller importance than a sword?"

"A princess is easier to get, because a princess is easier to make. A sword, far less a magic sword like Flamberge, cannot be fashioned without long training and preparation and special knowledge. But no man needs more than privacy and a queen's good will to make a princess."

"I confess, Monsieur Janicot, that your logic is indisputable. Well, when at the winter solstice you hold your Festival of the Wheel, I shall not sacrifice to you. That would be to relapse into the old evil ways of heathenry, a relapse for which is appointed an agonizing reproof, administered in realms unnecessary to mention, but doubtless familiar to you. However, I shall be glad to tender you a suitable Christmas present, since that sacred season falls at the same time."

"You may call it whatever you prefer. But it must be a worthy gift that one offers me at my Yule Feast."

"You shall have—not as a sacrifice, you understand, but as a Christmas present,—the greatest man living in France. You shall have no less a gift than the life of that weasel-faced prime minister who now rules France, the all-powerful Cardinal Dubois. For the rest, your bargain is reasonable: it contains none of those rash mortgagings of the soul, about which—if you will pardon my habitual frankness, Monsieur Janicot,—one has to be careful in all business dealings with your people. So let us subscribe this bond."

Janicot laughed: his traffic was not in souls, he said; and he said also that Florian, for a nobleman, was deplorably the man of business. None the less, Janicot now produced from his pocket a paper upon which the terms of their bargain happened, rather unaccountably, to be neatly written out: and they both signed this paper, with the pens and ink which Florian had not previously noticed to be laid there so close at hand, upon one of the tree stumps.

Then Janicot put up the paper, and remarked: "A thing done has an end. For the rest, these fellows will escort you to Brunbelois."

"And of what fellows do you speak?" asked Florian.

"Why, those servants of mine just behind you," replied Janicot.

And Florian, turning, saw in the roadway two very hairy persons in an oxcart, drawn by two brown goats which were as large as oxen; and yet Florian was certain no one of these things had been in that place an instant before. This Janicot, howsoever easy to see through had been all his traps for Florian, was beyond doubt efficient.

Florian said: "The liveries of your retainers tend somewhat to the capillary. None the less, I shall be deeply honored, monsieur, to be attended by any servants of your household."

Janicot replied: "Madame Mélusine has ordained against men and the living of mankind eternal banishment from the high place. Very well!"

He drew his sword, and without any apparent effort

he struck off the head of his brown horse. He set this head upon a stake, and he thrust the other end of the stake into the ground, so that the stake stood upright.

"I here set up," said Janicot, "a nithing post. I turn the post. I turn the eternal banishment against Madame Mélusine."

He waited for a moment. He was entirely brown: about him lilies bloomed, with a surprising splendor of white and gold: and the flowering at his feet was more red than blood.

He moved the stake so that the horse's head now faced the east, and Janicot said: "Also I turn this post against the protecting monsters of the high place, in order that they may all become as witless as now is this slain horse. I send a witlessness upon them from the nithing post, which makes witless and takes away the strength of the rulers and of the controlling gods of whatsoever land this nithing post be turned against. I, who am what I am, have turned the post. I have sent forth the Seeing of All, the Seeing that makes witless. A thing done has an end."

VI

Philosophy of the Lower Class

**F**LORIAN then parted from brown Janicot for that while; and Florian mounted his white horse, and he rode upward toward. the castle of Brunbelois, without further thought of the girl at Storisende whom logic had picked out to be his wife. Florian was followed by the oxcart which Janicot had provided. Florian found all the monsters lying in a witless stupor. So he fearlessly set upon and killed the black bleps and the crested strycophanês and the gray calcar.

He passed on upward, presently to decapitate the eale, which writhed its movable horns very remarkably in dying. Florian went on intrepidly, and despatched the golden-maned and -whiskered leucrocotta. The tarandus, farther up the road, proved more troublesome: this monster had, after its sly habit, taken on the coloring of the spot in which it lay concealed, so that it was hard to find; and, when found, its hide was so tough as to resist for some while the edge of Florian's sword. The thin and flabby neck of the catoblepas was, in contrast, gratifyingly easy to sever. Indeed, this was in all respects a contemptible monster, dingily colored, and in no way formidable now that its eyes were shut.

Florian's heroic butchery was well-nigh over: so he passed on cheerily to the next turn in the road; and in that place a moment later the bright red mantichora was impotently thrusting out its sting in the death agony, a sudden wind came up from the west, and the posture of the sun was changed.

Having dauntlessly performed these unmatched feats, the champion paused to reward himself with a pinch of snuff. The lid of his snuffbox bore the portrait of his dear friend and patron, Philippe d'Orléans, and it seemed odd to be regarding familiar features in these mischancy uplands. Then Florian, refreshed, looked about him. Three incredibly weather-beaten sheep were grazing to his right: to the left he saw, framed by the foliage upon each side of and overhanging the green roadway, the castle of Brunbelois.

Thus one by one did Florian cut off the heads of the seven wardens, with real regret—excepting only when he killed the catoblepas,—that his needs compelled him to destroy such colorful and charming monsters. The two remarkably hairy persons, without ever speaking, lifted each enormous head, one by one, into the cart. The party mounted within eyeshot of Brunbelois thus triumphantly. And at Brunbelois, where the old time yet lingered, the hour was not afternoon but early morning: and at the instant Florian slew the mantichora all the persons within the castle had awakened from what they thought was one night's resting.

Now the first of the awakened Peohtes whom Florian encountered was a milkmaid coming down from Brunbelois with five cows. What Florian could see of her was pleasantly shaped and tinted. He looked long at her.

"To pause now for any frivolous reason," reflected Florian, "or to disfigure in any way the moment in which I approach my life's desire is of course unthinkable—"

Meanwhile the milkmaid looked at Florian. She smiled, and her naturally high coloring was heightened.

"—So I do not pause for frivolous reasons. I pause because one must be logical. For, now that I think of it, to rescue people from enchantment is a logical proceeding only when one is certain that this rescuing involves some positive gain to the world. Do you drive on a little way, and wait for me," said Florian, aloud, to his hirsute attendants, "while I discover from this enticing creature what sort of persons we have resurrected."

The hairy servants of Janicot obeyed. Florian, very spruce in bottle-green and silver, dismounted from his white horse, and in the ancient roadway now overgrown with grass, held amicable discourse with this age-old milkmaid. She proved to be a virgin not wholly unsophisticated. And when they parted, each had been agreeably convinced that the persons of one era are much like those of another.

Florian thus came to the gates of Brunbelois logically reassured that he had done well in reviving such persons, even at the cost of destroying charming monsters and of the labor involved in removing so many heads. He counted smilingly on his finger-tips, but such was his pleased abstraction that he miscalculated, and made the total eight.

He found that, now the enchantment was lifted, Brunbelois showed in every respect as a fine old castle of the architecture indigenous to fairy tales. Flags were flying from the turrets; sentinels, delightfully shiny in the early morning sunlight, were pacing the walls, on the look-out for enemies that had died four hundred years ago; and at the gate was a night-porter, not yet off duty. This porter wore red garments worked with yellow thistles, and he seemed dejected but philosophic.

"Whence come you, in those queer dusty clothes?" inquired the porter, "and what is your business here?"

"Announce to King Helmas," said Florian, as he brushed the dust from his bottle-green knees, and saw with regret that nothing could be done about the grass-stains, which, possibly, had got there when he knelt to cut off the tarandus' head,—"announce to King Helmas that the lord of Puysange is at hand."

"You are talking, sir," the porter answered, resignedly, "most regrettable nonsense. For the knife is in the collops, the mead is in the drinking-horn, the eggs are upon the toast, the minstrels are in the gallery, and King Helmas is having breakfast."

"None the less, I have important business with him—"

"Equally none the less, nobody may enter at this hour unless he be the son of a king of a privileged country or a craftsman bringing his craft."

"Parbleu, but that is it, precisely. For I bring in that wagon very fine samples of my craft."

The porter left his small grilled lodge. He looked at the piled heads of the monsters, he poked them with his finger, and he said mildly,—

"Why, but did you ever!"

Then he returned to the gate.

"Now, my friend," said Florian, with the appropriate stateliness, "I charge you, by all the color and ugliness of these samples of my craft, to announce to your king that the lord of Puysange is at the gate with tidings, and with proof, that the enchantment is happily lifted from this castle."

"So there has been an enchantment. I suspected something of the sort when I came to, after nodding a bit like in the night, and noticed the remarkably thick forest which had grown up around us."

Florian observed, to this degraded underling who seemed not capable of appreciating Florian's fine exploits, "Well, certainly you take all marvels very calmly."

The sad porter replied that, with a reigning family so given to high temper and sorcery, the retainers of Brunbelois were not easily astounded. Something in the shape of an enchantment had been predicted in the kitchen only last night, after the great quarrel between Madam Mélusine and her father—

"My friend," said Florian, "that was not last night. You speak of a disastrous family jar in which the milk of human kindness curdled several centuries ago. Since then there has been a magic laid on Brunbelois: and the spell was lifted only to-day."

"Do you mean, sir, that I am actually several hundred and fifty-two years old?"

"Somewhere in that November neighborhood," said Florian. And he steeled himself against the other's outburst of horror and amazement.

"To think of that now!" said the porter. "I certainly never imagined it would come to that. However, it is always a great comfort to reflect it hardly matters what happens to us, is it not, sir?"

You could not but find in this stubborn unwillingness to face the magnitude of Florian's exploits, something horribly prosaic and callous. Yet, none the less, Florian civilly asked the man's meaning. And the dejected porter replied:

"It is just a sort of fancying, sir, that one wanders into after watching the stars, as I do in the way of business, night after night. One gets to reading them and to a sort of glancing over of the story that is written in their courses. Yes, sir, one does fall into the habit, injudiciously perhaps, but then there is nothing else much to do. And one does not find there quite, as you might put it, the excitement over the famousness of kings and the ruining of empires that one might reasonably look for. And one does not find anything at all there about porters, I can assure you, sir, because they are not important enough to figure in that story. There is no more writing in the stars about night-porters than there is about bumblebees; and that is always a great comfort, sir, when one feels low-spirited. Because I would not care to be in that story myself, for it is not light pleasant reading."

"A pest! so you inform me, with somewhat the gay levity of an oyster, that you can read the stars!"

The porter admitted dolefully, "One does come to it, sir, in my way of business."

"And how many chapters, I wonder, are written in the heavens about me?"

The porter looked at Florian for some while. The porter said, now even more dolefully:

"I would not be surprised if there was a line somewhere about you, sir. For your planet is Venus, and her people do get written about in an excessive way, there is no denying it. And I would not care to be one of them, myself, but of course there is no accounting for tastes, even if any man anywhere had any say in the matter."

"Parbleu, you may be right about my planet," said Florian, smiling for reasons of his own. "Yet, as an artless veteran of the first and second Pubic Wars, I do not see how you can be certain."

"Because of your corporature, sir," replied the porter. "He that is born under this planet is of fair but not tall stature, his complexion being white but tending a little to darkness. He has fine black hair, the brows arched, the face pretty fleshy, a cherry lip, a rolling wandering eye. He has a love-dimple in his cheek, and shows in all as one desirous of trimming and making himself neat and complete in clothes and body. Now these things I see in your corporature and in the fretfulness with which you look at the grass-stains on your knees. So your planet is evident."

"That is possible, your speech has a fine ring of logic, and logic is less common than hens' teeth. Upon what sort of persons does this honorable planet attend?"

"If you could call it attending, sir— For I must tell you that these planets have a sad loose way of not devoting their really undivided attention to looking after the affairs of any one particular gentleman, not even when they see him most magnificent in bottle-green and silver."

"They are as remiss, then, as you are precise. So do you choose your own verb, and tell me—"

"Sir," replied the porter, "I regret to inform you that the person whom Venus governs is riotous, expensive, wholly given to dissipation and lewd companies of women and boys. He is nimble in entering unlawful beds, he is incestuous, he is an adulterer, he is a mere skip-jack, spending all his means among scandalous loose people: and he is in nothing careful of the things of this life or of anything religious."

Florian brightened. "That also sounds quite logical, —in the main,—for you describe the ways of the best-thought-of persons since the old King's death. And one of course endeavors not to offend against the notions of one's neighbors by seeming a despiser of accepted modes. Yet I must protest to you, my friend, you err in the article of religion—"

"Oh, if you come hither to dispute about religion," said the porter, "the priests of Llaw Gyffes will attend to you. They love converting people from religious errors, bless you, with their wild horses and their red-hot irons. But, for one, I never argue about religion. You conceive, sir, there is an entire chapter devoted to the subject, in the writing we were just talking over: and I have read that chapter. So I say nothing about religion. I like a bit of fun, myself: but when you find it there, of all places, and on that scale—" Again the dejected porter sighed. "However, I shall say no more. Instead, with your permission, Messire de Puysange, I shall just step in, and send up your news about the enchantment."

This much the porter did; and Florian was left alone to amuse himself by looking about. Through the gateway he saw into a court paved with cobblestones. Upon each side of the gate was an octagonal granite tower with iron-barred windows: each tower was three stories in height, and the battlements were coped with some sort of rather bright red stone.

Then Florian, for lack of other diversions, turned and looked idly down the valley, toward Poictesme. There he saw something distinctly odd. A mile-long bridge was flung across the west, and over it passed figures. First came the appearance of a bear waddling upon his hind legs, followed by an ape, and then by a huddled creature with long legs. Florian saw also an unclothed woman, who danced as she went: over her head fluttered a bird, and by means of a chain she haled after her a sedentarily disposed pig. An old man followed her, dressed in faded blue, and he carried upon his arm a basket. Last came a shaggy beast, resembling a dog, and barking, it seemed, at all.

These figures were like clouds in their station and in their indeterminable coloring and vague outline, but their moving was not like the drifting of clouds: it was the walking of living creatures. Florian for an instant wondered as to the nature and the business of these beings that were passing over and away from Poictesme. He shrugged. He believed the matter to be no concern of one whose interests overhead were all in the efficient hands of Holy Hoprig.

VII

Adjustments of the Resurrected

THEY brought Florian to Helmas the Deep-Minded, where the King sat on a daïs with his Queen Pressina. The King was stately in scarlet and ermine: his nose too was red, and to his crown was affixed the Zhar-Ptitza's silvery feather. Florian found his appearance far more companionable than was that of the fat Queen (one of the water folk), whose skin was faintly blue, and whose hair was undeniably green, and whose little mouth seemed lost and discontented in her broad face.

Beside them, but not upon the dark red daïs, sat the high-priest of Llaw Gyffes, a fine looking and benevolent prelate, in white robes edged with a purple pattern of quaint intricacies: he wore a wreath of mistletoe about his broad forehead; and around and above this played a pulsing radiancy.

To these persons Florian told what had happened. When he had ended, the Queen said she had never heard of such a thing in her life, that it was precisely what she had predicted time and again, and that now Helmas could see for himself what came of spoiling Mélusine, and letting her have her own way about everything. The wise King answered nothing whatever.

But the high-priest of Llaw Gyffes asked, "And how did you lift this strong enchantment?"

"Monsieur, I removed it by the logical method of killing the seven monsters who were its strength and symbol. That they are all quite dead you can see for

yourself,—if I may make so bold as to employ her
Majesty's striking phrase—by counting the assortment
of heads which I fetched hither with me."

"Yes, to be sure," the priest admitted. "Seven is
seven the world over: everywhere it is a number of
mystic potency. It follows that seven severed heads
must predicate seven corpses; and such proofs are indisputable, as far as they go—"

Still, he seemed troubled in his mind.

Then Helmas, the wise King, said, "It is my opinion
that the one way to encounter the unalterable is to do
nothing about it."

"Yes," answered his wife, "and much that will help
matters!"

"Nothing that any man does anywhere, my dear,"
said the wise King, "helps matters. All matters are
controlled by fate and chance, and these help themselves unrestrainedly, to whatever they have need of.
These two it is that have taken from me a lordship that
had not its like in the known world, and have made
the palaces that we used to be feasting in, it still seems
only yesterday, just little piles of rubbish, and they
have puffed out my famousness the way that when any
man gets impudent a widow does a lamp. These two it
is that leave me nothing but this castle and this crevice
in the hills where the old time yet lingers. And I accept
their sending, because there is no armor against it, but
I shall keep my dignity by not letting even fate and
chance upset me with their playfulness. Here the old
time shall be as it has always been, and here I shall
continue to do what was expected of me yesterday.
And about other concerns I shall not bother, but I
shall leave everything, excepting only my self-respect,
to fate and chance. And I think that Hoprig will agree
with me it is the way a wise man ought to be acting."

"Hoprig!" reflected Florian, looking at the halo.

"But what the devil is my patron saint doing at Brunbelois disguised as the high-priest of Llaw Gyffes?"

"I am thinking over some other matters," replied Hoprig, to the King, "and it is in my thinking that nobody could manage to kill so many monsters, and to release us from our long sleeping, unless he was a sorcerer. So Messire de Puysange must be a sorcerer, and that is very awkward, with our torture-chamber all out of repair——"

"Ah, monsieur," said Florian, reproachfully, "and are these quite charitable notions for a saint to be fostering? And, oh, monsieur, is it quite fair for you to have been sleeping here this unconscionable while, when you were supposed to be in heaven attending to the remission of people's sins?"

Hoprig replied: "What choice had I or anybody else except to sleep under the Nis magic? For the rest, I do not presume to say what a saint might or might not think of the affair, because in our worship of Llaw Gyffes of the Steady Hand——"

"But I, monsieur, was referring to a most famous saint of the Christian church, which has for some while counted the Dukes of Puysange among its communicants, and is now our best-thought-of form of worship."

"Oh, the Christians! Yes, I have heard of them. Indeed I now remember very well how Ork and Horrig came into these parts preaching everywhere the remarkable fancies of that sect until I discouraged them in the way which seemed most salutary."

Florian could make nothing of this. He said,——

"But how could you, of all persons, have discouraged the spreading of Christianity?"

"I discouraged them with axes," the Saint replied, "and with thumbscrews, and with burning them at the stake. For it really does not pay to be subtle in dealing with people of that class: and you have to base your appeal to their better nature upon quite obvious arguments."

"My faith, then, how it came about I cannot say, Monsieur Hoprig; but for hundreds upon hundreds of years you have been a Christian saint."

"Dear me!" the Saint observed, "so that must be the explanation of this shining all around my head. I noticed it of course. Still, I have been troubled before by indigestion, and our minds have been rather preëmpted since we woke up— But, dear me, now, I am astounded, and I know not what to say. I do say, though, that this is quite extraordinary news for you to be bringing a well-thought-of high-priest of Llaw Gyffes."

"Nevertheless, monsieur, for all that you have never been anything but a high-priest of the heathen, and a persecutor of the true faith, I can assure you that you have, somehow, been canonized. And I am afraid that during the long while you have been asleep your actions must have been woefully misrepresented. Monsieur," said Florian, hopefully, "at least, though, was it not true about your being in the barrel?"

"Why, but how could ever you," the Saint marveled, "have heard about that rain-barrel? The incident, in any case, has been made far too much of. You conceive, it was merely that the man came home most unexpectedly; and, since all husbands are at times and in some circumstances so unreasonable—"

"Ah, monsieur," said Florian, shaking his head, "I am afraid you do not speak of quite the barrel which is in your legend."

"So I have a legend! Why, how delightful! But come," said the Saint, abeam with honest pleasure, and with his halo twinkling merrily, "come, be communicative; be copious, and tell me all about myself."

Then Florian told Hoprig of how, after Hoprig's supposed death, miracles had been worked at Hoprig's putative tomb, near Gol, and how this legend and that legend had grown up around his memory, and how these things had led to Hoprig's being canonized. And Florian alluded, also, with perfect tact but a little ruefully, to those fine donations he had been giving, year in and year out, to the Church of Holy Hoprig, under the impression that all the while the Saint had been, instead of snoring at Brunbelois, looking out for Florian's interests in heaven. And Hoprig now seemed rather pensive, and he inquired more particularly about his tomb.

"I shall take this," the Saint said, at last, "to be the fit reward of my tender-heartedness. The tomb near Gol of which you tell me is the tomb in which I buried that Horrig about whom I was just talking, after we had settled our difference of opinion as to some points of theology. Ork was so widely scattered that any formal interment was quite out of the question. My priests are dear, well-meaning fellows. Still, you conceive, they are conscientious, and they enter with such zeal into the performance of any manifest if painful duty—"

Florian said: "They exhibited the archetypal zeal becoming to the ministers of an established church in the defense of their vested rights. They were, with primitive inadequacy, groping toward the methods of our Holy Inquisition and of civilized prelates everywhere—"

"—So they were quite tired out when we passed on to Horrig's case. I do not deny that I was perhaps unduly lenient about Horrig. It was the general opinion that, tired as we were, this blasphemer against the religious principles of our fathers ought to be burned at the stake, and have his ashes scattered to the winds. But I was merciful. I had eaten an extremely light breakfast. So I merely had him broken on the wheel and decapitated, and we got through our morning's work, after all, without delaying dinner: and I gave him a very nice tomb indeed, with his name on it in capital letters. Dear me!" observed Holy Hoprig, with a marked increase of his benevolent smile, "but how drolly things fall out! If the name had not been in capital letters, now, I would probably never have been wearing this halo which surprised me so this morning when I went to brush my hair—"

"But what," said the Queen, "has happened to make things fall out so drolly, though it is really quite becoming, with your fine, high complexion?"

"Why, madame," replied the Saint, "I take it that, with the passage of years, the tail of the first R in the poor dear fellow's name was somewhat worn away. So, when such miracles began to occur at his tomb as customarily emanate from the tombs of martyrs to any faith which later is taken up by really nice people, here were tangible and exact proofs, to the letter, of the holiness of Hoprig. In consequence, this Christian church has naturally canonized me."

"That was quite civil of them of course, if this is considered the best-thought-of church. But, still," the Queen said, doubtfully, "the miracles must have meant that noisy and fearfully vulgar Horrig was right, and you were wrong."

"Certainly, madame, it would seem so, as a matter of purely academic interest. For now that his church is so well-thought-of everywhere and has canonized me, I must of course turn Christian, if only to show my appreciation of the compliment. So the church is not lessened in membership and there is no possible harm done."

"But in that case, although in any social way, of course, yet, even so, he is gone now, poor fellow, and it does not at all alter the fact that it was Horrig who was meant to have been made a saint of."

"Now I, madame, for one, cherish humility too much to dare assert any such thing. For the ways of

Providence are proverbially inscrutable: and it may well be that the abrasion of the tail of that R was also, in its quiet way, a direct intervention of Heaven to reward my mercifulness in according Horrig a comparatively pleasant martyrdom."

"Yes, but it was he, after all, who had to put up with that martyrdom, on a dreadfully depressing rainy morning, too, I remember, whereas you get sainthood out of the affair without putting up with anything."

"Do I not have to put up with this halo? How can I now hope to go anywhere after dark without being observed? Ah, no, madame, I greatly fear this canonization will cost me a host of friends by adorning my visits with such conspicuous publicity. Nevertheless, I do not complain. Instead, I philosophically recognize that well-bred women must avoid all ostentation, and that the ways of Providence are inscrutable."

"That is quite true," observed King Helmas, at this point, "and I think that nothing is to be gained by you two discussing these ways any more. The poets and the philosophers in every place have for a long while now had a heaviness in their minds about Providence, and the friendly advice which they have been giving to Providence is not yet all acted upon. So let us leave Providence to look out for itself, the way we would if Providence had wisdom teeth. And let us turn to other matters, and to hearing what reward is asked by the champion who has rescued us from our long sleeping."

"I too," replied Florian, "if I may make so bold as to borrow the phrase used by your Majesty just now —that phrase by which I was immeasurably impressed, that phrase which still remains to me a vocalization of supreme wisdom in terms so apt and striking—"

"Wisdom," said the King, "was miraculously bestowed upon me a great while ago as a free gift, which I have done nothing to earn and deserve no credit for not having been able to avoid. And my way of talking, and using similes and syntax,—along with phraseology and monostiches and aposiopesis and such-like things, —is another gift, also, which I employ without really noticing the astonishment and admiration of my hearers. So do you not talk so much, but come to the point."

"I too, then, in your Majesty's transcendent phrase, shall do what was expected of me yesterday. I ask the hand of the King's daughter in marriage."

"That is customary," wise Helmas said, with approval, "and you show a very fine sense of courtesy in adhering to our perhaps old-fashioned ways. Let the lord of Puysange be taken to his betrothed."

VIII

At the Top of the World

OU will find her," they had said, "yonder,"—and, pointing westerly, had left him. So Florian went unaccompanied through the long pergola overgrown with grapevines, toward the lone figure at the end of this tunnel of rustling greenness and sweet odors. A woman waited there, in an eight-sided summer-house, builded of widely spaced lattice-work that was hidden by vines. Through these vines you could see on every side the fluttering bright gardens of Brunbelois, but no living creature. This woman and Florian were alone in what was not unlike a lovely cage of vines. Florian seemed troubled. It was apparent that he knew this woman.

"I am flesh and blood," the woman said,—"as you may remember."

"Indeed, I have been singularly fortunate—But upon reflection, I retract the adverb. I have been marvelously fortunate; and I have no desire to forget it."

"She also, the girl yonder, is flesh and blood. You will be knowing that before long."

Florian looked at this woman for some while. "Perhaps that is true. I think it is not true. I have faith in the love which has endured since I was but a child. If that fails me, I must die. And I shall die willingly."

He bowed low to this woman, and he passed on, through the summer-house, and out into the open air. He came thus to a wall, only breast high, and opened the gate which was there, and so went on in full sunlight, ascending a steepish incline that was overgrown with coarse grass and with much white clover. Thus Florian came to the unforgotten princess and to that beauty which he in childhood had, howsoever briefly, seen. There was in this bright and windy place, which smelled so pleasantly of warm grass, nothing except a low marble bench without back or carving. No trees nor any bushes grew here: nothing veiled this place from the sun. Upon this sunlit mountain-top was only the bench, and upon the bench sat Melior, waiting.

She waited—there was the miracle,—for Florian de Puysange.

Behind and somewhat below Florian were the turrets and banners of Brunbelois, a place now disenchanted, but a fair place wherein the old time yet lingered. Before him the bare hillside sank sheer and unbroken, to the far-off tree-tops of Acaire: and beyond leagues of foliage you could even see, not a great number of miles away, but quite two miles below you, the open country of Poictesme, which you saw not as anything real and tangible but as a hazed blending of purples and of all the shades that green may have in heaven. Florian seemed to stand at the top of the world: and with him, high as his heart, stood Melior. . . .

And it was a queer thing that he, who always noticed people's clothes, and who tended to be very critical about apparel, could never afterward, in thinking about this extraordinary morning, recollect one color which Melior wore. He remembered only a sense of many interwoven brilliancies, as if the brightness of the summer sea, and of the clouds of sunset, and of all the stars, were blended here to veil this woman's body. She went appareled with the splendor of a queen of the old days, she who was the most beautiful of women that have lived in any day. For, if so far as went her body, one could think dazedly of analogues, nowhere was there anything so bright and lovely as was this woman's countenance. And it was to the end that he might see the face of Melior raised now to him, he knew, that Florian was born. All living had been the prologue to this instant: God had made the world in order that Florian might stand here, with Melior, at the top of the world.

And it seemed to Florian that his indiscretions in the way of removing people from this dear world, and of excursions into strange beds, and of failures to attend mass regularly, had become alienate to the man who waited before Melior. All that was over and done with: he had climbed past all that in his ascent to this bright and windy place. Here, in this inconceivably high place, was the loveliness seen once and never forgotten utterly, the loveliness which had made seem very cheap and futile the things that other men wanted. Now this loveliness was, for the asking, his: and Florian found his composure almost shaken, he suspected that the bearing suitable to a Duke of Puysange was touched with unbecoming ardors. Logic did not climb so high as he had climbed.

Besides, it might be, he had climbed too near to heaven. For nothing veiled this unimaginably high place from heaven; and God, seeing him thus plainly, would be envious. That was the thought which Florian put hastily out of mind. . . .

He parted his lips once or twice. This was, he joyously reflected, quite ridiculous. A woman waited: and Florian de Puysange could not speak. Then words came, with a sort of sobbing.

"My princess, there was a child who viewed you once in your long sleeping. The child's heart moved with desires which did not know their aim. It is not that child who comes to you."

"No, but a very gallant champion," she replied, "to whom we all owe our lives."

He had raised a deprecating hand. It was trembling. And her face seemed only a blurred shining, for in his eyes were tears. It must be, Florian reflected, because of the wind: but he did not believe this, nor need we.

"Princess, will you entrust to me, such as I am, the life I have repurchased for you? I dare make no large promises, in the teeth of a disastrously tenacious memory. Yet, there is no part in me but worships you, I have no desire in life save toward you. There has never been in all my life any real desire save that which strove toward you."

"Oh, but, Messire Florian," the girl replied, "of course I will be your wife if you desire it."

He raised now both his hands a little toward her. She had not drawn back. He did not know whether ths was joy or terror which possessed him: but it possessed him utterly. His heart was shaking in him, with an insane and ruthless pounding. He thought his head kept time to this pounding, and was joggling like the head of a palsied old man. He knew his finger-tips to be visited by tiny and inexplicable vibrations.

"If only I could die now—!" was in his mind. "Now, at this instant! And what a thought for me to be having now!"

Instead, he now touched his disenchanted princess. Yet their two bodies seemed not to touch, and not to have moved as flesh that is pulled by muscles. They seemed to have merged, effortlessly and without volition, into one body.

In fine, he kissed her. So was the affair concluded.

IX
Misgivings of a Beginning Saint

WHAT Florian remembered, afterward, about Brunbelois seemed rather inconsequential. It was, to begin with, a high place, a remarkably high place. In the heart of the Forest of Acaire, arose a mountain with three peaks, of which the middle and lowest was cleared ground. Here stood the castle of Brunbelois, beside a lake, a lake that was fed by springs from the bottom, and had no tributaries and no outlet. Forests thus rose about you everywhere except in the west, where you looked down and yet further down, over the descending tree-tops of Acaire, and could see beyond these the open country of Poictesme.

Now in this exalted and cleared space wherein stood Brunbelois, there was nothing between you and the sky. You were continually noting such a hackneyed matter as the sky. You saw it no longer as a dome, but as, quite obviously now, an interminable reach of space. You saw the huge clouds passing in this hollowness, each inconceivably detached and separate in the while that one cloud passed tranquilly above and behind the other, sometimes at right angles, sometimes traveling in just the opposite direction. It troubled you to have nothing between you and a space that afforded room for all those currents of air to move about in, so freely, so utterly without any obstruction. It made Puysange seem small. And at night the stars also no longer appeared tidily affixed to the sky, as they appeared to be when viewed from Bellegarde or Paris: the stars seemed larger here, more meltingly luminous, and they glowed each in visible isolation, with all that space behind them. It had not ever before occurred to Florian that the sky could be terrible: and he began somewhat to understand the notions of the gray-haired porter who had watched this sky from Brunbelois, night after night, alone.

And Florian remembered Brunbelois as being a silvery and rustling place. A continuous wind seemed to come up from the west. The forests rising about you everywhere except in the west were never still, you saw all day the gray underside of the leaves twinkling restlessly, and you heard always their varying but incessant murmur. And small clouds too were always passing, borne by this incessant wind, very close to you, drifting through the porches of the castle, trailing pallidly over the grass, and veiling your feet sometimes, so that you stood knee-deep in a cloud: and the sunlight was silvery rather than golden. And under this gentle but perpetual wind the broad lake glittered ceaselessly with silver sparklings.

Moreover, the grass here was thick with large white blossoms, which grew singly upon short stalks without any leaves, and these white flowers nodded in an unending conference. They loaned the very ground here an unstable silveriness, for these flowers were not ever motionless. Somtimes they seemed to nod in sleepy mutual assent, sometimes the wind, in strengthening, would provoke them to the appearance of expressing diminutively vigorous indignation. And humming-birds were continually flashing about: these were too small for you to perceive their coloring, they went merely as gleams. And white butterflies fluttered everywhither as if in an abstracted light reconnoitering for what they could not find. And you were always seeing large birds high in the air, drifting and wheeling, as it seemed, in an endless searching for what they never found.

So Florian remembered, afterward, in the main, the highness and the silveriness and the instability of the place that he now went about exultingly with nothing left to wish for. He hardly remembered, afterward, what he and Melior did or talked of, during the days wherein Brunbelois prepared for their wedding: time and events, and people too, seemed to pass like bright shining vapors; all living swam in a haze of happiness. Florian now thought little of logic, he thought nothing of precedent; he thrust aside the implications of his depressing discovery as to his patron saint: he stayed in everything light-headedly bewildered through hourly contemplation of that unflawed loveliness which he had for a quarter of a century desired. He was contented now; he went unutterably contented by that beauty which he in childhood had, howsoever briefly, seen, and which nothing had since then availed ever quite to put out of his mind. He could not, really, think about anything else. He cared about nothing else.

Still, even now, he kept some habit of circumspection; no man should look to be utterly naïf about his fifth wife. So when St. Hoprig contrived to talk in private with Melior, down by the lake's border, Florian, for profoundly logical reasons, had followed Hoprig. Florian, for the same reasons, stood behind the hedge and listened.

"It is right that you should marry the champion who rescued us all," said the voice of Hoprig, "for rules ought to be respected. But I am still of the opinion that nobody could have disposed of so many monsters without being an adept at sorcery."

"Why, then, it seems to me that we ought to be very grateful for the sorcery by which we profit," said the sweet voice of Melior. "For, as I so often think—"

"As goes the past, perhaps. The future is another matter. It is most widely another matter, for us two in particular."

"You mean that as his wife I must counsel my husband to avoid all evil courses—"

"Yes, of course, I mean that. Your duty is plain enough, since a wife's functions are terrestrial. But I, madame! I am, it appears, this young man's patron saint, and upon his behavior depends my heavenly credit. You will readily conceive I thus have especial reason to worry over the possibility that Messire de Puysange may be addicted to diabolic practices."

"Is it certain, my poor Hoprig, that you are actually a Christian saint? For, really, when one comes to think—!"

"There seems no doubt of it. I have tried a few miracles in private, and they come off as easily as old sandals. It appears that, now I am a saint, I enjoy, by approved precedents, all thaumaturgic powers, with especial proficiency in blasting, cursing and smiting my opponents with terrible afflictions; and have moreover the gift of tongues, of vision and of prophecy, and the power of expelling demons, of healing the sick, and of raising the dead. The situation is extraordinary, and I know not what to do with so many talents. Nor can anybody tell me here. In consequence, I must go down into the modern world of which Messire de Puysange brings such remarkable reports, and there I can instruct myself as to the requirements of my new dignity."

"So you will leave Brunbelois with us, I suppose, and then we shall all—"

"I do not say that: I do not promise you my company. Probably I shall establish a hermitage somewhere, once I have seen something of this later world, and shall live in that hermitage as becomes a Christian saint. Here, you conceive, everyone knows me too well. Quite apart from the conduct of my private affairs,—in which I could not anticipate that sanctity might be looked for,—people would be remembering how I preached against these Christian doctrines, exposed them by every rule of logic, and exterminated their upholders. Such memories would result in a depressing atmosphere of merriment. No saint could thrive in such an atmosphere. But down yonder, I daresay, I might manage tolerably well."

"I hope you will let depraved women alone," said the voice of Melior, "because, as you ought with proper shame to remember—"

"My princess, let us not over-rashly sneer at depraved women. They very often have good hearts, they have attested their philanthropy in repeated instances, and I have noticed that the deeper our research into their private affairs, the more amiable we are apt to find their conduct. In any case, as touches myself, a saint is above all carnal stains and, I believe, diseases also. But it was about other matters I wished to speak with you. I am, I repeat, suspicious of this future husband of yours. Sorcerers have an ill way with their wives, and deplorable habits with their children; and your condition, in view of your fine health and youth, may soon be delicate. I shall ask for a revelation upon these points. Whatever impends, though, my princess, Holy Hoprig will always be at hand to watch over you both."

"So you will establish your hermitage at Bellegarde? For in that event—"

"Again, madame, you go too fast. I do not know about that either. In the environs of Bellegarde, they tell me, is a church devoted to my worship, and Messire de Puysange considers—inexplicably, I think,— that it might unsettle the faith of my postulants to have me appear among them. It seems more to the point that this Bellegarde is a retired place in the provinces, with no gaming parlors, and, Messire de Puysange assures me, but one respectable brothel—"

"Then Bellegarde would not suit you—"

"No, of course not: for I would find ampler opportunities to put down the wicked, and to implant good seed, in large cities, which are proverbially the haunts of vice. In any case, do you take this ring. It was presented to me as a token of not unearned esteem and admiration, by a lady who had hitherto found men contemptible: and at my request—tendered somewhat hastily, but to the proper authorities,—this ring has been endowed with salutary virtues. The one trait of the holy ring which concerns us just now is its recently acquired habit of giving due warning whenever danger threatens its wearer. Dear me, now, how complete would have been my relaxation if only in my pagan days I had possessed such a talisman to put on whenever I undressed for bed! In any case, should the ring change, then do you invoke me."

"And you will come with your miracles and your blightings and your blastings! My poor Hoprig, I think you do Messire de Puysange a great wrong, but I will keep the ring, for all that. Because, while you may be utterly mistaken, and no doubt hope you are as much as I do, still, the ring is very handsome: and, besides, as I so often think—"

"Do not be telling me your thoughts just now," replied the voice of the Saint, "for I can hear the bugle calling us to supper. There is also another precaution I would recommend, a precaution that I will explain to you this evening, after we have eaten and drunk," said Hoprig, as they went away together.

Then Florian, after waiting a discreet while, came from behind the hedge. Florian looked rather thoughtful as he too walked toward the castle.

Sunset was approaching. The entire heavens, not

merely the west, had taken on a rose-colored glare. Unbelievably white clouds were passing very rapidly, overhead but not far-off, like scurrying trails of swan's down and blown powder puffs. The air was remarkably cool, with rain in it. The diffused radiancy of this surprising sunset loaned the graveled walkway before him a pink hue: the lawns about him, where the grass was everywhere intermingled with white blossoms, had, in this roseate glowing which flooded all, assumed a coldly livid tinge. To Florian's left hand, piled clouds were peering over the mountain like monstrous judges, in tall powdered wigs, appraising the case against someone in Florian's neighborhood.

He shrugged, but his look of thoughtfulness remained. It was distinctly upsetting to have one's patron saint, in place of contriving absolution for the past,—a function which that recreant Hoprig had never, after all, attended to,—now absolutely planning mischief for the future.

X

Who Feasted at Brunbelois

 LORIAN had been married so often that he had some claim to be considered a connoisseur of weddings: and never, he protested, had assembled to see him married a more delightful company than the revelers who came from every part of Acaire now that the magic was lifted from these woods.

Acaire was old, it had been a forest since there was a forest anywhere: and all its denizens came now to do honor to the champion who had released them from their long sleeping. The elves came, in their blue low-crowned hats; the gnomes, in red woolen clothes; and the kobolds, in brown coats that were covered with chips and sawdust. The dryads and other tree spirits of course went verdantly appareled: and after these came fauns with pointed furry ears, and the nixies with green teeth and very beautiful flaxen hair, and the duergar, whose loosely swinging arms touched the ground when they walked, and the queer little rakhna, who were white and semi-transparent like jelly, and the Bush Gods that were in Acaire the oldest of living creatures and had quite outlived their divinity. From all times and all mythologies they came, and they made a tremendous to-do over Florian and over his fine exploits, which had rescued them from yet more centuries of sleeping under Mélusine's enchantment.

He bore his honors modestly. But Florian delighted to talk with these guests, who came of such famous old families: and they told him strange tales of yesterday and of the days before yesterday, and it seemed to him that many of these stories were not quite logical. Few probabilities thrived at Brunbelois. Meanwhile the Elf Dwarfs danced for him, pouring libations from the dew pools; the Strömkarl left its waterfall in the forest, to play very sweetly for Florian upon the golden harp whose earlier music had been more dangerous to hear; and the Korrid brought him tribute in the form of a purse containing hair and a pair of scissors. And it was all profoundly delightful.

"I approve of the high place," said Florian, upon the morning of his marriage: "for here I seem to go about a more heroic and more splendid world than I had hoped ever to inhabit."

"Then, why," asked Helmas, "do you not remain at Brunbelois, instead of carrying off my daughter to live in that low sort of place down yonder? Why do you two not stay at Brunbelois, and be the King and Queen here after I am gone?"

Florian looked down from the porch where they were waiting the while that Queen Pressina finished dressing. From this porch Florian could see a part of the modern world, very far beneath them. He saw the forests lying like dark flung-by scarves upon the paler green of cleared fields; he saw the rivers as narrow shinings. In one place, very far beneath them, a thunderstorm was passing like—of all things, on this blissful day,—a drifting bride's-veil. Florian saw it twinkle with a yellow glow, then it was again a floating white long veil. And everywhere the lands beneath him bathed in graduations of vaporous indistinction. Poictesme seemed woven of blue smokes and of green mists. It afforded no sharp outline anywhere as his gazing passed outward toward the horizon. And there all melted bafflingly into a pearl-colored sky: the eye might not judge where, earth ending, heaven began in that bright and placid radiancy.

It was droll to see this familiar, tedious, quite commonplace Poictesme as a land so lovely, when you knew what sort of men and women were strutting and floundering through what sort of living down there. It would be pleasant to remain here at high Brunbelois, and to be a king of the exalted old time that lingered here and nowhere else in all the world. But Florian remembered his bargain with brown Janicot, and Florian knew that in this high place he could not keep faith with Janicot: and it was as if with the brightness of Florian's day-dreaming already mingled the shining of the sword with which Florian was to carry out his part of the bargain. Flamberge awaited him somewhere in those prosaic lowlands of 1723, down yonder.

Therefore, as became a man of honor, Florian said, resolutely: "No, your majesty, my kingdom may not be of this world. For my duty lies yonder in that other world, wherein I at least shall yet have many months of happiness before that happens which must happen."

"So you are counting upon many months of happiness," the King observed. "Your frame of mind, my son-in-law, is so thoroughly what it should be that to me it is rather touching."

"A pest! And may one ask just what, exactly, moves your majesty toward sadness!"

"I am moved by the reflection that there is no girl anywhere but has in her much of her mother, messire my son-in-law. However, my dear wife is already dressed, I perceive, and is waiting for us, after having detained us hardly two hours. So let us be getting to the temple."

"Very willingly!" said Florian.

He wondered a little at the blindness of fathers, but he was unutterably content. And straightway he and Melior were married, in the queer underground temple of the Peohtes, according to the marriage rites of Llaw Gyffes.

Melior that morning wore upon her lovely head a wreath of thistles, and about her middle a remarkable garment of burnished steel fastened with a small padlock: in her hand she carried a distaff, flax and a spindle. And the marriage ceremony of the Peohtes, while new to Florian, proved delightfully simple.

First Melior and Florian were given an egg and quince pear: he handed her the fruit, which she ate, and the seeds of which she spat out; he took from her the egg and broke it. Holy Hoprig, who had tendered his resignation as the high-priest of Llaw Gyffes, but whose successor had not yet been appointed, then asked the bridegroom a whispered question.

Florian was astonished, and showed it. But he answered, without comment,—

"Well, let us say, nine times."

Hoprig divided a cake into nine slices, and placed these upon the altar. Afterward Hoprig cut the throat of a white hen, and put a little of its blood upon the feet of Melior and Florian. The trumpets sounded then, as King Helmas came forward, and gave Florian a small key.

Part Two

The End
of Light Winning

————◂◆▸————

"En femme, comme en tout, je veux suivre ma
    mode. . . .
Et j'ay beny le Ciel d'avoir trouvé mon faict,
Pour me faire une femme au gré de mon souhait."

XI
Problems of Beauty

T was conceded even by the younger and most charming ladies of the neighborhood that the new Duchess of Puysange was quite good looking. The gentlemen of Poictesme appeared, literally, to be dazzled by any prolonged consideration of Melior's loveliness: otherwise, as Florian soon noted, there was no logical accounting for the discrepancy in their encomia. Enraptured pæans upon her eyes, for example, he found to differ amazingly and utterly in regard to such an important factor as the color of these eyes. This was, at mildest, a circumstance provocative of curiosity.

Florian therefore listened more attentively to what people said about his fifth wife; and he thus discovered that his fellows' ecstasies over Melior's hair and shape and complexion were not a whit less inconsistent. These envious babblers were at one in acclaiming as flawless the beauty which he had intrepidly fetched down from the high place: yet when their compliments touched any single feature of this loveliness these gentlemen seemed not to be talking about the same woman. Either her perfection actually did dazzle men so that they were bewilderedly aware of much such a beguiling and intoxicating brightness as Florian, on looking back, suspected Melior to have been in his own eyes before he married her, or, else, the appearance of this daughter of the Léshy was not to all persons the same. Well, this was queer: but it was not im-

73

portant. Florian at least was in no doubt as to his wife's appearance or as to his right to glory in it.

So Florian tended to let this riddle pass unchallenged, and to quarrel with nothing, for Florian was very happy.

He could not have said when or why awoke the teasing question if, after all, this happiness was greater than or different from that which he had got of Aurélie or Hortense or Marianne or Carola? Being married to a comparative stranger was, as always, pleasant; it was, in act, delightful: but you had expected, none the less, of the love which had miraculously triumphed over time and all natural laws some sharper tang of bliss than ordinarily flavored your honeymoons. Still, at thirty-five, you were logical about the usual turning-out of expectations. And you were content: and Melior was beautiful; and among the local nobility this new Duchess of Puysange had made friends everywhere, and she was everywhere admired, howsoever puzzlingly all male persons seemed to word their praise of her loveliness.

The newly married pair had journeyed uneventfully from Brunbelois to Florian's home. Those mute and hairy servants of Janicot had brought Melior's trunks in their cart; and St. Hoprig too came with them through Acaire, but no further. Florian had at last persuaded him of how untactful it would be for Hoprig to disrupt a simple and high-hearted faith that had thrived for so many hundred years, by appearing at Bellegarde in person. Florian had pointed out the attendant awkwardnesses, for the fetich no less than for the devotees. And Hoprig, upon reflection, had conceded that for a saint in the prime of life there were advantages in traveling incognito.

So the holy man left them at the edge of the forest. "We shall meet again, my children," the Saint had said, with a smile, just as he vanished liked a breaking bubble. It seemed to Florian that his heavenly patron had become a little ostentatious with miracles, but Florian voiced no criticism. Still, he considered the evanishment of the two hairy persons and their monstrous goats, an evanishment quite privately conducted in the stable to which they had withdrawn after uncarting Melior's trunks, to be in much better taste.

But Florian picked no open fault with Hoprig nor with anyone, for Florian was content enough just now. He began to see that his notions about Melior had been a trifle extravagant, that the strange loveliness which he had been adoring since boyhood was worn by a creature whose brilliance was of the body rather than of the intellect: however, he had not married her in order to discuss philosophy; and, with practice, it was easy enough to pretend to listen without really hearing her.

All this was less worrying, less imminent, than the trouble he seemed in every likelihood about to have with his brother, on account of Raoul's damnable wife. For Madame Marguerite de Puysange, as Florian now heard, was infuriated by his failure to appear at Storis-ende upon the twentieth of July, the day upon which he had been due to marry her sister: nor by learning that he had married somebody else was the unconscionable virago soothed. She considered a monstrous affront had been put upon them all, a deduction which Florian granted to be truly drawn, if that mattered. What certainly mattered was that the lean woman had no living male relatives. She would be at her husband to avenge this affront by killing Florian: and dear, plastic, good-natured Raoul so hated to deny anybody anything that the result of her coaxing and tears and nagging would probably be a decided nuisance. . . .

"That ring with the three diamonds in it," Florian had said, "is deplorably old-fashioned—"

"Yes, I suppose it is, sweetheart: but it was given me

by a dear friend, and you know the sort of things they pick out, and, besides, I like to have it keeping me in mind of how ridiculously the best-meaning people may be mistaken sometimes," his Melior had answered,—very happily, and nuzzling a very wonderfully soft cheek against his cheek.

So he had let the matter stand. . . .

It was a nuisance, too, this news which Florian had received as to the great Cardinal Dubois, whom Florian had promised—as he regretted now to remember, in carelessly loose terms,—to offer as a Christmas present to Janicot. It appeared that during Florian's stay at Brunbelois the over-gallant Cardinal had been compelled to submit to an operation which deprived him of two cherished possessions and shortly afterward of his life. His death was a real grief to Florian, not as in itself any loss, but because, with Dubois interred at St. Roch, the greatest man living in France when Christmas came would be the Duc d'Orléans.

Florian had long been fond of Philippe d'Orléans, and Florian loathed the thought of making a present of his friend's life to a comparatively slight and ambiguous acquaintance like Janicot. There seemed no way out of it, however, for Florian had in this matter given his word. But he regretted deeply that he had thus recklessly promised the greatest man in the kingdom instead of specifically confining himself to that selfish Dubois, who could without real self-denial have lived until December, and who could so easily have furthered everybody's well-being by restricting his amours to ladies of such known piety and wholesomeness and social position as made them appropriate playfellows for a high prince of the Church.

But all this was spilt milk. What it came to in the upshot was that Florian, through his infatuation for Melior, was already in a fair way to lose his most intimate and powerful friend and his only legitimate brother. It was a nuisance, for Florian disliked annoying either one of them, and thus to be burdened with the need of bereaving yourself of both appeared a positive imposition. But we cannot have all things as we prefer them in this world, his common-sense assured him: and, in the main, as has been said, the incidental disappointments, now that he had attained his life's desire, were tepid and not really very deep.

For Melior was beautiful; after months of intimacy and fond research he could find no flaw in her beauty: and in other respects she proved to be as acceptable a wife as any of his own marrying that he had ever had. If she was not always reasonable, if sometimes indeed she seemed obtuse, and if she nagged a little now and then, it was, after all, what past experience had led him to expect alike in marriage and liaisons. The rapture which he had known at first sight of her, the rapture of the mountain-top, was not, he assured himself, a delusion of which he had ever expected permanence. . . .

"But this remarkably carved staff, my darling—?"

"Oh, it was one of my sister Mélusine's old things. I would not be in the least surprised if it were magical— And while we are speaking about sisters, Florian, I do wish that black-faced one of yours would not look at me so hard and then shrug, because she has done it twice, in quite a personal way—"

"Marie-Claire is a strange woman, my pet."

But that fretted him. He knew so well why Marie-Claire had shrugged. . . .

No, he had never, really, expected the rapture of the mountain-top to be permanent. Besides, he need not expect permanency of Melior. It was sad, of course, that when she had borne him a child, the child must be disposed of, and the mother must vanish, in accordance with Florian's agreement with Janicot. But there was always some such condition attached to marriage between a mortal and any of the Léshy, or some abstention set like a trap whereinto the unwary mortal was sure to flounder, and so lose the more than mortal helpmate. The union must always, in one way or another, prove transitory, as was shown by the sad history of the matrimonial ventures of Melior's own sister, and of the knight Helias, and by many other honorable old precedents.

And Florian now began to see that if the Melior whom he had adored since boyhood were thus lost to him in the fulltide of their love and happiness,—for these were still at fulltide, he here assured himself,—then he would retain only pleasant and heartbreaking and highly desirable memories. A great love such as his for his present wife ought, by all the dictates of good taste, to end tragically: to have it dwindle out into the mutual toleration of what people called a happy marriage would be anticlimax, it would be as if one were to botch a sublime and melifluous sonnet with a sestet in prose.

Melior, so long as she stayed unattainable, had provided him with an ideal: and Melior, once lost to him, once he could never hear another word of that continuous half-witted jabbering,—or, rather, he emended, of this bright light creature's very diverting chat,—then his high misery would afford him even surer ground for a superior dissatisfaction with the simple catering of nature. So the company of his disenchanted princess, her company just for the present, could be endured with a composure not wholly saddened by that dreadful and permanent bereavement which impended.

He reasoned thus, and was in everything considerate and loving. His devotion was so ardent and unremittent, indeed, that, when Florian left Bellegarde, Melior was forehandedly stitching and trimming baby-clothes. This was at the opening of December, and he was going to court in answer to a summons from the great Duke of Orléans.

"It is rather odd," observed Florian, "that I go at Philippe's expressed desire. Yet one knows that shrewd old saying as to the gods' preliminary treatment of those whom they wish to destroy."

"Still, if you ask me," observed his wife,—not looking at him, but at her sewing,—"I think it is much better not to talk about the gods any more than is necessary, and certainly not in that exact tone of voice—" The break in speech was for the purpose of biting a thread.

You saw, as she bent over this thread, the top of her frilly little lace cap efflorescent with tiny pink ribbons. You saw, as she looked up, that Melior was especially lovely to-day in this flowing pink robe à la Watteau over a white petticoat and a corsage of white ribbons arranged in a sort of ladder-work. There was now about her nothing whatever of the mediæval or the outré: from the boudoir cap upon her head to the pink satin mules upon her feet, this Melior belonged to the modern world of 1723: and the whiteness and the pinkness of her made you think about desserts and confectionery.

"But what exact tone of voice," asked Florian, smiling with lenient pride in his really very pretty duchess, "does my darling find injudicious?"

"Why, I mean, as if you were looking at something a great way off, and smelled something you were not quite certain you liked. To be sure, now that we are both good Christians, we know that the other gods are either devils or, else, illusions that never existed at all —Father Joseph has the nicest possible manners, and just the smile and the way of talking that very often remind me of Hoprig, and qualifies him to teach any religion in the world, even without stroking both your hands all the time, but in spite of that, as I told him only last Saturday, he will not ever speak out quite plainly about them—"

"About your lovely hands, madame?"

"Now, monsieur my husband, what foolish questions you ask! I mean, about whether they are devils or illusions. Because, as I told him frankly—"

"Ah, now I comprehend. Yet, surely, these abstruse questions of theology—"

She was looking at him in astonishment. "Why, but not in the least. I am not interested in theology, I merely say that a thing is either one way or the other: and, as I so often think, nothing whatever is to be gained by beating about the bush instead of being our own candid natural selves, and confessing to our ignorance, even if we happen to be priests, where ignorance is no disgrace—"

"Doubtless, my dearest, you intend to convey to me—"

"Oh, no, not for one instant!" And this bewitching seamstress was virtually giggling, quite as if there were some logical cause for amusement. "Anybody who called that dear old soft-soaper stupid would be much more mistaken, monsieur my husband, than you suspect. I merely mean that is one side of the question, a side which is perfectly plain. The other is that, as I have told him over and over again, it is not as if I had ever for a moment denied that Father and Mother are conservative, but quite the contrary—"

Florian said: "Dearest of my life, I conjecture you are still referring to your confessor, the good Father Joseph. Otherwise, I must admit that, somehow, I have not followed the theme of your argument with an exactness which might, perhaps, have enabled me to form some faint notion as to what you are talking about "

And again the loveliest face in the world was marveling beneath that very pleasing disorder of little pink ribbons. "Why, I was talking about Father Joseph, of course, and about my wanting to know how my parents at their time of life could be expected to take up with new ideas. Oh, and I kept at him, too: because, even if they are worshiping devils up at Brunbelois, and doing something actually wicked when they sacrifice to Llaw Gyffes a few serfs that are past their work and are no use to anybody, and no real pleasure to themselves,—which is a side you have to look at,—it would be a sort of comfort to be certain of the worst. Whereas, as for them, the poor dears, as I so often say, what you do not know about does not worry you—"

"I take it that you mean—"

"Exactly!" Melior stated, with the most sagacious of nods. "Though, for my part, I feel it is only justice to say that such devils as my sister Mélusine used to have in now and again, in the way of sorcery, were quite civil and obliging. So far as looks go, it is best to remember in such cases that handsome is as handsome does, and I am sure they did things for her that the servants would never have so much as considered—"

"But, still—"

"Oh, yes, of course, we all know what a problem that is, at every turn, with your kindness and your consideration absolutely wasted: and in fact, as I so often think, if I could just have two rooms somewhere, and do my own cooking—" Another thread was bitten through by the loveliest teeth in the world.

"You aspire to such simple pleasures, my wife, as are denied to a Duchess of Puysange. No, one must be logical. We have the duties of our estate. And among these duties, as I was just saying, I now discover the deplorable need of absenting myself from the delights of your society and conversation—"

"I shall miss you, monsieur my husband," replied Melior, abstractedly holding up a very small undershirt, and looking at it as if with the very weightiest of doubts, "of course. But still, it is not as if I cared to be traveling now, and, besides, there really is a great deal of sewing to be done for months to come. And with everything in this upset condition, I do hope that—if by any chance you are sitting on that other pair of scissors? I thought they must be there. Yes, I do hope that you will be most careful in this affair, because I already have enough to contend with. You ought to send the lace at once, though: and I suppose we might as well have pink yarn and ribbons, since the chances are equal in any event—"

"But in what affair, delight of my existence, are you requesting me to be careful?"

"Why, how should I know?" And Melior, he perceived, had still the air of one who is dealing patiently with an irrational person. "It is probably a very good thing that I do not, since you are plainly up to something with your friend Orléans which you want nobody to find out about. All men are like that: and, for my part, I have no curiosity whatever, because, as I so often think, if everybody would just attend to their own affairs—"

He bowed, and, murmuring, "Your pardon, madame!" he left her contentedly sewing. It seemed to Florian a real pity that a creature in every way so agreeable to his eye should steadily betray and tease his ear. He did not find that, as wives average, his Melior was especially loquacious: it was, rather, that when she discoursed at any length, with her bewildering air of commingled self-satisfaction and shrewdness, he could never make out quite clearly what she was talking about: and as went intelligence, his disenchanted princess seemed to him to rank somewhere between a magpie and a turnip.

This, upon the whole, adorable idiocy might have made it appear, to some persons, surprising that Melior should divine, as she had so obviously divined, that Florian, in going to Philippe d'Orléans, was prompted by motives which discretion preferred to screen. But Florian had learned by experience that your wives very often astound you by striking the target of your inmost thinking, fair and full, with just such seemingly irrational shots of surmise. You might call it intuition or whatever else you preferred: no husband of any at all lengthy standing would be quick to call it accident. Rather, he would admit this to be a faculty which every married woman manifested now and then: and he would rejoice that, for the health of the world's peace, such clairvoyancy was intermittent. Florian esteemed it to be just one of the inevitable drawbacks of matrimony that the most painstaking person must sometimes encounter discomfortable moments when his wife appears to be looking over his secret thoughts somewhat as one glances over the pages of a not particularly interesting book. So the experienced husband would shrug and would await this awkward moment's passing, and the return of his wife's normal gullibility and charm.

Melior, too, then, had her instants of approach to wifely, if not precisely human, intelligence. And Melior was beautiful. There was no flaw anywhere in her beauty. This Florian repeated, over and over again, as he prepared for travel. Here, too, one must be logical. That ideal beauty which he had hopelessly worshiped, and had without hope hungered for, ever since his childhood, was now attained: and the goddess of his long adoration was now enshrined in, to be exact, the next room but one, already hemming diapers for their anticipated baby. Nobody could possibly have won nearer to his heart's desire than Florian had come; he had got all and more than his highest dreaming had aspired to: and so, if he was now sighing over the reflection, it must be, he perceived, a sigh of content.

Then he kissed his wife, and he rode away from Bellegarde, toward the vexatious duties which awaited him at court. Florian stopped, of course, to put up a prayer, for the success of his nearing venture into homicide, at the Church of Holy Hoprig. That ceremonial Florian could not well have omitted without provoking more or less speculation as to why the Duke of Puysange should be defaulting in a pious custom of long standing; nor, for that matter, without troubling his conscience with doubts if he was affording the country-side quite the good example due from one of his rank.

Through just such mingled considerations of expediency and duty had Florian, since his return from Brunbelois, continued his giving to this church with all the old liberality, if with somewhat less comfort to himself. It was a nuisance to reflect that so many irregularities which Florian had believed compounded, to everybody's satisfaction, had never been attended to at all by his patron saint. It was annoying to know that the church had got, and was continuing to get, from the estate of Puysange so many pious offerings virtually for nothing. Even so, replied logic, what was to be gained by arousing criticism or by neglecting your religious duties in a manner that was noticeable? Let us adhere to precedent, and then, if we can no longer count assuredly on bliss in the next world, we may at least hope for tranquillity in this one.

So Florian, for the preservation of the local standards, now put up a fervent prayer to his patron saint in heaven; and reflected that, after all, the actual whereabouts, and the receptivity to petitions, of Holy Hoprig was none of Florian's affair. A little wonder, however, about just where the Saint might be doing what, was, Florian hoped, permissible, since he had found such wondering not to be avoided.

ow that Florian came out of the provinces, he wished to take matters in order. Not merely a snobbish pride of race led him to give his own family affairs precedence to those of the Bourbons. It was, rather, that Florian yet had a day to wait before the coming of the winter solstice. He was unwilling to waste these twenty-four hours, because Florian looked with some uneasiness toward the inevitable encounter with his wife-ridden brother, and Florian was desirous to get this worry off his mind. For, a thing done, as Janicot had mentioned, has an end. . . .

Florian therefore made inquiries as to where Raoul was passing that evening; and the two brothers thus met, as if by chance, at the home of the Duc de Brancas The circle of Monsieur de Brancas was not gallant toward women, and his guests were gentlemen in middle age, most of whom came each with a boy of about seventeen or thereabouts

Florian was grieved when, as he approached the group clustered about the big fireplace, he saw with what ceremony Raoul bowed. Raoul had fattened, he seemed taller, he was to-night superb in this crimson coat, with huge turned-back cuffs,—that must be the very latest mode,—and in this loose gold-laced white waistcoat, descending to the knees, and unfastened at the bottom. Raoul had the grand air of their father a tall man was always so much more impressive But it was apparent that the dear fellow's abominable wife had been at her mischief-making.

"Monsieur the Duke," Raoul began, affably, "this encounter is indeed fortunate."

"To encounter Monsieur the Chevalier," replied Florian, with quite as sweet a stateliness, but feeling rather like a bantam cock beside this big Raoul, "is always a privilege."

People everywhere were listening now: this gambit hardly seemed fraternal. The well-bred elderly friends of Monsieur de Brancas, to be sure, made a considerate pretence at going on with their talk, but most of the scented and painted boys had betrayed their lower social degree by gaping openly: and Florian knew he was in for an unpleasant business.

"—For I am wondering if you have heard, monsieur," the Chevalier went on, "that the Comte d'Arnaye has spread the report that at Madame de Nesle's last ball I appeared with two buttons missing from my waistcoat?"

"I really cannot answer for the truth of such gossip, monsieur,"—thus Florian, with high civility,—"since I have not seen my uncle for some time."

"Ah, ah! so the Comte d'Arnaye is your uncle!" Raoul seemed gravely pleased. "That is excellent, for, inasmuch as I cannot readily obtain satisfaction for this calumny from your uncle, who has retired into the provinces for the winter, I can apply to you."

Florian said, with careful patience: "I am delighted, monsieur, to act as his representative. In that capacity I can assure you whoever asserted Monsieur d'Arnaye declared the waistcoat in which you attended the last ball of Madame de Nesle to be deficient in two buttons, or in one button, or in a half-stitch of thread, has told a lie."

Raoul de Puysange frowned. "Diantre! it was my own cousin, the Count's youngest son, who was my informant; and since my cousin, monsieur, as you are well aware, is little more than a child—"

"You should have the less trouble, then," said Florian, vexed by his brother's pertinacity, "in horsewhipping the brat for his silly falsehood."

"Come, Monsieur the Duke, but I cannot have my cousin called a liar, far less listen to this talk of horsewhipping one who is of my blood. I must ask satisfaction for these affronts, and I will send a friend to wait upon you."

Florian looked sadly at his brother. But the Duc de Puysange shrugged before a meddlesome and quite unimportant person.

Florian answered: "I am well content, Monsieur the Chevalier. Only, to save time, I would suggest that your friend go direct to the Vicomte de Lautrec, since he is here to-night, and since I have promised him that he should second me in my next affair."

The two brothers bowed and parted decorously, having thus arranged a public quarrel in which Mademoiselle de Nérac was in no way involved. The instant's tension was over, and the guests of Monsieur de Brancas thronged hastily through the corridor,—which was rather chilly, because all the outer side of this corridor was builded of stained glass,—and went into the little private theatre, where the fiddles were already tuning for the overture of a new and tuneful burletta that dealt with The Fall of Sodom The curtain by and by rose on the civic revels, and the rest of the evening passed merrily.

After the first act, while the scenery was being shifted so as to represent Lot's cave in the mountains, all details of the fraternal duel were arranged by Messieurs de Lautrec and de Soyecourt. Tall lean Monsieur de Soyecourt had, as a cousin, been prompt to insist upon his right to act for Raoul in an encounter so sure to be discussed everywhere.

Shortly after midnight,—at which hour the other guests of Monsieur de Brancas went into the Salon des Flagellants to amuse themselves at a then very fashionable game which you played with little whips —the two brothers left the hôtel with their seconds. A surgeon had been sent for, and he accompanied them and the five girls, whom the Vicomte de Lautrec had caused to be fetched from La Fillon's, to a house near the Port Maillot, where all indulged in various pleasantries until morning.

The wine here proved so good, the girls were so amiable and accomplished, that by daylight Florian had mellowed into an all-embracing benevolence, and he proposed to compound the affair. The suggestion roused an almost angry buzz of protest.

Lautrec was demanding, of the company at large, would you have me, who was married only last week, staying out all night, with no better excuse than that I was drunk with these charming girls? Why, I was committed to three rendezvous last night, and if there be no duel I shall have trouble with a trio of ladies of the highest fashion. Nor is it, put in the Marquis de Soyecourt,—whose speaking was always somewhat indistinct, because of the loss of all his upper front-teeth, —nor is it kind of you, my dear, to wish to deprive us of taking part in a business which will make so much noise in the world: brothers do not fight every day, this affair will be talked about. I quite agree with Lautrec that your whim is foolish and inconsiderate. Besides, Raoul was saying reprovingly, the honor of our house is involved. To have a Puysange cry off from a duel would be a reflection upon our blood that I could not endure—

"What is honor," replied Florian, half-dazedly hearing all this chatter, "what is honor, O my dear, to the love which has been between us?"

The Chevalier looked half-shocked at this sort of

talk: but he only answered that Hannibal and Agamemnon had been very pretty fellows in their day while it lasted; so too the boys who had loved each other at Storisende and Bellegarde. Let the dead rest. No, to go back now was impossible, without creating a deal of adverse comment, in view of the publicity of their quarrel.

Florian sighed, half wearied, half vexed, by the remote sound of his brother's talking; and Florian replied: "That is true. One must be logical. You three are better advised than I, Raoul; and we of Puysange dare not offend against the notions of our neighbors."

The gentlemen then went into the park. They walked toward the old Château de Madrid. There had been a very light fall of snow. It felt like sand underfoot as you walked. Florian reflected it was droll that oak-trees should retain so many bronze leaves thus late in winter. They quite overshadowed this place, and made the snow look bluish.

The gentlemen prepared for their duel. Each of the four was armed with two pistols and a sword. When all was ready, Raoul fired at once, and he wounded Florian in the left arm. It hurt. The little brother whose face was always smudged would never have hurt you.

At Florian's side, Lautrec had fallen, dead. The bullet of the Marquis de Soyecourt had by an incredible chance struck the Vicomte full in the right eye, piercing the brain.

"Name of a name!" observed the troubled Marquis, who was unwounded, "but here is another widow to be consoled,—when I had aimed too at his ear! That is the devil of this carousing all night, and then coming to one's duels with shaken nerves. But how fare our sons of Œdipus?"

The Marquis turned, and what he saw was sufficiently curious.

Florian had winced when hit, thus for an instant

spoiling his aim, but he at once lowered his pistol, and he shot this tall man who had nothing to do with his little brother, neatly through the breast. Raoul de Puysange fired wildly with his second pistol, and now drew his sword as if to rush upon Florian, who merely shifted the yet loaded pistol to his uncrippled right hand, and waited. But Raoul had not advanced two paces when Raoul fell.

Florian dropped the undischarged pistol, and went to his brother. This thin snow underfoot was like scattered sand, and your treading in it was audible.

"You have done for me, my dear," declared the Chevalier.

And Florian was perturbed. He wished, for all that his arm was hurting him confoundedly, to reply whatever in the circumstances was the correct thing, but he could think of no exact precedent. So he put aside the wild fancy of responding, "Am I my brother's keeper?" and to this stranger at his feet he said, with a quite admirable tremor wherein anguish blended nicely with a manly self-restraint:

"Raoul, you are the happier of us two. Do you forgive me?"

"Yes," replied the other, "I forgive you." Raoul gazed up fondly at his brother. Raoul said, with that genius for the obviously appropriate which Florian always envied, "I feel for you as I know you do for me."

Thus speaking, Raoul de Puysange looked of a sudden oddly surprised. His nostrils dilated, he shivered a little, and so died.

Florian turned sadly to the gaunt Marquis de Soyecourt. "You spoke of the sons of Œdipus, Antoine. But many other eminent persons have been fratricides. There was Romulus, and Absalom in Holy Writ, and Sir Balen of Northumberland, and several of the Capets and the Valois. King Henry the First of England, a very wise prince, also put his brother out of the way, as did Constantius Chlorus, a most noble patron of the Church. Whereas all Turkish Emperors—"

"Oh, have done with your looking for precedents!" said the Marquis. "What we should look for now, my dear, is horses to get us away from this sad affair. For one, I am retiring into the provinces, to spend Christmas at my venerable father's château at Beaujolais, where I shall be more comfortable than in the King's prison of the Bastille. And I most strongly advise you to imitate me."

"No," Florian said, gently, "these are but the first fruits of the attainment of my desire. For, as you remind me, Antoine, Christmas approaches; and at court I still have some unfinished business."

XIII

Debonnaire

THEREAFTER Florian went to the Duke Orléans, with two motives. One was the obvious necessity of obtaining a pardon for having killed the Chevalier: Florian's other motive was the promise given to brown Janicot that he should have for his Christmas present, upon this day of the winter solstice, the life of the greatest man in the kingdom. The greatest man in the kingdom, undoubtedly, was Philippe of Orléans, the former Regent, now prime minister, and the next heir to the throne. The King was not a man but a child of thirteen. One must be logical. Florian regretted the loss of his friend, for he was unfeignedly fond of Orléans, but a promise once given by a Puysange was not to be evaded.

He must get the pardon first. Florian foresaw that the granting of a pardon out of hand for his disastrous duel would seem to the Duke of Orléans an action liable to involve the prime minister in difficulties. Florian thought otherwise, in the light of his firm belief that to-morrow Orléans would be oblivious of all earthly affairs, but this was not an argument which Florian could advance tactfully. Rather, he counted upon the happy fact that Florian's services in the past were not benefits which any reflective statesman would care to ignore. Yes, the pardon would certainly be forthcoming, Florian assured himself, this afternoon, as he rode forth in his great gilded coach, for his last chat, as he rather vexedly reflected, with all-powerful

Philippe of Orléans, whom people called Philippe the
Débonnaire.

"So!" said the minister, when they had embraced,
"so, they tell me that you have married again, and that
you killed your brother this morning. I am not pleased
with you, Florian. These escapades will come to no
good end."

"Ah, monseigneur, but I like to take a wife occa-
sionally, whereas you prefer always to borrow one. It
is merely a question of taste, about which we need not
quarrel. As to this duel, I lamented the necessity, your
Highness, as much as anybody. But these meddling
women—"

"Yes, yes, I know," replied Orléans, "your sister-
in-law talks too much. In fact, as I recall it, she talks
even in her sleep."

"Monseigneur, and will you never learn discretion?"

"I am discreet enough, in any event, to look upon
fratricide rather seriously. So I am sending you to the
Bastille for a while, Florian, and indeed the lettre de
cachet ordering your imprisonment was made out an
hour ago."

Florian at this had out the small gold box upon
whose lid was painted a younger and far more amiable
looking Orléans than frowned here in the flesh,—in a
superfluity of flesh,—and Florian took snuff. It was always a good way of gaining time for reflection. . . .
Wine and cakes were set ready upon the little table.
Philippe was probably expecting some woman. There
had been no lackeys in the corridor which led to this
part of the château. Philippe always sent them away
when any of his women were to come in the daytime.
Yes, one was quite alone with this corpulent, black-
browed and purple-faced Philippe, in this quiet room,
which was like a pimpled gilt shell of elaborately
carved woodwork, and which had bright panels everywhere, upon the walls and the ceiling, representing,

very explicitly indeed, The Triumphs of Love. Such solitude was uncommonly convenient; and one might speak without reticence. . . .

Florian put up his snuff-box, dusted his fingertips, and said: "I regret to oppose you in anything, monseigneur, but for me to go to prison would be inconvenient just now. I have important business at the Feast of the Wheel to-morrow night."

Since Philippe had lost the sight of his left eye he cocked his head like a huge bird whenever he looked at you intently. "You had best avoid these sorceries, Florian. I have not yet forgotten that fiend whom your accursed lieutenant evoked for us in the quarries of Vaugirard—" Orléans paused. He said in a while, "Before that night and that vision of my uncle's deathbed, I was less ambitious, Florian, and more happy."

"Ah, yes, poor old Mirepoix!" said Florian, smiling. "What a preposterous fraud he was, with his absurd ventriloquism and stuffed crocodiles and magic lanterns! However, he foretold very precisely indeed the extraordinary series of events which would leave you the master of this kingdom: and I had not the heart to see the faithful fellow exposed as an ignoramus who talked nonsense. So I was at some pains to help his prophesying come true, and to make you actually the only surviving male relative at the old King's deathbed."

"Let us speak," said Orléans, with a vexed frown, "of cheerier matters. Now, in regard to your imprisonment—"

"I was coming to your notion of a merry topic. This visit to the Feast of the Wheel is about a family matter, your Highness, and is imperative. So I must keep my freedom for the while: and I must ask, in place of a lettre de cachet, a pardon in full."

"Instead, Florian, let us have fewer 'musts' and

more friendliness in this affair." Orléans now put his arm about Florian. "Come, I will delay your arrest until the day after to-morrow; you shall spend the night here, my handsome pouting Florian; and you shall be liberated at the end of one little week in the Bastille."

Florian released himself, rather petulantly. "Pardieu! but I entreat you to reserve these endearments for your bedchamber! No, you must find some other playfellow for to-night. And I really cannot consent to be arrested, for it would quite spoil my Christmas."

Orléans, rebuffed, said only, "But if I continue to ignore your misbehaviors, people will talk."

"That is possible, your Highness. It is certain that, under arrest, I also would become garrulous."

"Ah! and of what would you discourse?"

Florian looked for a while at his red-faced friend beyond the red-topped writing table.

Florian said: "I would talk of the late Dauphin's death, monseigneur; of the death of the Duc de Bourgogne; of the death of the little Duc de Bretagne; and of the death of the Duc de Berri. I would talk of the death of every one who stood, once, between you and your present ranking in this kingdom. I would talk, in fine, about those inexplicable, fatal illnesses among your kinsmen, which of a sudden made you, who were nobody of much consequence the master of France and the next heir to the throne."

Orléans said nothing for a time. Speaking, his voice was quiet, but a little hoarse. "It is perhaps as well for you, my friend, that my people have been dismissed. Yes, I am expecting Madame de Phalaris, who is as yet amusingly shamefaced about her adulteries. So there is nobody about, and we may speak frankly. With frankness, then, I warn you that it is not wholesome to threaten a prince of the blood, and that if you continue in this tone you may not long be permitted to talk anywhere, not even in one of the many prisons at my disposal."

"Ah, your Highness, let us not speak of my death, for it is a death which you would deplore."

"Would I deplore your death?" Orléans' head was now cocked until it almost lay upon his left shoulder. "It is a fact of which I am not wholly persuaded."

"Monseigneur, mere self-respect demands that one's death should rouse some grief among one's friends. So I have made certain that your grief would be inevitable and deep. For I am impatient of truisms—"

"And what have truisms to do with our affair?"

"The statement that dead men tell no tales, your Highness, is a truism."

"Yes; and to be candid, Florian, it is that particular truism of which I was just thinking."

"Well, it is this particular truism I have elected to deride. My will is made, the disposing of my estate is foreordered, and every legacy enumerated. One of these legacies is in the form of a written narrative: it is not a romance, it is an entirely veracious chronicle, dealing with the last hours of four of your kinsmen; and it is bequeathed to a fifth kinsman, to your cousin, the Duc de Bourbon. Should I die in one of your prisons, monseigneur,—a calamity which I perceive to be already foreshadowed in your mind,—that paper would go to him."

The Duke of Orléans considered this. There had been much whispering; mobs in the street had shouted, "Burn the poisoner!" when Orléans passed: but this was different. Once Bourbon had half the information which Florian de Puysange was able to give, there would be, of course, no question of burning Orléans, since one does not treat a prince of the blood like fuel: but there would be no doubt, either, of his swift downfall nor of his subsequent death by means of the more honorable ax.

Orléans knew all this. Orléans also knew Florian. In consequence Orléans asked,—

"Is what you tell me the truth?"

"Faith of a gentleman, monseigneur!"

Orléans sighed. "It is a pity. By contriving this conditional post-mortem sort of confession to the devil-work you prompted, you have contrived an equally devilish safeguard. Yes, if you are telling the truth, for me to have you put out of the way would be injudicious. And you do tell the truth, confound you! Broad-minded as you are in many ways, Florian, you are a romantic; and I have never known you to break your given word or to voice any purely utilitarian lie. You are positively queer about that."

"I confess it," said Florian, frankly. "Puysange lies only for pleasure, never for profit. But what do my foibles matter? Let us be logical about this! What does anything matter except the plain fact that we are useful to each other? I do not boast, but I think you have found me efficient. You needed only a precipitating of the inevitable, a little hastening here and there of natural processes, to give you your desires. Well, four of these accelerations have been brought about through the recipes of a dear old friend of mine, through invaluable recipes which have made you the master of this kingdom. It is now always within your power, without any real trouble, to remove the scrofulous boy whose living keeps you from being even in title King of France. Yes, I think I have helped you. Some persons would in my position be exigent. But all I ask is your name written upon a bit of paper. I will even promise you that your mercifulness shall create no adverse comment, and that to-morrow people shall be talking of something quite different."

And Florian smiled ingratiatingly, the while that he fingered what was in his waistcoat pocket, and reflected that all France would very certainly have more than enough to talk about to-morrow.

"This dapper imp, in his eternal bottle-green and silver, will be the ruin of me," Orléans observed. But he had already drawn a paper from the top drawer: and he filled it in, and signed it, and he pushed it across the red-topped writing table, toward Florian.

"I thank you, monseigneur, for this favor," said Florian, then, "and I long to repay it by making you King of France. Let us drink to Philippe the Seventh!"

"No," said Orléans,—"let us drink if you will, now that a woman is coming, but I have no thirst for kingship. I play with the idea, of course. To be a king sounds well, and I once thought— But it would give me no more than I already have of endless nuisances to endure. As matters stand, I can make shift with the discomforts of being a great personage, because I know that I can, whenever I like, lay aside my greatness. I can at will become again a private person, and I can find a host of fools eager to fill my place. But from the throne there is no exit save into the vaults of St. Denis. So I procrastinate, I play with the idea of putting the boy out of the way, and I play with the idea of resigning my ministry, but I do nothing definite until to-morrow."

"There are many adages that speak harshly of procrastination," said Florian, as he poured and, with his back to Orléans, flavored the wine which was set ready. "Logic is a fine thing, monseigneur: and logic informs me that no man is sure of living until to-morrow."

"But it is no fun being a great personage," Orléans lamented, as he took the tall, darkly glowing glass. "I have had my bellyful of it: and I find greatness rather thin fare. I am master of France, indeed I may with some show of reason claim to be master of Europe. I used to think it would be pleasant to rule kingdoms;

but you may take my word for it, Florian, the game is not worth the candle. There are times," said Orléans, as lazily he sipped the wine which Florian had just seasoned, "there are times when I wish I were dead and done with it all."

"That, your Highness, will come soon enough."

"Yes, but do you judge what I have to contend with!"

And Orléans at once launched into a bewailing of his political difficulties.

Florian kept a polite pose of attention, without exactly listening to these complaints about Parliament's obstinacy, about Alberoni's and Villeroy's plottings in their exile, about the sly underminings of Fréjus, about what the legitimated princes were planning now, about Bourbon, about Noailles, about the pig-headedness of the English Pretender, about the empty Treasury— Of these things Philippe was talking, in a jumble of words without apparent end or meaning. But Florian thought of a circumstance unrelated to any of these matters, with a sort of awed amusement.

"All this to make a maniac of me," the minister went on, "and with what to balance it? Anything I choose to ask for, of course. But then, Florian, what the deuce is there in life for one to ask for at forty-nine? I was once a joyous glutton: now I have to be careful of my digestion. I used to stay drunk for weeks: now one night of virtually puritanic debauchery leaves me a wreck to be patched up by physicians who can talk about nothing but apoplexy. Florian, let us drink again, for this talk of death leaves my throat dry. . . . Women no longer rouse any curiosity. I know so well what their bodies are like that an investigation is tautology: and half the time I go to bed with no inclination to do anything but sleep. Not even my daughters, magnificent women that you might think them—"

"I know," said Florian, with a reminiscent smile.

"—Not even they are able to amuse me any more. No, my friend, I candidly voice my opinion that there is nothing in life which possession does not discover to be inadequate: we are cursed with a tyrannous need for what life does not afford: and we strive for various prizes, saying 'Happiness is there,' when in point of fact it is nowhere. They who fail in their endeavors still have in them the animus of desire: but the man who attains his will cohabits with an assassin, for, having it, he perceives that he does not want it; and desire is dead in him, and the man too is dead. Florian, let us drink, since you persist in talking about death. Florian, be advised by me; and do you avoid greatness as you should—and by every seeming do not, —the devil!"

So Philippe d'Orléans also, thought Florian, had got what he wanted, only to find it a damnable nuisance. Probably all life was like that. Over-high and over-earnest desires were inadvisable. It was a sort of comfort to reflect that poor Philippe at least would soon be through with his worries. . . .

A bell rang; and Florian, rising, said: "I shall heed your advice, monseigneur— But that bell perhaps announces an arrival about which I should remain in polite ignorance?"

"Yes, so let us—at forty-nine, alas!—let us drink again. Yes, it is Madame de Phalaris. We are to try what Aretino and Romano can suggest for our amusement, before I go up to my hour's work with the King. So be off with you through the private way, for it is a very modest little bitch."

Florian passed through the indicated door, but he did not quite close it. Instead, he waited there, and he saw the entrance of charming tiny Madame de Phalaris, whom Orléans greeted with tolerable ardor.

"So you have come at last, you delicious rogue, to end my expounding of moral sentiments. And with what fairy tale, bright-eyed Sapphira, will you explain your lateness?"

"Indeed, your Highness," said the lady, who had learned that in these encounters the Duke liked to be heartened with some gambit of free talk, "indeed, your question reminds me that only last night I heard the most diverting fairy tale. But it is somewhat—"

"Yes?" said the Duke.

"I mean, that it is rather—"

"But I adore that especial sort of fairy story," he announced. "So, after this one glass, of course we must have it, and equally of course we must spare our mutual blushes."

Thus speaking, Orléans sat at her feet, and he leaned back his head a bit tipsily between her knees, so that neither could see the face of the other. Her lithe white fingers stroked his cheeks, caressing those great pendulous red jaws: and her sea-green skirts, flowered with a pattern of slender vines, were spread like billows to each side of him.

"There was once," the lady began, "a king and a queen—"

"I know the tale," said Orléans, with a forlorn hiccough,—"they had three sons. Two of them failed in their quests, but the third prince succeeded in everything, and he was damnably bored by everything. I know the tale only too well—"

He desisted from speaking. But he was making queer noises.

"Highness—!" cried Madame de Phalaris.

She had risen in alarm; and as she rose, the Duke's head fell to the crimson-covered footstool at her feet. He did not move, but lay quite still, staring upward; and his foreshortened face, as Florian saw it, was now of a remarkable shade of purple among the elaborate dark curls of Orléans' peruke.

There was for a moment utter silence. You heard

only the gilded clock upon the red chimney piece. Then Madame de Phalaris screamed.

Nobody replied. She rang wildly at the bell cord beside the writing table. You could hear a remote tinkling, but nothing else. The shaking woman lifted fat Orléans, and propped him against the chair in which a moment ago she had been cajoling him. Philippe of Orléans sprawled thus, more drunken looking than Florian had ever seen him in life: the corpse was wholly undignified. The head of him whom people had called Philippe the Débonnaire had fallen sideways, so that his black peruke was pushed around and hid a third of his face. The left eye, the eye with which Philippe had for years seen nothing, yet leered at the woman before him.

She began again to scream. She ran from the room, and Florian could now just hear her as she ran, still screaming, about the corridors in which she could find nobody. It sounded like the squeaking of a frightened rat.

Florian came forward without hurry, for there was no pressing need of haste. Florian quite understood that Orléans had dismissed all his attendants, so that Madame de Phalaris might come to him unobserved: her husband was a notionary man. After a little amorous diversion with the lady, Orléans had meant to go up that narrow staircase yonder, for an hour's work with the young King. . . . It was odd to reflect that poor Philippe would never go to the King nor to any woman's bed, not ever any more; odd, too, that anyone could be thus private in this enormous château wherein lived several thousand persons. At all events, this privacy was uncommonly convenient. . . .

So Florian reflected for an instant, after his usual fashion of fond lingering upon what life afforded of the quaint. . . . It was certainly very quaint that history should be so plastic. He had, with no especial effort or discomfort, with no real straining of his powers, changed the history of all Europe when he transferred this famous kingdom of France and the future of France from the keeping of Philippe to guardians more staid. Probably Monsieur de Bourbon would be the next minister. But whoever might be minister in name, the Bishop of Fréjus, the young King's preceptor, would now be the actual master of everything. Well, to have taken France from a debauchee like this poor staring gaping Philippe here,—Florian abstractedly straightened the thing's peruke,—to give control of France to such an admirable prelate as André de Fleury was in all a praiseworthy action. It was a logical action. . . .

Then Florian performed unhurriedly the rite which was necessary, and there was a sign that Janicot accepted his Christmas present. It was not a pleasant sign to witness, nor did they who served Janicot appear to be squeamish. After this came two hairy persons, not unfamiliar to Florian, and these two removed as much as their master desired of Philippe d'Orléans. They answered, too, in a fashion no whit less impressive because of their not speaking, the questions which Florian put as to the proper manner of his coming to Janicot and the Feast of the Wheel. Then they were not in this room: and Florian, somewhat shaken, also went out of this room, not as they had gone but by way of the little private door.

It was a full half-hour, Florian learned afterward, before Madame de Phalaris returned with a cortège of lackeys and physicians. These last attempted to bleed Duke Philippe, but found their endeavors wasted: La Tophania's recipes were reliable, and to all appearance he had for some while been dead of apoplexy. The obscene toy discovered, hanging about his neck, when they went to undress him, surprised nobody: the Duke had affected these oddities.

When the physicians made yet other discoveries, a trifle later, they flutteringly agreed this death must, without any further discussion, be reported to have arisen from natural causes. "Monsieur d'Orléans," said one of them, jesting with rather gray lips, "has died assisted by his usual confessor."

Florian had of course not needed to amass good precedents for putting out of life anybody who was to all intents a reigning monarch. As he glanced back at history, this seemed to him almost the favorite avocation of estimable persons. So, as Florian rode leisurely away in his great gilded coach, leaving behind him the second fruits of the attainment of his desire, if he lazily afforded a side thought to Marcus Brutus and Jacques Clément and Aristogeiton and Ehud the Benjamite, and to a few other admirable assassins of high potentates, it was through force of habit rather than any really serious consideration. For the important thing to be considered now was how to come by the sword Flamberge, for which Florian had, that day, paid.

XIV

Gods in Decrepitude

 OT one of the ambiguous guardians of the place in any way molested Florian in that journey through which he hoped to win the sword Flamberge. His bearing, which combined abstraction with a touch of boredom, discouraged any advances from phantoms, and made fiends uneasily suspect this little fellow in bottle-green and silver to be one of those terrible magicians who attend sabbats only when they are planning to kidnap with strong conjurations some luckless fiend to slave for them at unconscionable tasks. That sort of person a shrewd fiend gives a wide berth: and certainly nobody who was not an adept at magic would have dared venture hereabouts, upon this night of all nights in the year, the guardians reasoned, without considering that this traveler might be a Puysange. So Florian passed to the top of the hill, without any molestation, in good time for the beginning of the Feast of the Wheel.

When Florian came quietly through the painted gate, the Master was already upon the asherah stone receiving homage. The scene was well lighted with torches which flared bluishly as they were carried about by creatures that had the appearance of huge dark-colored goats: each of these goats bore two torches, the first being fixed between its horns, and the second inserted in another place. Florian stood aside, and watched these venerable rites of unflinching osculation and widdershins movings and all the rest of the ritual. One respected of course the motives which took visible form in these religious ceremonies, but the formulæ seemed to Florian a bit primitive.

So he sat upon a secluded grass bank, beyond the light of the blue torches, and waited. It was quaint, and pathetic too in a way, now that the communicants were reporting upon their unimaginative doings since the last Sabbat. The Master listened and advised upon each case. To Florian it appeared a rather ridiculous pother over nothing, all this to-do about the drying up of a cow or the unfitting of a bridegroom for his privileges or the sapping away of some one's health. Florian inclined to romanticism even in magic, whose proper functions he did not consider to be utilitarian or imitative of real life. It seemed to him mere childish petulancy thus to cast laborious spells to hasten events which would in time have happened anyhow, through nature's unprompted blunderings, when the obvious end of magic should be to bring about chances which could not possibly happen. But the Master had an air of taking it all quite seriously.

Nor were the initiations much more diverting, howsoever dreadfully painful they must be to the virgin novitiates. Florian could not but think that some more natural paraphernalia would be preferable, would be more logical, than that horrible, cold and scaly apparatus. It was interesting, though, to note what disposition was made of the relics of Philippe d'Orléans: and in the giving of four infants also, by the old ritual, Florian took a sort of personal concern, and he watched closely, so as to see just how it was done. He was relieved to find it a simple enough matter, hardly more difficult than the gutting of a rabbit, once you had by heart the words of the invocation. Florian assumed that Janicot would in due course supply the woman whose body must serve as the altar, and Florian put the matter out of mind.

Besides, to one with his respect for ancient custom and precedent, the fertility rites now in full course were interesting: he imagined that to a professed and not prudish antiquary they would be of absorbing interest, coming down, as these ceremonies did unaltered, from the dwarf races that preceded mankind proper. Still, as a whole, the Feast of the Wheel was rather tedious, Florian declared to his large neighbor. Florian had just noticed that others sat on this secluded grass bank, to both sides of him, in a twilight so vague that he could only see these other watchers of the feast were of huge stature and had unblinking shining eyes.

Yes, this dim person assented, these modern ways lacked fervor and impressiveness: and matters had been infinitely better conducted, he said, in the good old days when the Sabbat was held in blasphemy against him.

Florian, really interested at last, asked questions. It developed that this shadowy watcher was called Marduk. He had once been rather widely esteemed, by he had no notion how many millions of men, as the overlord of heaven and all living creatures, in whose hands were the decrees of fate, and as the bright helper and healer from whom were hid no secrets. Apsu yonder had in those fine days conducted his blasphemies, Marduk repeated, with considerably more splendor and display. Yes, the times worsened, the thing was now done meagrely. Apsu had never been really the same, said Marduk,—with a dry chuckle, like the stirring of a dead leaf,—since Apsu lost his wife. She was called Tiamat: and, say what you might about her—

"I quite agree with you. He was a far more dashing rogue," put in another half-seen shape, "in the good times when I was the eternal source of light, the up-holder of the universe, all-powerful and all-knowing, and when nobody anywhere except that rascal Anra-Mainyu was bold enough to talk back to Ahura-Mazda. Yes, the times worsen in every way: and even his effrontery flags, if that is any comfort."

"Oh, for that matter," said a third, "This Vukub-Ka-kix was at hand with his impudence when the Old Ones covered with Green Feathers first came out of the waters and tried to make men virtuous. He was then a splendid rogue. I found him annoying, of course, but wonderfully amusing. Now the times wor-sen: and the adversary of all the gods of men no longer has such opponents as used to keep him on his mettle."

"Each one of you," marvelled Florian, "gives the Master a new and harder christening! And what, mon-sieur," asked Florian, of the last speaker, "May be your name?"

The third dim creature answerel, "Xpiyacoc."

"Ah, now I understand why you should be the most generous to the Master in the matter of cacophony! I take it that you also have retired from a high position in the church. And I am wondering if all you veteran gods are assembled upon half-pay"—here Florian dis-creetly jerked a thumb skyward, "to conspire?"

"No," said a fourth,—who, like that poor Philippe, had only one eye,—"it is true we look to see put down the gods who just now have men's worship. But we do not conspire. We are too feeble now; and the years have taken away from us even all our anger and malev-olence. It was not so in the merry days when the little children came to me upon spear points. Now the times worsen: and they can but make the best of very poor times up yonder, as we do here." The speaker seemed to listen to that thing in the appearance of a raven perched on his shoulder, and he then said: "Besides, wise Huginn tells me that the reign of any god is an ephemeral matter hardly worth fretting over. I fell. They will fall. But neither fact is very important, says wise Huginn."

And about the Master these dim watchers preferred not to talk any more. He had denied them, they said, when they were kings of heaven and of man's worship and terror: and the Master had always maintained his cult against whatever god was for the moment supreme. He had never been formidable, he had never shown any desire toward usurping important powers. He had remained content to assert himself Prince of this world, whoever held the heavens and large stars: and while he had never meddled with the doings of any god in other planets, here upon Earth he had displayed such pertinacity that in the end most rulers of the universe let him alone. And now their omnipotence had passed, but the Master's little power—somehow —endured. The old gods found it inexplicable; but they were under no bonds to explain it; and it was not worth bothering about: nor was anything else worth bothering about, said they, whom time had freed of grave responsibilities.

And Florian mildly pitied their come-down in life, and their descent into this forlorn condition, but felt himself, none the less, to be sitting among ne'er-do-wells, and to be in not quite the company suited to a nobleman of his rank. So it was really a relief when the Master's religious services were over, and when, with the coming of red dawn, his servants departed, trooping this way and that way, but without ever ascending far above earth as they passed like sombre birds. The Master now stood unattended upon the asherah stone.

Florian then nodded civilly to the fallen gods, and

left them. Florian came forward and, removing his silver-laced green hat with a fine stately sweep, he gave Janicot that ceremonious bow which Florian reserved for persons whose worldly estate entitled them to be treated as equals by a Duke of Puysange.

XV

Dubieties of the Master

 "OME," said Janicot, yawning in the dawn of Christmas Day, "but here is our romantic lordling of Puysange, to whom love is divine, and the desired woman a goddess."

Florian did not at once reply. He had for the instant forgotten his need of the sword Flamberge. For on account of the requirements of the various ceremonies, Janicot, except for a strip of dappled fawn-skin across his chest, was not wearing any clothes, not even any shoes. Florian had just noticed Janicot's feet. But Florian was too courteous to comment upon personal peculiarities: for this only is the secret of all good-breeding, he reflected, not ever to wound the feelings of anybody, in any circumstances, without premeditation. So his upsetment was but momentary, and was not shown perceptibly, he felt sure, by that gasp which politeness had turned into a sigh.

"But what the deuce," said Janicot then, "is this a proper groan, is this the appropriate countenance, for one whose love has overridden the by-laws of time and of nature and even of necromancy?"

"Ah, Monsieur Janicot," answered Florian, "gravity everywhere goes arm-in-arm with wisdom, and I am somewhat wiser than I was when we last talked together. For I have been to the high place, and my desires have been gratified."

"That is an affair of course, since all my friends

have all their desires in this world. What cannot be with equal readiness taken for granted is the fact that you appear on that account to be none the happier."

"Merriment," replied Florian, "is a febrile passion. But content is quiet."

"So, then, you are content, my little duke?"

"The word 'little,' Monsieur Janicot, has in its ordinary uses no uncivil connotations. Yet, when applied to a person—"

"I entreat your pardon, Monsieur the Duke, for the ill-chosen adjective, and I hastily withdraw it."

"Which pardon, I need hardly say, I grant with even more haste. I am content, then, Monsieur Janicot. I have achieved my heart's desire and I find it"—Florian coughed,—"beyond anything I ever imagined. But now, alas! the great love between my wife and me draws toward its sweet fruition, and one must be logical. So I comprehend—with not unnatural regret,—that my adored wife will presently be leaving me forever."

"Ah, to be sure! Then you have already, in this brief period, passed from the pleasures of courtship to the joys of matrimony—?"

"Monsieur, I am a Puysange. We are ardent."

"—And she is already—?"

"Monsieur, I can but repeat my remark."

"Eh," replied Janicot, "you have certainly spared no zeal, you have not slept, in upholding the repute of your race: and this punctilious and loving adherence to the fine old forthright customs of your fathers affects me. There remains, to be sure, our bargain. Yet I am honestly affected, and since this parting grieves you so much, Florian, some composition must be reached—"

"It is undeniable," said Florian, with a reflective frown, "that my most near acquaintances address me—"

"I accept the reproof, I withdraw the vocative noun,

and again I entreat your pardon, Monsieur the Duke."

"I did not so much voice a reproof, Monsieur Janicot, as a sincere lament that I have never enjoyed the privilege of your close friendship." And Florian, too, bowed. "I was about to observe, then, that a gentleman adheres in all to all his bargains. So I can in logic consider no alteration of our terms, though you comprehend, I trust, how bitter I find their fulfilment."

"Yes," Janicot responded, "it is precisely the amount of your grief which I begin to comprehend. Its severity has even brought on a bronchial irritation which prevents your speaking freely: and indeed, one might have foreseen this."

"—So I have come to inquire how I am to get the sword Flamberge, which, as you may remember, must figure in the ceremony of—your pardon, but I really do appear to have contracted a quite obstinate cough in the night air,—of giving you your honorarium by the old ritual."

Janicot for a moment reflected. "You have sacrificed—"

"Monsieur, pray let us be logical! I have offered you no sacrifice. I have participated in no such inadvisable custom of heathenry. I must remind you that this is Christmas; and that I, naturally, elect to follow our Christian custom of exchanging appropriate gifts at this season of the year."

"I again apologize, I withdraw the verb. You have made me a Christmas present, then, of the life of a person of some note and mightiness, as your race averages. So it is your right to demand my aid. Yet there is one at your home, in an earthen pot, who could have procured for you the information, and very probably the sword too, without your stirring from your fireside and adored wife. It appears to me odd that, with so few months of happiness remaining, you should absent yourself from the sources of your only joy."

Florian's hand had risen in polite protest. "Ah, but, Monsieur Janicot, but in mere self-respect, one would not employ the power of which you speak, unless there were some absolute need. Now, for my part, I have always found it simple enough to get what I wanted without needing to thank anyone for help except myself. And Flamberge too is a prize that I prefer to win unaided, at the trivial price of a slight token of esteem at Christmas. I prefer, you conceive," said Florian, as smilingly he reflected upon the incessant carefulness one had to exercise in dealing with these fiends, "I prefer to settle the affair without incurring humiliating and possibly pyrotechnic obligations to anybody."

Janicot replied: "Doubtless, such independent sentiments are admirable. And it shall be as you like—"

"Still, Monsieur Janicot," said Florian, with just the proper amount of heartbreak in his voice. "is it not regrettable that this cruel price should be exacted of me?"

"Old customs must be honored, and mine are oldish. Besides, as I recall it, you suggested the bargain, not I."

"Yes, because I know that gifts from you are dangerous. Why, but let us be logical! Would you have me purchase an ephemeral pleasure at the price of my own ruin, when I could get it at the cost of somewhat inconveniencing others?"

"You say that my gifts are dangerous. Yet, what do you really know about me, Florian? Again I entreat your pardon, Monsieur the Duke, but, after all, our acquaintance progresses."

"I know nothing about you personally, Monsieur Janicot, beyond the handsomeness of your generosity. I only know the danger of accepting a free gift from any fiend; and you I take to be, in cosmic politics, a leader of the party in opposition."

Janicot looked grave for a moment. He said:

"No, I am not a fiend, Monsieur the Duke; nor, for that matter, does your current theology afford me any niche."

"Well, then," asked Florian, with his customary fine frankness, "If you are not the devil, what the devil are you!"

Janicot answered: "I am everything that was and that is to be. I am the Prince of this world. Never has any mortal been able to discover what I am. Never has any god been able to destroy me."

"Ah, monsieur, that sounds well, and, quite possibly, it means something. Of that I know no more than a frog does about toothache, but I do know they call you the adversary of all the gods of men—"

"Yes," Janicot admitted, rather sadly, "I have been hoping, now for a great while, that men would find some god with whom a rational person might make terms, but that seems never to happen."

"Monsieur, monsieur!" cried Florian, "pray let us have no scepticism—!"

"Scepticism also is a comfort denied to me. Men have that refuge always open. But I have in my time dealt with too many gods to have any doubt about them. No, I believe, and I shudder with distaste."

"Come, now, Monsieur Janicot, religion and somewhere to go on Sundays are quite necessary amenities—"

Janicot was surprised. "Why, but, Monsieur the Duke, can it be true that you, as a person of refinement, approve of worshiping goats and crocodiles and hawks and cats and hippopotami after the Egyptian custom?"

"Parbleu, not in the least! I, to the contrary—"

"Oh, you admire, then, the monkeys and tigers, in whose honor the men of India build temples?"

"Not at all. You misinterpret me—"

"Ah, I perceive. You approve, instead, of those gods

of Greece and Rome, who went about earth as bulls and cock cuckoos and as sprinklings of doubloons and five franc pieces, when they were particularly desirous of winning affection?"

"Now, Monsieur Janicot, you very foolishly affect to misunderstand me. One should be logical in these grave matters. One should know, as the whole world knows, that the Dukes of Puysange care nothing for the silly fables of paganism, and that, ever since the great Jurgen begot us, for five centuries, we of Puysange have been notable and loyal Christians."

Janicot said: "For five whole centuries! Jahveh also, being so young a god, must think that a long while; and doubtless he feels honored by these five centuries of patronage."

"Well, of course," said Florian, modestly, "As one of the oldest families hereabouts, we find that our example is apt to be followed. But we ourselves think little of our long lineage, we have grown used to it, we think that logically it is only the man himself who matters: and I confess, Monsieur Janicot, that it seems almost droll to see you impressed by our antiquity."

"I!" said Janicot. Then he said: "For all that, I am impressed. Yes, men are really wonderful. However, let that pass. So it is Jahveh of whom you approve. You confess it. Why, then, I ask you, as one logical person addressing another—"

"A pest! logic is a fine thing, but let us not put these matters altogether upon the ground of logic," said Florian, in some haste, as a large tumble-bug climbed on the rock, and sat beside Janicot.

"—I ask you," Janicot continued, "as one person of good taste addressing another—"

"It is not wholly an affair of connoisseurs. Let us talk about something else."

"—For you have this Jahveh's own history of his

exploits all written down at his own dictation. I allow him candor, nor, for one so young, does he write badly. For the rest, do these cruelties, these double-dealings, these self-confessed divine blunders and mis-calculations, these subornings of murders and thefts and adulteries, these punishments of the innocent, not sparing even his own family—"

Florian yawned delicately, but without removing his eyes from the tumble-bug. "My dear Monsieur Janicot, that sort of talk is really rather naïve. It is, if you will pardon my frankness, quite out of date now that we have reached the eighteenth century."

"Yes, but—"

"No, Monsieur Janicot, I can consent to hear no more of these sophomoric blasphemies. I must tell you I have learned that in these matters, as in all matters, it is better taste to recognize some drastic regeneration may be necessary without doing anything about it, and certainly without aligning ourselves with the foul anar-chistic mockers of everything in our social chaos which in making for beauty and righteousness—"

"Why, but, Monsieur the Duke," said Janicot, "but what—!"

"I must tell you I perceive, in honest sorrow, that with a desire for fescennine expression you combine a vulgar atheism and an iconoclastic desire to befoul the sacred ideas of the average man or woman, collectively scorned as the bourgeoisie—"

"Yes, doubtless, this is excellent talking. Still, what—?"

"I must tell you also that I very gravely suspect you to be one of those half-baked intellectuals who confuse cheap atheism, and the defiling of other men's altars, with deep thinking; one of those moral and spir-itual hooligans who resent all forms of order as an en-croachment upon their diminutive, unkempt and unsavory egos; one of the kind of people who relish nasty books about sacred persons and guffaw over the amours of the angels."

"Yes, I concede the sonority of your periods; but what does all this talking mean?"

"Why, monsieur," said Florian, doubtfully, "I do not imagine that it means anything. These are merely the customary noises of well-thought-of-persons in reply to the raising of any topic which they prefer not to pursue. It is but an especially dignified manner of saying that I do not care to follow the line of thought you suggest, because logic here might lead to uncomfortable conclusions and to deductions without honorable precedents."

"Ah, now I understand you," said Janicot, smiling. He looked down, and stroked the tumble-bug, which under his touch shrank and vanished. "I should have noticed the odor before; and, as it is, I confess that, in this frank adhesion to your folly without pretending it is anything else, I recognize a minim of wisdom. So let us say no more about it. Let us return to the question of that sword with which you, as a loyal servant of him who also came not to bring peace, but a sword, have need to sever your family ties. Those persons just behind you were very pretty swordsmen in their day: and I imagine that they can give you all the necessary information as to the sword Flamberge."

XVI

Some Victims of Flamberge

 T was really no affair of Florian's, how vaguely-hued and quaintly appareled persons happened to be standing just behind him. They had not been there a moment ago: but Janicot seemed partial to these small wonder-workings, and such foibles, while in dubious taste, did not greatly matter.

So Florian was off again with his silver-laced hat, and Florian saluted these strangers with extreme civility. And Florian inquired of the gray and great-thewed champion if he knew of the whereabouts of Flamberge; and this tall man answered:

"No. It was a fine sword, and I wore it once when I had mortal life and was very young. But I surrendered this sword to a woman, in exchange for that which I most desired. So I got no good of Flamberge, nor did anyone else so far as I could ever hear, for there is a curse upon this sword."

"A curse, indeed!" said Florian, somewhat astonished. "Why, but I have always been told, monsieur, that the wearer of Flamberge is unconquerable."

"That I believe to be true. Thus the wearer of Flamberge can get all his desires, and he usually does so: and, having them, he understands that the sword is accursed."

"And did you too get your desire in this world, monsieur, and perceive the worth of it?"

"My boy, there is a decency in these matters, and an

indecency. I got my desire. And having it, I did not complain. Let that suffice."

With that, the speaker picked up his shield, upon which you saw emblazoned a rampant and bridled stallion; and this tall, gray, squinting, military looking man was there no longer.

Then came a broad and surly person, in garments of faded scarlet, and with gems dangling from his ears, and he said: 'From him, who was in his day a Redeemer, the sword came to my mother, and from her to me, and with it I slew my father, as was foreordained. And the sword made me unconquerable, and I went fearing nobody, and I ruled over much land, and I was dreaded upon the wide sea. And the sword won for me the body of that woman whom I desired, and the sword won for me long misery and a snapped backbone and sudden ruin."

"A pest!" said Florian. "So you also, monsieur, were the victim of your own triumph!"

"Not wholly," the other answered. "For I learned to envy and to admire that which I could not understand. That is something far better worth learning than you, poor shallow-hearted little posturer, are ever likely to suspect."

And now came a third champion, who said: "From him, who was in his day a most abominable pagan and a very gallant gentleman as well, the sword came to me. And I cast it into the deep sea, because I meant to gain my desire unaided by sorcery and with clean hands. And I did get my desire."

"And did you also live unhappily ever afterward"

"Our marriage was as happy as most marriages. My love defied Time and Fate. Because of my love I suffered unexampled chances and ignominies, and I performed deeds that are still rhymed about; and in the end, through my unswerving love, I got me a wife who was as good as most wives. So I made no complaint, but, instead, I made her a fair husband, as husbands go."

And Florian nodded. "I take your meaning. There was once a king and a queen. They had three sons. And the third prince succeeded in everything— Your faces and your lives are strange to me. But it is plain all four of us have ventured into the high place, that dreadful place wherein a man attains to his desires."

Then said another person: "That comes of meddling with Flamberge. Now my weapon was, at least upon some occasions, called Caliburn. And I ventured into a great many places, but I was careful of my behavior in all of them."

"Did you thus attain your desire, monsieur?"

"Never, my lad, although I had some narrow shaves. Why, once there was only a violet coverlet between me and destruction, but I was poet enough to save myself."

"Parbleu, now that is rather odd! For I first saw my wife—I mean, my present duchess,—asleep beneath a violet coverlet."

"Ah," said the other, drily, "so that is where you sought a woman to be, of all things, your wife! Then you are braver than I: but you are certainly not a monstrous clever fellow."

"Well, well!" said Florian, "so the refrain of this obsolescent quartet is a jingle-jangle of shallow and cheap pessimism: and the upshot of the matter is that Flamberge is lost somewhere in the old time, and that I know not how to come to it."

"That is easy," said the fifth person, the only one who now remained. "You must adventure as they once adventured, who were your forefathers, and you must go with me, who am called Horvendile, into Antan. For nowadays I am Lord of the Marches of Antan—"

"Were those evaporating gentlemen my forefathers?" asked Florian. "And how does one go into the Antan of whose Marches you are the overlord?"

"They were," answered Horvendile. "And one goes in this way." He explained the way, and the need for traveling on it.

And Florian looked rather dubious and took snuff. He saw that Janicot had vanished from the asherah stone, with that ostentatious simplicity the brown creature seemed to affect. Then Florian shrugged, and said he would go wherever Horvendile dared go, since this appeared now the only chance of coming by the sword Flamberge.

"And as for those who were my forefathers, and begot me, I would of course have said something civil, to express my appreciation of their exertions, if I had known. But between ourselves, Monsieur Horvendile, I would have preferred to meet some of the more imposing progenitors of Puysange,—say, heroic old Dom Manuel or the great Jurgen,—instead of these commonplace people. It is depressing to find any of one's own ancestors just ordinary persons, persons too who seem quite down in the mouth, and with so little life in them—"

"To be quite ordinary persons," replied Horvendile, "is a failing woefully common to all men and to the daughters of all men, nor does that foible shock anybody who is not a romantic. As for having very little life in them, what more do you expect of phantoms? The life that was once in these persons today endures in you. For it is a truism—preached to I do not, unluckily, know how many generations,—that the life which informed your ancestor, tall Manuel the Redeemer, did not perish when Manuel passed beyond the sunset, but remained here upon earth to animate the bodies of his children and of their children after them."

"But by this time Manuel must have the progeny of a sultan or of a town bull—"

"Yes," Horvendile conceded, "in a great many bodies, and in countless estates, that life has known a largish number of fruitless emotions. At least, they appear to me to have been rather fruitless. . . . And to-day that life wears you, Monsieur de Puysange, as its temporary garment or, it may be, as a mask: to-morrow you also will have been put by. For that is always the ending of the comedy."

"Well, so that the comedy wherein I figure be merry enough—"

"It is not ever a merry comedy," replied Horvendile, "though, for one, I find it amusing. For I forewarn you that the comedy does not vary. The first act is the imagining of the place where contentment exists and may be come to; and the second act reveals the striving toward, and the third act the falling short of, that shining goal,—or, else, the attaining of it, to discover that happiness, after all, abides a thought farther down the bogged, rocky, clogged befogged, heart-breaking road."

"Ah, but," said Florian, "these reflections are doubtless edifying, since they combine gloom with verbosity and no exact meaning. Still, it is not happiness I am looking for, but a sword to which all this philosophizing brings us no step nearer. No, it is not happiness I seek. For through that sword, when I have got it, will come such misery as I cannot bear to think of, since its sharp edge must sever me irrevocably from that perfect beauty which I have adored since boyhood. None the less, I have given my word; and these old phantoms have unanimously reassured me that it is better to have love end at full tide. So let us be logical, and let us go forward, Monsieur Horvendile, as merrily as may be possible."

XVII

The Armory of Antan

HE way to Antan was woman-haunted, and it was made difficult by darkness and obstacles and illusions; and the main three who guarded that cedar-shadowed way were called Glaum of the Haunting Eyes and Tenjo of the Long Nose and Maya of the Fair Breasts. But these warders did not greatly bother Horvendile, who passed them by the appointed methods and through means which Florian found remarkable if not actually indelicate. Yet you were not allowed, said Horvendile, to travel on the road of gods and myths. And therefore in no other way than through these cedargroves and through the local customs might you win to Freydis, whom love brought out of Audela to suffer as a mortal woman, and whom the druids and satirists had brought, through Sesphra's wicked aid, to Antan. Thus had she come to reign in Antan, as the Queen Consort of the Master Philologist, and to attest her ardor to do harm and to work great mischief.

Now this part of Antan was a queer place, all cloudiness and grayness, but full of gleamings which reminded you of sparks that linger insecurely among ashes: and there were no real noises, not even when you talked. And when Horvendile had departed, you asked this gray and dimly golden woman if the sword Flamberge was to be come by anywhere in madame's most charming and tasteful residence? She replied, a shadow speaking with the shadow of a voice, that it was perhaps somewhere in her armory: and she then led the way into a misty place wherein were all those famous swords whereby came many deaths and a little fame.

Very curious it was to see them coldly shining in the mistiness, and to handle them. Here was long Durandal, with which Sir Roland split a cleft in the Pyrenees; and beside it hung no less redoubtable Haulte-Claire, with which Sir Oliver had held his own against Durandal and Durandal's fierce master, in that great battling which differed from other military encounters by resulting in something memorable and permanent, in the form of a proverb. Here was Lancelot's sword Aroundight, here was Ogier's Courtain, and Siegfried's Balmung. One saw in this dim place the Cid's Colada, Sir Bevis's Morglay, the Crocea Mors of Cæsar, and the Joyeuse of Charlemagne. Nor need one look in vain for Curtana and Quernbiter, those once notable guardians of England and Norway, nor for Mistelstein, nor Tizona, nor Greysteel, nor Angurvadel, nor any other charmed sword of antiquity. All were here: and beside Joyeuse was hung Flamberge; for Galas made both of them.

Well, you estimated, Flamberge was by no means the handsomest of the lot: but it would serve your turn, you did not desire to seem grasping. And since madame appeared somewhat oversupplied with cutlery—

Indeed that was the truth, as Freydis could not deny, in the thin tones which people's voices had in Antan, since not only these patrician murderers harbored here. Here too were death's plebeian tools in every form. Here were Italian stilettos heaped with Malay krisses, the hooked Turkish scimitar with the Venetian schiavona; curved Arab yataghans, sabres that Yoshimitzu had tempered, the Albanian cutlass, and the notched blades of Zanzibar; the two-handed

claymores of Scotland, the espada of the Spanish mata-
dor, the scalping-knives of the Red Indians and the
ponderous glaives of executioners: swords from all cities and all kingdoms of the world, from Ferrara and
Toledo and Damascus, from Dacia and Peru and Mus-
covy and Babylon.

To which you replied that, while you had never
greatly cared for the cataloguing method in literature,
you allowed its merits in conversation. These crisp little résumés indicated a really firm grasp of the subject.
For the rest, it was most interesting to note what ingenuity people had displayed in contriving how to kill
one another.

Freydis assented as to men's whole-heartedness in
malignity, but was disposed to view without optimism
the support it got from human ingenuity. She considered these swords in any event to be outmoded lumber,
as concerned the needs of anybody who really desired
to do harm and work any actually great mischief.

Still, you, whose speaking seemed even to you a
whisper in the grayness, declined to be grasping: and
Flamberge would serve your turn. Therefore it was
vexatious that, instead of gracefully presenting you
with the sword, the Queen of Antan went through a
gray vague corridor, wherein upon a table lay a hand-
ful of rusty iron nails and a spear, and then into another twilit place.

Here, as you hastily observed, were madame's pistols, cannons, culverins, grenades, musketoons, harque-
busses, bombs, petronels, siege-guns, falconets, car-
bines, and jingals, and swivels. Yes, it was most interesting.

Freydis looked at you somewhat queerly: and it
was, again, as outmoded lumber that she appraised this
arsenal. Then Freydis almost proudly showed the
weapons which she had in store for men's needs when
men should go to war to-morrow, and such assistants

would further every patriot's desire to do harm and work great mischief. And you felt rather uncomfortable to see the sleek efficiency of these gleaming things in this ambiguous place.

Yes, they were very interesting, and, beside them, Flamberge certainly seemed inadequate. Still, you admitted, you had never been grasping: and Flamberge would serve your turn.

It was really maddening how the woman kept turning to irrelevant matters. These engines of destruction, although ingenious and devastating toys within their limits, should not be regarded over-seriously. A million or so persons, or at most a few nations, could be removed with these things, but that was all. So speaking, she passed into a room wherein were books,—but not many books—and four figures modelled in clay, as she told you, by old Dom Manuel very long ago. It was more important, her thin talking went on, that as occasion served she was sending into the world these figures, to follow their six predecessors, to each one of whom she had given a life empoisoned with dreams, with dreams which were immortal, and were so contagious that they would infect still other dreamers and yet others eternally, and thus would make living as unhappy and as morbid a business as dying. What were these dreams? she was asked: and she in turn asked, Why should I tell you? Your own dream is quite different, nor may you escape it. This must suffice: that the dreams I send are the most subtle and destructive of poisons, and do harm and work great mischief, in that they enable men to see that life and all which life can afford is inadequate to human desires.

This seemed rather unwholesome talk. To evade it tactfully, the four changelings as yet unborn were examined, with civil comments: and indeed there was about one little hook-nosed figure a something which quite took the fancy. He reminds me of a parrot, was your smilingly tendered verdict: and Freydis, with her habitual tired shrugging, replied that others, later, would detect, without much reticence, a resemblance to that piratical and repetitious bird.

Now then, all this was very interesting, most interesting, and you really regretted having to revert to the topic of the sword Flamberge— Freydis had not made up her mind: she might or might not give the sword, and her deciding must pivot upon what harm you meant to do with it. Her visitor from the more cheery world of daylight was thus forced to make a clean breast of why he needed Flamberge, the only sword which may spill the blood of the Léshy, so that he might give, by the old ritual, his unborn child, and rid himself of his wife.

Whereupon Queen Freydis expressed frank indignation, because the child would by this plan be rescued from all, and the woman from much, sorrow. Could even a small madman in bottle-green and silver suppose that the Queen of Antan, after centuries of thriving malevolence, was thus to be beguiled into flagrant philanthropy?

But that which you had suggested was not, in the long run, philanthropy, you insisted. It was depressing to have to argue about anything in this gray, vague, gleaming, endless place, wherein you seemed only to whisper: and you were, privately, a little taken aback by the unaccustomed need to prove an action, not amply precedented and for the general good, but the precise contrary. Aloud,—though not actually aloud, but in the dim speech one uses in Antan,—you contended that when a man thus rid himself of his wife he did harm and worked great mischief, because the spectacle made all beholders unhappy. Women, of course, had obvious reasons for uneasiness lest the example be followed generally: and men were roused to veritable frenzies of pious reprovings when they saw the thing which they had so often thought of doing accomplished by somebody else.

Did married men, then, at heart always desire to murder their wives? was what Freydis wondered. No, you did not say that: not always; some wives let weeks go by without provoking that desire. And to appearances, most men became in the end more or less reconciled to having their wives about. Still, let us not go wholly by appearances. Let us be logical! Whom does any man most dislike?

Freydis had settled down, with faint golden shimmerings, upon a couch which was covered with gray cushions, and she meditated. What person does any man most dislike? Why, Freydis estimated, the person who most frequently annoys him, the person with whom he finds himself embroiled in the most bitter quarrels, the person whose imperfections are to him most glaringly apparent, and, in fine, the person who most often and most poignantly makes him uncomfortable.

Just so, you assented: and in the life of any possible married man, who was that person? The question was rhetorical. You did not have to answer it, any more than did most husbands. None the less, you esteemed it a question which no married man had failed to consider, if gingerly and as if from afar, if only with the mere tail of his mental eye, in unacknowledged reveries. It was perhaps the memory of these cloistered considerations which made married men acutely uncomfortable when any other man disposed of his wife without all this half-hearted paltering with the just half-pleasant notion that some day she would go so far as to make justifiable— A gesture showed what, as plainly as one could show anything in this vague endlessness of grays and gleamings. No; madame might depend upon it, to assist any gentleman in permanently disposing of his wife was not, in the long run, philanthropy.

It really did make the majority of other husbands uncomfortable, whether through envy or whether through a conscience-stricken recalling of unacknowledged reveries, you did not pretend to say.

All that might be true enough, Freydis admitted, from her dim nook among the gray cushions, without alluring her into the charitable act of freeing a child from the sorrows and fatigues of living.

Ah, but here again, madame must not reason so carelessly, nor be misled by specious first appearances. Let us, instead, be logical! The child, knowing nothing, would not know what it was escaping: and it would not be grateful, it would derive no æsthetic pleasure from the impressive ceremony of giving by the old ritual, it would even resent the moment's physical pain. But the beholders of the deed, and all that heard of it, would be acutely uncomfortable, since the father who secured for his child immunity from trouble and annoyance, did harm and worked great mischief by setting an example which aroused people to those frenzies evocable by no other prodigy than a display of common-sense.

For people would turn from this proof of paternal affection, to the world from which the child was being removed: and people would be unhappy, because, with all their natural human propensity for fault-finding tugging them toward denunciation, nobody would be able to deny the common-sense of rescuing a child from discomforts and calamities. What professional perjurer anywhere, madame, whether in prison or politics or the pulpit, could muster the effrontery to declare life other than a long series of discomforts diversified only by disasters? What serene, what wholly untroubled person could you encounter anywhere outside of homes for the insane? What dignity was possible in an arena we entered in the manner of urine and left in the shape of ordure? What father endowed with any real religious faith could, after the most cursory glancing over of the sufferings which men got gratis in this life and laboriously earned in the next, could then appraise without conscience-stricken remorse the dilemma in which he had placed his offspring?

Well, to see thus revealed the one sure way of rescuing the child from this disastrous position, and to know himself too much a poltroon to follow the example of which his judgment and all his better instincts approved, was a situation that, madame, must make every considerate parent unhappy, through the one manner in which alone might every man be made really miserable,—by preventing him from admiring himself any longer.

For parents would look, too, toward the nearest police officer and toward the cowardice in their own hearts: and these commingled considerations would prevent many fathers from doing their plain duty. They would send many and it might be the hapless majority of fathers to bed that night with clean hands, with the pallid hands of self-convicted dastards: and self-contempt would make these fathers always unhappy. No, here again, madame might depend upon it that to assist a gentleman in this giving, by the old ritual, of his offspring was not, in the long run, and whatever the deed might seem to a first glance, philanthropy. It did some good: one could not deny that: but, after all, the child was absolutely the only person who profited, and through the benefits conferred upon the child was furthered the greatest ill and discomfort for the greatest number, who, here as in every other case, replied to any display of common-sense with frenzies that did harm and everywhither splutteringly worked mischief.

And you spoke with such earnestness, and so much logic, that in the end the vaguely golden Queen of Antan smiled toward you through the gray mist, and said that you reminded her of her own children. You were enamored of words, you delighted in any nonsense which was sonorous. You were like all her children, she told you, the children whom, in spite of herself, she pitied. Here Freydis sighed.

Pity has kindred, you stated. Freydis leaned back among the gray cushions of her couch, so as to listen in perfect ease, and she bade you explain that saying.

And as you sat down beside her, Puysange arose to the occasion. Here was familiar ground at last, the ground on which Puysange thrust forward with most firmness. And you reflected that it would be inappropriate to lament, just now, that not even in Antan did a rigidity of logic seem to get for anyone the victory which you foresaw to be secured by your other gifts. . . .

When Florian left Antan, the needed sword swung at his thigh.

XVIII

Problems of Holiness

THUS it was not until Handsel Monday that Florian took the serious step which led from the realm in which Queen Freydis ruled, to the world of every day; and Florian found there, standing on the asherah stone upon which Janicot had received homage, no other person than Holy Hoprig.

"So I catch you creeping out of Antan," observed the Saint, and his halo glittered rather sternly. "I shall not pry into your actions there, because Antan is not a part of this world, and it is only your doings in this world which more or less involve my heavenly credit. Upon account of that annoying tie I now admonish you. For now we enter a new year, and this is the appropriate season for making good resolutions. It would be wise for you to make a great many of them, my son, for I warn you that I am a resolute spiritual father, and do not intend to put up with any wickedness now that you return to the world of men."

This was to Florian a depressing moment. He had been to a large deal of trouble to get the sword Flamberge, upon whose powers depended his whole future. And the instant he had it, here in his path was a far stronger power, with notions which bid fair to play the very devil with Florian's plans. Now one could only try what might be done with logic and politeness.

"Your interest in my career, Monsieur Hoprig, affects me more deeply than I can well express; and I shall treasure your words. Still, Monsieur Hoprig, in view of your own past, and in view of all your abominable misdeeds as a priest of heathenry, one might anticipate a little broadmindedness—"

"My past is quite good enough for any saint in eternity, and so, my son, ought not to be sneered at by any whippersnapper of a sorcerer—"

"Putting aside your delusion as to my necromantic accomplishments, I had always supposed, monsieur, that the living of a saint would be distinguished by meritorious actions, by actions worthy of our emulation. And so—!"

Hoprig sat down, sitting where Janicot had sat, and Hoprig made himself comfortable. When all was redisposed, and the luxurious scratching was over, the Saint remarked:

"That is as it may be. People get canonized in various ways, and people, if you have ever noticed it, are human—"

"Still, for all that, monsieur—"

"—With human frailties. Now my confrères, I find since the extension of my acquaintance in heavenly circles, are no exception to this rule. St. Afra, the patroness of Augsburg, was for many years a courtesan in that city, conducting a brothel in which three other saints, the blessed Digna, Eunomia and Eutropia, exerted themselves with equal vigor and viciousness. St. Aglae and St. Boniface for a long while maintained an illicit carnal connection. St. Andrea of Corsini conducted himself in every respect abominably until his mother dreamed that she had given birth to a wolf, and so, of course, converted him. As for St. Augustine, I can but blush, my dear son, and refer you to his Confessions—"

"Still, monsieur, I think—"

"You are quite wrong. St. Benedict led for fifteen years a sinful life, precisely as St. Bavon was a profligate for fifty. St. Bernard Ptolemei was a highly successful lawyer, than which I need say no more—"

"Yet, monsieur, if I be not mistaken—"

"You are mistaken," replied Hoprig. "The Saints Constantine and Charlemagne committed every sort of atrocity and abomination, excepting only that of parsimony to the Church. St. Christopher made a pact with Satan, and St. Cyprian of Antioch also was, like you, my poor child, a most iniquitous sorcerer—"

"Let us go no further in the alphabet, for there are twenty-six letters, of which, I perceive, you have reached only the third. I was merely about to observe," said Florian, at a venture, "that you, after living dishonestly—"

"Now, if you come to that, St. George of Cappadocia was an embezzler. St. Guthlac of Croydon was by profession a cut-throat and a thief—"

"—After," continued Florian, where guessing seemed to thrive, "after your being involved in I know not how many escapades with women—"

"Whom I at worst accompanied in just the physical experiments through which were graduated into eternal grace St. Margaret of Cortona, St. Mary the Egyptian, St. Mary the Penitent, St. Mary Magdalene, and I cannot estimate how many other ladies now canonized."

"—And, worst of all, after your persecuting and murdering of real Christians—"

"St. Paul stones Stephen the Protomartyr; St. Vitalis of Ravenna and St. Torpet of Pisa both served under Nero, that arch-persecutor of the faithful; and St. Longinus conducted the Crucifixion. No, Florian: no, I admit that at first I was a trifle uncertain. For I did remember some incidents that were capable of misconstruction and exaggeration, and people talk too much upon this side of the grave for burial quite to cure them of the habit. But since moving more widely among the dead and blessed elect, it has been extremely gratifying to find my past as blameless as that of most other holy persons."

"—You, after all these enormities, I say, have been canonized by the lost tail of an R, and through mistake have been fitted out with a legend in which there is no word of truth—"

"The histories of many of my more immaculate confrères have that same little defect. St. Hippolytus, who never heard of Christianity, since he lived, if at all, several hundred years before the Christian era, was canonized by a mistake. St. Filomena's legend rests upon nothing save the dreams of a priest and an artist, who were thus favored with, one regrets to note, quite incompatible revelations. The name of St. Viar was presented for beatification because of a time-disfigured tombstone, like mine, a stone upon which remained only part of the Latin word *viarum;* and two syllables of a road-inspector's vocation were thus esteemed worthy of being canonized. The record of St. Undecimilla was misread as relating to eleven thousand virgins, and so swelled the Calendar with that many saints who were later discovered never to have existed. No, Florian, mistakes seem to occur everywhere, in awarding the prizes of celestial as well as earthly life: but not even those of the elect who have without any provocation been thrust into the highest places of heaven ought to complain, for one never really gains anything by being hypercritical."

"Why, then, monsieur, I say that all these legends—"

"You are quite wrong. They are excellent legends. I know that, for one, I have been moved to tears and to the most exalted emotions of every kind through considering my own history. What boy had ever a more edifying start in life than that ten years of meditation in a barrel? It was not a beer barrel either, I am sure, for stale beer has a vile odor. No, Florian, you may depend upon it, that barrel had been made aromatic by a generous and full-bodied wine, by a rather sweetish wine, I think—"

"Yes, but, monsieur—"

Still Hoprig's rolling voice went on, unhurriedly and very nobly, and with something of the stateliness of an organ's music: and in the Saint's face you saw unlimited benevolence, and magnanimity, and such deep and awe-begetting wisdom as seemed more than human.

And Hoprig said: "Wonder awakens in me when I consider my travels, and stout admiration when I regard the magnificence of my deeds. Why, but, my son, I defied two emperors to their pagan faces, I sailed in a stone trough beyond the sunset, I killed five dragons, I forget how many barbarous tribes I converted, and I intrepidly went down into Pohjola and into the fearful land of Xibalba, among big tigers and blood-sucking bats, to the rescue of my poor friend Hork! Now I consider these things with a pride which is not selfish, but with pride in the race and in the religion which produces such heroism: and I consider these things with tears also, when I think of my steadfastness under heathen persecution. Do you but recall, my dear child, what torments I endured! I was bound to a wheel set with knives. I was given poison to drink. I was made to run in red-hot iron shoes. I was cast into quicklime — But I abridge the list of my sufferings, for it is too harrowing. I merely point out that the legend is excellent."

"But, monsieur, this legend is not true."

"The truth, my son," replied the Saint, "is that which a person, for one reason or another, believes. Now if I had really been put to the horrible inconvenience of doing all these splendid things, and they had been quite accurately reported, my legend would to-day be precisely what it is: it would be no more or less than the fine legend which piety has begotten upon imagination. You will grant that, I hope?"

"Nobody denies that. It is only—"

"Then how can it to-day matter a pennyworth whether or not I did these things?" asked the Saint, reasonably.

"Well, truly now, Monsieur Hoprig, the way you put it—"

"I put it, my son, in the one rational way. We must zealously preserve those invigorating stories of the heroic and virtuous persons who lived here before our time so gloriously, because people have need of these excellent examples. It would be a terrible misfortune if these stories were not known everywhere, and were not always at hand to hearten everybody in hours of despondency by showing what virtuous men can rise to at need. These examples comfort the discouraged with a sentiment of their importance as moral beings and of the greatness of their destinies. So, since the actual living of men has at no time, unluckily, afforded quite the necessary examples, the philanthropic historian selects, he prunes, he colors, he endeavors, like any other artist, to make something admirable out of his raw material. The miracles which the painter performs with evil-smelling greases, the sculptor with mud, and the musician with the intestines of a cat, the historian emulates through the even more unpromising medium of human action. And that is as it should be: for life is a continuous battle between the forces of good and evil, and news from the front ought to be delivered in the form best suited to maintain our morale. Yes, it is quite as it should be, for fine beliefs do everybody good."

"Parbleu, monsieur, I cannot presume to argue with you; but this sort of logic is unsettling. It is also unsettling to reflect that all the magnificent gifts I have been offering to your church were sheer waste, since you have not been at your post attending to the forgiveness of my irregularities. You conceive, monsieur, I had kept very exact accounts, with an equitable and even generous assessment for every form of offence; and to find that all this painstaking has gone for nothing has upset my conscience."

"That is probable. Still, I suspect that famous conscience of yours is as much good to you upset as in any other position."

"Well, but, monsieur, now that my other troubles seem in every likelihood to approach a settlement," said Florian, caressing the pommel of Flamberge, "what would you have me do about rectifying my unfortunate religious status?"

The Saint looked now at Florian for a long while. In the great shining pale blue eyes of Hoprig was much of knowledge and of pity. "You must repent, my son. What are good works without repentance?"

"A pest! if that is all which is needful, I shall put my mind to it at once," said Florian, brightening. "And doubtless I shall find something to repent of."

"I think that more than probable. What is certain is that I have no more time to be wasting on you. I have given you my fair warning, in the most delicate possible terms, without even once alluding to my enjoyment of thaumaturgic powers and my especial proficiency in blasting, cursing and smiting people with terrible afflictions. I prefer, my dear child, to keep matters on a pleasant footing as long," the Saint said meaningly, "as may prove possible. So I have not in any way alluded to these little personal gifts. I have merely warned you quite affably that, for the sake of my celestial credit, I intend to put up with no wickedness from you; and I have duly called you to repentance. With these duties rid of, I can be off to Morven. After having seen, during the last five months, as much of this modern world as particularly appeals to a saint in the prime of life, I am establishing a hermitage in Upper Morven."

"And for what purpose, may one ask?" Florian was reflecting that Morven stood uncomfortably near to Bellegarde.

The Saint regarded Florian with some astonishment. "One may ask, to be sure, my son: but why should one answer?"

"Well, but, monsieur, this Upper Morven is a place of horrible fame, a place which is reputed still to be given over to sorcery—"

"I would feel some unavoidable compassion for any sorcerer that I caught near my hermitage: but, none the less, I would do my duty as a Christian saint with especial proficiency—"

"—And, monsieur, you would be terribly lonely upon Upper Morven."

It appeared to Florian that the Saint's smile was distinctly peculiar. "One need never be lonely," St. Hoprig stated, "when one is able to work miracles."

With that he slightly smacked his lips and vanished.

And Florian remained alone with many and firm grounds for depression, and with forebodings which caused him to look somewhat forlornly at the sword Flamberge. For there seemed troubles ahead with which Flamberge could hardly cope.

LORIAN did not at once set forth for Bellegarde, to make the utmost of the four months of happiness which he might yet hope to share with Melior. Instead, he despatched a very loving letter to his wife, lamenting that business matters would prevent his returning before February.

Meanwhile he had gone to the Hôtel de Puysange. Along with Clermont, Simiane, the two Belle-Isles, and all the rest of Orléans' fraternity of roués, Florian found himself evicted from Versailles. His rooms there had already been assigned to the de Pries, by the new minister, Monsieur de Bourbon, whom Florian esteemed to have acted with unbecoming promptness and ingratitude.

Florian, in any event, went to the Hôtel de Puysange, where he lived rather retiredly for a month. He did not utterly neglect his social duties between supper- and breakfast-time. But during the day he excused himself from participation in any debauchery, and save for three trivial affairs of honor,—in which Florian took part only as a second, and killed only one of his opponents, an uninteresting looking young Angevin gentleman, whose name he did not catch,—with these exceptions, Florian throughout that month lived diurnally like an anchorite.

Nobody could speak certainly of what went on in the daytime within the now inhospitable gates of the

Hôtel de Puysange, but the rumors as to Florian's doings were on that account none the less numerous.

It was public, in any event, that he had retained Albert Aluys, the most accomplished sorcerer then practising in the city. What these two were actually about at this time, behind the locked gates of the Hôtel de Puysange, remains uncertain, for Florian never discussed the matter. Aluys, when questioned,—though the value of his evidence is somewhat tempered by his known proficiency and ardor at lying,—reported that Monsieur the Duke made use of his services only to evoke the most famous and beautiful women of bygone times. That was reasonable enough: but, what the deuce! once these marvelous creatures were materialized and ready for all appropriate employment, then monseigneur asked nothing of the loveliest queens and empresses except to talk with him. It was not as if he got any pleasure from it, either: for after ten minutes of the prettiest woman's talking about how historians had misunderstood her with a fatuity equalled only by that of her husband and his relatives, and about what had been the true facts in her earthly life,—after ten minutes of these friendly confidences, monseigneur would shake his head, and would even groan outright, and would ask that the lady be returned to her last home.

Monseigneur, in point of fact, seemed put out by the circumstance that these ladies manifested so little intelligence. As if, a shrugging Aluys demanded of Heaven's common-sense, it were not for the benefit of humanity at large that all beautiful women were created a trifle stupid. The ladies whom one most naturally desired to seduce were thus made the most apt to listen to the seducer: for the good God planned the greatest good for the greatest number.

When February had come, and Florian might hope to share with Melior only three more months of happiness, Florian sent a letter to his wife to bewail the necessity of his remaining away from home until March. The rumors as to his doings were now less colorful but equally incredible. Yet nothing certainly was known of his pursuits, beyond the fact that Aluys reported they were evoking the dead persons who had been pre-eminent for their holiness and mental gifts and other admirable qualities; and that even by the most bright examples of human excellence Monsieur de Puysange appeared disappointed.

For he seemed, Aluys lamented, really not to have comprehended that when men perform high actions or voice impressive sentiments, this is by ordinary the affair of a few moments in a life of which the remainder is much like the living of all other persons. Monsieur de Puysange appeared to have believed that famous captains won seven battles every week, that authentic poets conversed in hexameters, and that profound sages did not think far less frequently about philosophy than their family affairs. As if too, Aluys cried out, it were not very pleasant to know the littlenesses of the great and the frailties of the most admirable! —Æschylos had confessed to habitual drunkenness, the prophet Moses stuttered, and Charlemagne told how terribly he had suffered with bunions. Monsieur de Puysange ought to be elated by securing these valuable bits of historical information, but, to the contrary, they seemed to depress him. He regretted, one judged, that his colloquies with the renowned dead revealed that human history had been shaped and guided by human beings. A romantic! was Aluys' verdict: and you cannot cure that. The gentleman will have an unhappy life.

"His wives die quickly," was hazarded.

"They would," Aluys returned: "and it makes for the benefit of all parties."

Upon the first day of March, when Florian could

hope at most to share only two more months of happiness with Melior, Florian sent a letter to his wife announcing the postponement until April of his homecoming. And throughout this month too he lived in equal mystery, except that toward the end of March he entertained a party of young persons at a supper followed by that form of debauch which was then most fashionable, a fête d'Adam.

"Let us not be epigrammatic," Florian had said, as they stripped at outset. "Love differs from marriage; and men are different from women: and a restatement of either of these facts is an epigram. It is understood that we are all capable of such revamping. So let us, upon this my birthnight, talk logically."

They discussed, in consequence, between the ardors of their sports, that new world and that new era which was upon them. For Europe was just then tidying up the ruin into which the insane ambition of one man, discredited Louis Quatorze, had plunged civilization. All the conventions of society had given way under the strain of war, so that the younger generation was left without any illusions. Those older people, who had so boggled matters, had been thrust aside in favor of more youthful and more vigorous exponents of quite new fallacies, and everyone knew that he was privileged to live at a period in the world's history hitherto unparalleled. So they had a great deal to talk over at supper, with the errors of human society at last triumphantly exposed, and with the younger generation at last permitted utter freedom in self-expression, and with recipes for all the needful social regeneration obtainable everywhere.

"We live," it was confidently stated, "in a new world, which can never again become the world we used to know."

Thus it was not until the coming of spring that Florian rode away from the Hôtel de Puysange, wherein he had just passed the first actually unhappy period of Florian's life. For this man had long and fervently cherished his exalted ideals: and since his boyhood the beauty of Melior and the holiness of Hoprig had been at once the criteria and the assurance of human perfectibility. To think of these two had preserved him in faith and in wholesome optimism: for here was perfect beauty and perfect holiness attained once by mankind, and in consequence not unattainable. To dream of these two had kept Florian prodigally supplied with lofty thoughts of human excellence. And these two had thus enriched the living of Florian with unfailing streams of soothing and ennobling poesy, of exactly the kind which, in Hoprig's fine phrase, was best suited to impress him with a sentiment of his importance as a moral being and of the greatness of man's destiny.

Now all was changed. Now in the Saint he found, somehow, a sort of ambiguity; not anything toward which one could plump a corporeal forefinger, but, rather, a nuance of some indescribable inadequacy. Florian could not but, respectfully, and with profound unwillingness, suspect that any daily living, hour in and hour out, with Holy Hoprig—in that so awkwardly situated hermitage upon Morven,—would bear as fruitage discoveries woefully parallel to the results of such intimacy with Melior.

And of Melior her husband thought with even more unwillingness. At Bellegarde he had found her, to the very last, endurable. But now that Florian was again at court, the exigencies of his social obligations had drawn him into many boudoirs. One could not be uncivil, nobody would willingly foster a reputation for being eccentric, with a mania for spending every night in the same bed. In fact, a husband who had lost four wives in a gossip-loving world had obvious need to avoid the imputation of being a misogynist. So Florian followed the best-thought-of customs; and in divers bedrooms had, unavoidably and logically, drawn comparisons.

For at this time Florian was brought into quite intimate contact with many delightful and very various ladies: with Madame de Polignac, just then in the highest fashion on account of her victory in the pistol duel she had fought with Madame de Nesle; with La Fillon, most brilliant of blondes,—though, to be sure, she was no longer in her first youth,—who was not less than six feet in height; with Madame du Maine (in her Cardinal's absence), who was the tiniest and most fairy-like creature imaginable; with La Tencin, the former nun, and with Emilie and La Souris, those most charming actresses; with Madame de Modena and the Abbess de Chelles, both of whom were poor Philippe's daughters; with dashing Madame de Prie, who now ruled everything through her official lover, Monsieur de Bourbon, and who in the apartments from which Florian had been evicted accorded him such hospitality as soon removed all hard feeling; and with some seven or eight other gentlewomen of the very finest breeding and wit. These ladies now were Florian's companions night after night: it was as companions that he compared them with Melior: and his deductions were unavoidable.

He found in no tête-à-tête, and through no personal investigation, any beauty at all comparable to the beauty of Melior. This much seemed certain: she was perhaps the most lovely animal in existence. But one must be logical. She was also an insufferable idiot: she was, to actually considerate eyes, a garrulous blasphemer who profaned the shrine of beauty by living in it: and Florian was tired of her, with an all-possessing weariness that troubled him with the incessancy of a physical aching.

Time and again, in the soft arms of countesses and abbesses of the very highest fashion, even there would

Florian groan to think how many months must elapse before he could with any pretence of decency get rid of that dreadful woman at Bellegarde. For the methods formerly available would not serve here: his pact with brown Janicot afforded to a man of honor no choice except to wait for the birth of the child that was to be Janicot's honorarium, of the dear child, already beloved with more than the ordinary paternal fondness, whose coming was to ransom its father from so much discomfort. No, it was tempting, of course, to have here, actually in hand, the requisite and unique means for killing any of the Léshy. But to return to Bellegarde now, and to replace that maddening idiotic chatter by the fine taciturnity of death, would be a reprehensible action, in that it would impugn the good faith of a Puysange. For to do this would be to swindle Janicot, and to evade an explicit bargain. One had no choice except to wait for the child's birth.

So Florian stood resolutely, if rather miserably, upon his point of honor. Inasmuch as a Puysange might not break faith, not even with a fiend, poor Florian must carry out his bargain with Janicot, so far as went the reach of Florian's ability. . . . He could foresee a chance of opposition. Melior might perhaps have other views as to the proper disposal of the child: and Melior certainly had the charmed ring which might, if she behaved foolishly with it, overspice the affair with a tincture of Hoprig's officiousness. And this at worst might result in some devastating miracle that would destroy Florian; and at best could not but harrow his conscience with the spectacle of a Duke of Puysange embroiled in unprecedented conflict with his patron saint. . . .

His conscience, to be sure, was already in a sad way. Ever since the reawakening of Hoprig, Florian had stayed quite profoundly conscience-stricken by the discovery that all the irregularities of his past remained unforgiven. That was from every aspect a depressing discovery. It had not merely a personal application: it revealed that in this world the most painstaking piety might sometimes count for nothing. It was a discovery which troubled your conscience, which darkened your outlook deplorably, and which fostered actual pessimism.

For what was he to do now? "Repent!" the Saint had answered: it was the sort of saying one expected of a saint, and indeed, from Hoprig, who was secure against eternity, such repartees were natural enough. The serene physician had prescribed, but who would compound, the remedy? Florian himself was ready to do anything at all reasonable about those irregularities which had remained unforgiven through, as he must respectfully point out to inquirers, no remissness of his; he quite sincerely wanted to spare Heaven the discomfort of having a Duke of Puysange in irrevocable opposition: but he did not clearly see how repentance was possible. The great majority of such offences as antedated, say, the last two years had, after putative atonements, gone out of his mind, just as one puts aside and forgets about receipted bills: he could not rationally be expected to repent for misdemeanors without remembering them. That was the deuce of having placed unbounded faith in this—somehow— ambiguous Hoprig and in Hoprig's celestial attorneyship.

Even such irregularities as Florian recalled seemed unprolific of actual repentance. Florian now comprehended that he—perhaps through a too careful avoidance of low company, perhaps, he granted, through a tinge of pharisaism,—had never needed to incite the funerals of any but estimable and honorable persons who were upon the most excellent footing with the Church. He could not, with his rigid upbringing, for one instant doubt that all these had passed from this unsatisfactory world to eternal bliss. He could not question that he had actually been the benefactor of these persons. The only thing he could be asked to repent of here was a charitable action, and to do that was, to anyone of his natural kindliness, out of all thinking.

His irregularities in the way of personal friendship, too, appeared, upon the whole, to have resulted beneficially. Girls and boys that he had raised from sometimes the most squalid surroundings, even rescuing them in some cases from houses of notorious ill fame, has passed from him to other friends, and had prospered. . . . Louison had now her duke, Henri his prince, and little Sapho her princess of the blood royal, —and so it went. All were now living contentedly, in opulence, and they all entertained the liveliest gratitude for their discoverer. You could not repent of having given the ambitious and capable young a good start in life. . . . Among Florian's married friends of higher condition, there was hardly one duchess or marquise or countess who was not glad to acknowledge that his passing had tinged the quiet round of matrimony with romance, had left a plenitude of pleasant memories, and not infrequently had improved the quality of her children. Here too he had in logic to admit he had scattered benefactions, of which no kindly-hearted person could repent. . . .

He had never, he rather wistfully reflected, either coveted or stolen anything worth speaking of: he might have had some such abominable action to repent of, if only he had not always possessed a plenty of money to purchase whatever he fancied. That over-well filled purse had also kept him from laboring upon the Sabbath, or any day. And it had, by ill luck, never even occurred to him to worship a graven image. . . .

Nor had it ever occurred to him to break his given word. Philippe, he remembered, had referred to that as being rather queer, but it did not seem queer to Florian: this was simply a thing that a Puysange did not do. The word of honor of a Puysange, once given, could not in any circumstances be broken: to Florian that was an axiom sufficiently obvious.

He had told many falsehoods, of course. . . . For an instant the reflection brightened him: but he found dejectedly, on looking back, that all these falsehoods appeared to have been told either to some woman who was chaste or to some husband who was suspicious, entirely with the view of curing these failings and making matters more pleasant for everybody. A Puysange did not lie with the flat-footed design of getting something for himself, because such deviations from exactness, somehow, made you uncomfortable; nor through fear, because a Puysange, quite candidly, did not understand what people meant when they talked about fear.

No, one must be logical. Florian found that his sins —to name for once the quaint term with which so many quaint people would, he knew, label the majority of his actions,—seemed untiringly to have labored toward beneficence. Florian was not prepared to assert that this established any general rule; for some persons, it well might be that the practice of these technical irregularities produced actual unhappiness: but Florian was here concerned just with his own case. And it did not, whatever a benevolent saint advised,—and ought, of course, in his exalted position to advise,—it did not afford the material for any rational sort of repentance. And to prevaricate about this deficiency, or to patch up with Heaven through mutual indulgence some not quite candid compromise, seemed hardly a proceeding in which Florian cared to have any part, or could justify with honorable old precedents. Say what you might, even though you spoke from behind the locked gates of paradise, Puysange remained Puysange; and wholly selfish and utilitarian lying made Puysange uncomfortable. . . .

In fine, Florian earnestly wanted to repent, where repentance was so plainly a matter of common-sense, and appeared to offer his only chance for an inexcruciate future: but the more he reflected upon such of his irregularities as he could for the life of him recollect, the less material they afforded him for repentance. No, one must be logical. And logic forced him to see that under the present divine régime there was slender hope for him. So his conscience was in these days in a most perturbed state: he seemed to be deriving no profit whatever from a wasted lifetime of pious devotion: and the more widely he and Aluys had conducted their investigations, the less remunerative did Florian everywhere find the pursuit of beauty and holiness.

XX

Smoke Reveals Fire

HUS it was not until the coming in of spring that Florian rode away from the Hôtel de Puysange, riding toward Bellegarde and the business which must be discharged. Florian went by way of Storisende, the home of his dead brother, for Florian's son still lived there, and Florian now felt by no means certain he would ever see the boy again, now that Holy Hoprig roosted over the Bellegarde to which Florian returned.

Florian came to Storisende unannounced, as was his usage. Madame Marguerite de Puysange and Raoul's children kept her chamber, with a refusal to see Florian which the steward, to all appearance, had in transmission considerably censored. Florian thought that this poor fellow faced somewhat inadequately the problem of the proper demeanor toward a great peer who had very recently killed your master; and that too much fidgeting marred a well-meant endeavor to combine the politeness appropriate to a duke with the abhorrence which many persons feel to be demanded by fratricide.

Meanwhile the father wished to know of his son's whereabouts. Monsieur the Prince de Lisuarte had left the house not long after breakfast, it was reported, and might not return until evening. Florian shrugged, dined alone, and went out upon the south terrace, walking downward, into gardens now very ill tended. Raoul had let the gardens fall from their old, well-remembered, sleek estate. . . .

So much of Florian's youth had been passed here that with Florian went many memories. He had made love to a host of charming girls in this place, in these gardens which were now tenantless and half ruined: and none of these girls had he been able to love utterly, because of his mad notions about Melior. He comprehended now of how much he had been swindled by this lunacy. His dislike of Melior—of that insufferable bright-colored imbecile,—rose hot and strong.

So many women had been to him only the vis-à-vis in a pleasurable coupling, when he might have got from them the complete and high insanity which other lads got out of loving! He remembered, for example, another April afternoon in this place, the April before his first marriage. . . . Yes, it had happened just yonder.

Florian turned to the right, passing the little tree from the East, which seemed no bigger now than he remembered it in boyhood; and then trampled through a thick undergrowth which hid what he remembered as a trim lawn. Raoul had really let the gardens fall into a quite abominable state. A person who had taken no better care of Storisende had not deserved to inherit such a fine property: and Florian remembered now with some compunction how easily, when he disposed of their father, he could also have disposed of their father's foolish will. But Florian too, as he admitted, had always spoiled Raoul.

Florian came to a boulder some four feet in height, before which stood a smaller rock that was flat-topped and made a natural seat. Both were overgrown with patches of gray-green lichen. He looked downward. Against the boulder, partly hidden by old withered leaves, lay two flat stones which were each near a foot in length and about an inch thick, two stones which Florian remembered.

He lifted these stones. Where they had lain, the ground showed dark and wet, and was perforated with small holes. The raising of the first stone disclosed a bloodless yellow centipede, which flustered and wavered into hiding among the close-matted dead leaves. Under the other stone, a great many ants were hastily carrying their small white eggs into these holes in the ground. Some twenty gray winged ants remained clustering together futilely. There was adhering to the under side of this second stone a clotted web. Florian saw the evicted spider, large and clumsy looking but very quick of movement, trundling away from molestation much as the centipede had fled.

It seemed to him that no life ought to be in this place; not even the life of insects should survive in this ruined haunt of memories. He set the two rocks at right angles to the boulder, just as he and a girl, who no longer existed anywhere, had placed them eighteen years ago. Moss had grown upon the boulder, so that the rocks did not fit against it so snugly as they had done once, but they stood upright now a foot apart. Florian gathered five fallen twigs, broke them, and piled the fragments in this space. From his pocket he took a letter, from the Abbess de Chelles, which he crumpled and thrust under the twigs. He took out flint and steel, and struck a spark, which fell neatly into the crevice between his left thumb and the thumbnail. The pensive gravity of his face was altered as he said "Damn!" and sucked at his thumb. Then he tried again, and soon had there just such a tiny fire as he and that dark-haired girl had once kindled in this place.

He sat there, feeding the small blaze with twigs and yet more twigs: and through his thinking flitted thoughts not wholly seized. But this fire was to him a poem. So went youth, and, by and by, life. Brief heat and bluster and brilliancy, a little noise, then smoke and ashes: then youth was gone, with all its sparkle and splutter. You were thirty-six: you still got love-letters from abbesses of the blood royal, but your heart was a skuttle of cold cinders. And all that which had been, in these gardens and in so many other places, did not matter to you. It probably did not matter to anybody, and never had mattered. Yes, like this tiny blazing here, so went youth, and, by and by, life. . . .

"Why, what the devil, my friend—!"

Someone was speaking very close at hand. Florian looked up, strangely haggard, looked into the face of his son Gaston. The young Prince de Lisuarte was not alone, for a little behind him stood a dark-haired staring peasant girl. She was rather pretty, in a fresh and wholesome way that acquitted her of rational intelligence; and her bodice, Florian noted, had been torn open at the neck. Well, after all, Gaston was sixteen. . . .

"My father!" the boy said now. But Florian observed with approval that the embarrassment was momentary. "This is in truth a delightful surprise, monsieur," Gaston continued. "We saw the smoke, and could not imagine what caused it here in the park—"

"So that," said Florian, "you very naturally investigated—"

He was reflecting that, after all, he was not answerable, and owed no explanation, to his son for making a small fire in the spring woods. That was lucky, for the boy would not understand the poetry of it. . . . Florian saw too with approval that the young woman had disappeared. For her to have remained would have been wholly tactless, since it would have committed him to some expression of elevated disapproval. . . . As it was, he needed only to rise and shake hands with this tall son of his, and then sit down again.

Gaston was rather picturesquely ugly; he indeed most inconsiderately aspersed his grandmother's memory by this injudicious resemblance to the late King of England whom rumor had credited with the begetting of Gaston's mother. Carola, though, had been quite pretty. Florian thought for a while of his first wife with less dislike than he had entertained toward her for years. Still, he perceived, he did not actually like this tall boy who waited before him, all in black. That would be for Raoul. . . .

"My son," said Florian, slowly, "I am on my way homeward to dispose of an awkward business in which there is an appreciable likelihood of my getting my death. So the whim took me to see you, it may be, for the last time."

"But, monsieur, if there is danger you should remember that I count as a man now that I am seventeen next month. I have already two duels to my credit, I must tell you, in which I killed nobody, to be sure, but gave very handsome wounds. So may I not aid in this adventure?"

"Would you fight, then, in my defence, Gaston?"

"Assuredly, monsieur."

"But why the devil should you? Let us be logical, Gaston! You loved that handsome hulking uncle of yours, not me, as people are customarily supposed to love their fathers; and I have recently killed him. Your damned aunt, I know, has been telling you that I ill-treated and murdered your mother also. To cap all, you have a great deal to gain by my death, for you are my heir. And I am too modest to believe that my engaging qualities have ever ensnared you into any personal affection."

The boy reflected. "No; there has been no love between us. And they say you are wicked. But I would fight for you. I do not know why."

Florian smiled. He nodded his head, in a sort of unwilling approval.

"We come of a queer race, my son. That is the reason you would fight in my cause. It is also a reason why we may speak candidly."

"Is candor, monsieur, quite possible between father and son?"

Florian liked that too, and showed as much. He said:

"All eccentricities are possible to our race. There are many quaint chronicles to attest this, for there has always been a Puysange somewhere or another fluttering the world. To-day I am Puysange. To-morrow you will be Puysange. So I sit here with my little blaze of spluttering twigs already half gray ashes. And you stand there, awaiting my departure, I will not ask how patiently."

"I regard you, monsieur, with every appropriate filial sentiment. But you can remember, I am afraid, just what that comes to."

"I remember most clearly. In these matters we are logical. So it is the defect of our race not ever to love anybody quite whole-heartedly; and certainly we are not so ill-advised as to squander adoration upon one another. Rather, we must restively seek everywhither for our desire, even though we never discover precisely what is this desire. That also, Gaston, is logic: for we of Puysange know, incommunicably but very surely, that this unapprehended desire ought to be gratified. It is this lean knowledge which permits us no rest, no complacent living in the usual drowsiness. . . ."

"They tell me, monsieur, that we derive this trait from that old Jurgen who was our ancestor, and from tall Manuel too, whose life endures in us of Puysange."

"I do not know. I talked lately with a Monsieur Horvendile, who had extreme notions about an Author who compiles an endless Biography, of the life that uses us as masks and temporary garments. . . . But I do not know. I only know that this life was given me by my father, without any knowledge as to what use I should preferably make of the unsought gift. I only know that I have handed on this life to you, on the same terms. Do with the life I gave you whatever you may elect. Now that I see you for the last time, my premonitions tell me, I proffer no advice. I shall not even asperse the effects of vice and evil-doing by protesting that I in person illustrate them. No: I am conscious of a little compassion for you, but that is all; I do not really care what becomes of you. So I proffer no advice."

"Therein, monsieur, at least, you do not deal with me as is the custom of fathers."

"No," Florian replied. "No: I find you at sixteen already fighting duels and tumbling wenches in the spring woods; and I spare you every appropriate paternal comment. For one thing, I myself had at your age indulged in these amusements; in fact, at your age, with my wild oats sown, I was preparing to settle down to quiet domesticity with your mother: and for another thing, I cannot see that your escapades matter. It is only too clear to me as I sit here, with my little blaze of spluttering twigs already half gray ashes, that in a while you and your ardors and your adversaries and your plump wenches will be picked bones and dust about which nobody will be worrying. These woods will then be as young as ever: and nobody anywhere will be thinking about you nor your iniquities nor your good actions, or about mine either; but whensoever April returns in this place there will still be anemones."

"Meanwhile I have my day, monsieur—"

"Yes," Florian agreed—"the bustling, restless and dissatisfying day of a Puysange. That is your right, it is your logical inheritance. Well, there has always been a Puysange, since Jurgen also made the most of day and night,—a Puysange to keep his part of the world a-twitter until he had been taught, with bruises and hard knocks, to respect the great law of living. Yes, there has always been a Puysange at that schooling, and each in turn has mastered the lesson: and I cannot see how, in the end, this, either, has mattered."

"But what, monsieur, is this great law of living?"

Florian for a moment stayed silent. He could see yonder the little tree from the East, already budding in the spring. He was remembering how, a quarter of a century ago, another boy had asked just this question just here. And living seemed to Florian a quite futile business. Men's trials and flounderings got them nowhither. A wheel turned, that was all. Too large to be thought about, a wheel turned, without haste and irresistibly. Men clung a while, like insects, to that wheel. The wheel had come full circle. Now it was not Florian but Florian's son who was asking of his father, "What is this great law of living?" And no response was possible except the old, evasive and cowardly answer. So Florian gave it. One must be logical, and voice what logic taught.

"Thou shalt not offend against the notions of thy neighbor," Florian replied,—"or not, at least, too often or too openly. I do not say, mark you, my son, but that in private, and with the exercise of discretion, one may cultivate one's faculties."

"Yes, but, monsieur, I do not see—"

"No," Florian conceded, with a smiling toward his tall son which was friendly but a little sad, "no, naturally you do not. How should you, infamous seducer of the peasantry, when this is a law which no young person anywhere is able to believe? Yet it is certain, dear child, that if you openly offend against these notions you will be crushed: and it is certain that if you honor them,—with, I am presupposing, a suitable appreciation of the charms of privacy and sympathetic companions,—then all things are permitted, and nobody will really bother about your discreet pursuing of your desires. A wise man will avoid, though, for his comfort's health, all over-high and over-earnest desires. . . . This is the knowledge, Gaston, which every father longs to communicate to his son, without caring to confess that his own life has been such as to permit the acquiring of this knowledge."

And the boy shook his head. "I understand your words. But your meaning, monsieur, I do not see. . . ."

Part Three

The End
of Lean Wisdom

"Ne point aller chercher ce qu'on fait dans la lune,
Et vous mesler un peu de ce qu'on fait chez vous,
Où nous voyons aller tout sans-dessus-dessous."

XXI

Of Melior Married

ow Florian returned to Bellegarde to face the disillusion appointed for every husband in passing from infatuation to paternity. His disenchanted princess now was hardly recognizable. Her face was like dough, her nose seemed oddly swollen; under and about the bloodshot eyes were repulsive yellow splotches. As for the bloated body, he could not bear to look at it. He was shaken with hot and sick disgust when he saw this really perfectly dreadful looking creature.

Perhaps, though, Florian reflected, he saw her through emotions which exaggerated every blemish unfairly. He knew all other pregnant women had seemed to him unattractive rather than actually loathsome. But here, here was the prize he had so long and fervently desired, the prize to gain which he had sacrificed those dearest to him in this world, and had parted with the comforting assurances of religion. . . . For, Melior, then, had flawless and unequalled beauty. So he had bought, at an exceedingly stiff price, this shining superficies, to learn almost immediately thereafter that she possessed not one other desirable quality. And now Melior had not even the thin mask of loveliness. Worse still, the beauty which he had worshipped since boyhood now existed nowhere. To purchase an hour or two of really not very remarkable entertainment, he had himself destroyed this beauty. . . .

"My love," said Florian, "now if only I were a conceited person, I would dare to hope that the long months since I last saw you have passed as drearily with you as with me."

He kissed her tenderly. Even the woman's breath was now unpleasant. It seemed to Florian that nothing was being spared him.

"Yes, that sort of talk is all very well," replied Melior. "But, Florian, I do think that, at a time when I have every right to expect particular attention and care, you might at least have made an effort to get home sooner, and not leave everything upon my shoulders, especially with all the neighbors everywhere pretending, whenever I come into the room, that they were not talking about your having killed your brother—"

"Yes, yes, a most regrettable affair! But what, sweetheart, had been going amiss at Bellegarde?"

"That is a pretty question for you to ask, with me in my condition, with all these other worries on top of it, about your friend Orléans. Because, knowing you as well as I do, Florian, and not being able to feel as you do that a prime minister is no more than a house fly or a flea,—and seeing quite well, too, how little you consider what my feelings naturally would be if they cut off your head—"

"Ah, but let us take one thing at a time, and for the present leave my head where it is. Do you mean that you have been unwell, my pet?"

"Have you no eyes in the head you keep talking about just to keep me upset? But I do not wonder you prefer not to look at me, now I am such a fright, and that is you men all over. Still, you might at least have the decency to remember who is responsible for it, and that much I must say."

"But, dearest, I have both the eyes about which you inquire, and in those doubtless partial orbs you happen not to look a fright. So I cannot quite follow you. No, let us be logical! There is a slight pallor, to be sure— But, no! No, dear Melior, upon the whole, I never saw you looking lovelier, and I wonder of what you are talking."

"I mean, you fool, that I am sick and miserable because now almost any day I am going to have a baby."

Florian was honestly shocked. He could remember no precedent among his mistresses of anybody's having put this news so bluntly: and when he recalled the behavior of his first wife in precisely these circumstances, he could not but feel that women were deteriorating. A wife endowed with proper sensibility would have hidden her face upon his shoulder, just as Carola had done, and would in this posture have whispered her awed surmise that Heaven was shortly to consign them a little cherub. But this big-bellied idiot appeared to have no sensibilities. "You fool, now almost any day I am going to have a baby!" was not a nice nor even a dignified way of announcing the nearness of his freedom.

But Florian's plump face was transfigured, as he knelt before his Melior, and very reverently lifted to his lips her hand. He slipped a cushion under his knee, made himself comfortable, and kneeling still, went on to speak of his bliss and of his love for her and of how sacred in his eyes appeared the marks of her condition. Shs listened: he could see that Melior was pleased; and he in consequence continued his gallant romanticizing.

For Florian really wanted to be pleasant to the woman; and was resolved politely to ignore even this last disillusionment, and to condone, as far as was humanly possible, the lack of consideration through which this dreadful creature had now added to stupidity and garrulity out-and-out physical ugliness.

But while Florian was talking he could see, too, that

the central diamond in the charmed ring that Melior wore was to-day quite black, like an onyx, so that he took care to keep it covered with his hand all the while he was talking about his adoration. Here was an appalling omen, a portent, virtually, of open conflict between Florian and his patron saint. The central stone of this ring had become as black and as bright and as inimical, looking as though, he reflected, one of the small eyes of Marie-Claire Cazaio started thence. This was a depressing sight: and it seemed to Florian quite vexingly illogical that the ring should change in this fashion when, after all, he was planning no harm against Melior.

When she had borne her child, he meant of course to carry out his bargain with brown Janicot,—a bargain that Florian considered an entirely private matter, and an affair with which Hoprig could not meddle without exhibiting absolute ill breeding. Then Melior would disappear, Florian did not know whither, to be sure, but her destination would be none of his selecting or responsibility. . . . A really logical ring would not call that contriving any harm against Melior. Even Holy Hoprig must be reasonable enough to see that much. So Florian for the while put aside his foreboding, and assured himself that, with anything like fair luck, he was on the point of getting rid of this dreadful woman forever. The reflection spurred him to eloquence and to the kindliness which Florian had always felt to be due his wives in their last hours.

XXII

The Wives of Florian

FLORIAN watched his Melior with a not unnatural care. She remained, to the eye, unperturbed, and was her usual maddening self throughout the evening: it seemed to him she must inevitably have noticed the changing of her ring; and in that event, he granted the woman's duplicity at least to be rather magnificent.

For Melior talked, on and on and on,—with that quite insupportable air of commingled self-satisfaction and shrewdness,—about Monsieur d'Aigremont's new liveries, which were the exact color, my dear, of Madame des Roches' old wig, the one she was wearing that day she drove in here in all that rain; and about how that reminded Melior of what a thunderstorm had come up only last Thursday, without the least warning; and about how Marie-Claire had been looking at Melior again in that peculiar way and ought not to be permitted to raise storms and cast spells that dried up people's cows.

Even so, Melior continued, milk was fattening and was not really good for you in large quantities, and, for one, she meant to give it up, though if you were intended to be fat you had in the end simply to put up with it, just as some persons got bald sooner than others, and no hair-dresser could help you, not even if he was as airy and as pleased with himself as that high-and-mighty François over at Manneville. Oh, yes, but

167

Florian must certainly remember! He was the very skinny one whom she had in two or three times last autumn, and who had turned out to be a Huguenot or a Jansenist or something of that sort, so that, people did say, the dear old Bishop was going to take the proper steps the very instant he was out again. That was the trouble, though, with colds at his age, you never knew what they might lead to at the moment you were least expecting it—

So her talking went, on and on and on, while Florian looked at the woman,—who was repulsive now even to the eye,—and he reflected: "And it was for this that I intrepidly assailed the high place, and slaughtered all those charming monsters! It was for this that I have sacrificed poor Philippe and my dear Raoul!"

Bed-time alone released him from listening to her; but not from prudent watchfulness.

That night he roused as Melior slipped from their bed. Through discreetly half-closed eyelids Florian saw her take from the closet that queer carved staff which had once belonged to her sister Mélusine. Now Melior for a while regarded this staff dubiously. She replaced it in the closet. She took up the night-light from the green-covered table beside the bed, and she passed out of the room.

He lay still for a moment, then put on his dressing-gown and slippers, and followed her. Melior turned, with her lamp, at the second corridor, and went out into the enclosed Thoignet Courtyard, skirted the well, and so disappeared through the small porch into the Chapel. Florian followed, quite noiselessly. The paved court was chilly underfoot: as he went into the porch a spray of ivy brushed his cheek in the dark.

Inside the Chapel three hanging lamps burned before the altar, like red stars, but they gave virtually no illumination. Florian saw that Melior had carried her yellow lamp into the alcove where his earlier wives were buried. She knelt there. She was praying, no doubt, for the intercession of that meddlesome Hoprig. Florian was rather interested. Then his interest was redoubled, for of a sudden the place was flooded with a wan throbbing bluish luminousness. The effigies upon the tombs of Florian's wives were changed; and the recumbent marble figures yawned and stretched themselves.

Thus, then, began the unimaginative working of Hoprig's holy ring, with a revamping of the affliction put upon Komorre the Cursed in the old nursery tale, Florian decided; and these retributory resurrections were rather naïve. He drew close his dressing-gown, and got well into the shadow of his great-grandfather's tomb, the while that his four earlier wives sat erect and looked compassionately at Melior.

"Beware, poor lovely child," said the likeness of Aurélie, "for it is apparent that Florian intends to murder you also."

"I was beginning to think he had some such notion," Melior replied, "for otherwise, of course, he would hardly be fetching home the sword Flamberge."

She had arisen from her knees, and there was in the composure with which she now sat sociably beside the ghost of Carola, on top of Carola's tomb, something that Florian found rather admirable. And he recalled too with admiration the innocence and the unconcern with which Melior had commented upon his having acquired such a delightfully quaint and old-fashioned looking sword. . . .

"Yes, for, my dear," said Carola, "you have permitted him to get tired of you. It was for that oversight he murdered all of us."

"But I have no time to put up with the man's foolishness just now, when I am going to have a baby," said Melior, with unconcealed vexation.

"Go seek protection of St. Hoprig," advised Hortense.

"And how may she escape," asked Marianne, "when

Florian's lackeys are everywhere, and Florian's great wolfhounds guard the outer courts?"

"She can give them the sweet-scented poison which destroyed me," said Carola. "But all the gates of Bellegarde are locked fast; and how could anyone climb down the unscalable high walls of the outer fortress?"

"By means of the strong silken cord which strangled me," answered Marianne.

"But who would guide her through the dark to sorcerous Upper Morven?"

"The molten lead which was poured into my ear," replied Aurélie, "will go before her glowing like a will-o'-the-wisp."

"And how can she, in her condition, make so long a journey?"

"Let her take the fine ebony cane which broke my skull," rejoined Hortense. "For now the cup of Florian's iniquity runs over, the hour of Florian's doom is struck, and the implements of his wickedness all revolt against him."

"Come now," said Melior, "there has been a great deal of nonsense talked. But you have at last, poor ghost, suggested something really practical, and something that had occurred to me also. Yes, you are entirely right, and your suggestion is most sensible, though, to be sure, it can hardly be ebony; for now that I am quite certain about Florian I simply owe it to my self-respect to leave him before he murders me too, and the easiest way to do that of course is to use my unfortunate and misguided sister's staff. But ebony, you know, is perfectly black—"

"Now of what staff can you be talking?"

"Why, but, my dear! As anybody at Brunbelois, even the veriest tidbits of children, could tell you, it was presented to Mélusine by one of the most fearful and ruthless demons resident in the Red Sea. It was the staff the poor darling always rode on. I do not, of course, mean him; in fact, I only saw him once, on a Saturday, when I was the merest child. And with all those scales, he could hardly expect anybody to call him a darling, even if you overlooked his having a head like a cat. Only much more so, of course, on account of his being larger. No, I meant that Mélusine rode on it—"

Now Florian was reflecting, "With what a lovely air of innocence she lied to me about that staff!" And Aurélie was saying, ineffectively, "Yes, but—"

"—Not as a steady thing, of course, but when she was about some particularly important enchantment, and wanted to make an impression. Mélusine was accomplished, and all that, and nobody denies it, but, if you ask me about being vain, then I can only say that, sister or not, I believe in being truthful. And as for leaving her things about helter-skelter, even the crown jewels—for Mélusine was the oldest of us girls, and Father always spoiled her quite terribly, and Mother never cared especially for dressing up,—why, we all know what clever people are in that way: and I need only say that I found this very staff stuck away in a cupboard, like an old wornout broom—"

Said Marianne, "Yes, but—"

"—When I was getting my things together to leave Brunbelois. And, much as I hate to contradict anybody, it has a distinctly red tinge, so that it could not possibly be ebony. So, what with all the talk, and Hoprig's suspicions about Florian, it simply occurred to me that this staff was not the sort of thing my dear father would care to be stirring up unpleasant old memories with, by seeing it, after all his trouble with Mélusine. For, even if Hoprig had been quite wrong, still, marriage, as I so often think, is really just a lottery—"

"Yes, but," said Hortense, "but, but, but! one needs to know the charm that controls the staff—"

"My dear creature! But you are Hortense, are you not? Yes, I remember Florian told me all about you:

and after the manner in which he has behaved to me, I am perfectly willing to believe that he misrepresented you in every way. Even if you used to make it a regular habit of flying at people's throats like that, I know how many entirely well-meaning women simply do not realize what an annoyance it is for any one person to want to do all the talking—"

"I think so too, but—"

"Oh, I am not in the least offended, my dear. It is merely that, as I was telling you, Hortense, my sister Mélusine was one of the most potent sorceresses in the known world, and so utterly devoted to her art that hardly a day passed without at any rate a little parlor conjuring. And I used often to be playing in the corner with my building blocks and my dolls when she was at her practising. If I were to tell you half the things I have witnessed with my own eyes, you simply would not believe a word of it. Yes, Mélusine was quite accomplished, there is no denying that. And as I was saying, you know how children are, and how often they surprise you when you had no notion they were paying the least attention. Yes, as I often think, it is the littlest pitchers that have the largest ears—"

"If you know how the cantraps run, then, to be sure—"

"Why, but," said Melior, now with her air of one who is dealing patiently with an irrational person, "but everybody knows if it is not the *Eman hetan* charm, it has to be either the *Thout tout a tout* or the *Horse and hattock* one. And so, I do hope, you see my feeling in the matter. Because, of course, appreciating as I do the perfectly well-meant suggestions of every one of you, still nobody in my delicate condition exactly likes to go about sliding down ropes and poisoning the servants, not to speak of the dogs, who, after all, are not responsible for their master's doings, and walking nobody knows how many miles in the dark. So I shall go to

Hoprig more carefully, and quickly too, upon the demon's staff, vexatious as it is not to be remembering his name. I distinctly remember there was a Z in it, because there always seemed to me something romantic about a Z, and that he had talons like an eagle; but it was not Bembo, or Celerri, or El-Gabal— No, it has quite gone out of my mind, but, in any event, I am much obliged to all of you. And no doubt it will come back to me the moment I stop trying to remember—"

Thus speaking, Melior arose from the tomb, and left the Chapel reflectively. A brief silence followed, a silence that was broken by Marianne. She said,—

"Poor Florian!"

"He had his faults of course," assented Hortense, "But really, to a person of any sensibility— Do peep, my love, and tell me if my skirts are down properly—"

Now Florian came forward, as statelily as anybody can walk in bedroom slippers, just as his wives were settling back, each as her sculptor had arranged her, upon their various tombs.

"Dear ladies," said he, "I perceive with real regret that not even death is potent enough to allay your propensities for mischief making."

"Oh, oh!" they cried, each sitting very erect, "here is the foul murderer!"

"Parbleu, my pets, what grievance, after all, have you against me? Are you not happier in your present existence than when you lived with me?"

"I should think so, indeed!" replied Carola, indignantly. "Why, wherever do you suppose we went to?"

"I do not inquire. It is a question raised by no widower of real discretion: he merely inclines in this, as in most matters, to be optimistic. Yet come now, let us be logical! Is it quite right for you four to complain against me, and to harbor actual animosity, on account of what was in the beginning just the natural result of my rather hasty disposition, and in the end my quadruple misfortune? Do you, Carola, for example, honestly believe that, after having been blessed with your affection, I could ever be actually satisfied with Melior?"

"For one, I certainly see nothing in her. And I really do think, Florian—"

"Nor I, either," said Aurélie, "nor could any rational person. And for your own good, I must tell you quite frankly, Florian—"

"Though, heaven knows," said Marianne, "it is not as if any of us could envy the poor idiot for being your wife—"

"It is merely that one cannot help wondering," said Hortense, "that even you should have had no more sense or good taste—"

So for an instant the sweet voices were like a choir of birds in fourfold descant: and they thrilled him with remembered melodies, vituperative and plaintive and now strangely dear. Then came the changing. All, Florian saw in that queer bluish light, were pitiably eager to talk about Melior, and to explain to him exhaustively just what a fool he had been, and how exactly like him was such behavior. But the magic of Hoprig's revivifying ring was spent: and color and flexibility were going away from the pretty bodies, so that their lips could but move stiffly and feebly now, without making the least noise. It was really heart-breaking, Florian thought, to see these lovely women congeal into stone, and be thus petrified upon the verge of candors which would have completely freed their minds.

Then that strange throbbing bluish light was gone: and Florian was alone in the dark Chapel where only three dim lamps were glowing like red stars. An ordinary person would have estimated that this gloom did but very inadequately prefigure Florian's future. But a Puysange knew perfectly where next to apply for help against any and all saints.

XXIII

The Collyn in the Pot

FLORIAN went from the Chapel to the secret chamber which nobody else cared to enter. At this last pinch he was resolved to enlist in his defence that power which was at least as strong as Hoprig's power. So Florian carried with him wine and wafers.

He opened a wicker basket, wherein was an earthen pot. Inside this pot lay, upon strips of white and black wool, a small, very smooth dun-colored creature that had the appearance of a cat. Florian with a green-handled little knife pricked the end of his ring-finger until he got the necessary blood; and presently the Collyn of Puysange had opened her yellow eyes and was licking daintily her lips so as to lose no drop of the offering. Florian fed her also with the wine and wafers.

"Whither," asked Florian then, "will the staff carry Melior?"

The Collyn answered, in a tiny voice: "To the hut which is between Amneran and Upper Morven. For that hut is the outpost of romance, and is as near as the demon's staff may dare approach to the hermitage of Holy Hoprig."

"Where is that hermitage?"

"Upon Upper Morven, upon the highest uplands of Morven, between a thorn-tree and an ash-tree, and beneath an oak-tree."

"What is my patron saint doing in this place?"

"Master, I also keep away from these saints. But it

175

is rumored that this Hoprig is now somewhat recklessly exercising the privileges of sainthood; that his
doings are not very favorably looked down upon; and
that the angels, in particular, are complaining because
of his frequent demands on them."

"That does not sound at all well," said Florian,
"and certainly there is no precedent for the wife of a
Puysange consorting with people who annoy the angels."

The Collyn yawned: and for a while she looked at
Florian somewhat as ordinary cats regard a mouse-
hole.

"Master, I would not bother about this last wife.
Why should you count so scrupulously one woman
more or less on the long list?"

"It is not the woman I wish to keep. Faith of a gentleman, no! But I must keep my plighted word."

"Master," said the cool and tiny voice, "you are
thrusting yourself into a dangerous business. For this
woman is now under Hoprig's protection, and the
powers of these saints are not to be despised."

"That is true, but I must hold to my bargain with
Monsieur Janicot. The pious old faith that made my
living glad has been taken away from me, the dreams
that I preserved from childhood have been embodied
for my derision. I see my admirations, and my desires
for what they are, and this is a spectacle before which
crumbles my self-conceit. The past, wherein because of
these empoisoned dreams I stinted living, has become
hateful: and of my hopes for the future, the less said
the better. All crumbles, Collyn: but Puysange remains
Puysange."

"I wonder, now," the cat asked, innocently, "if that
means anything?"

"Yes, Collyn," Florian answered: "it means that I
shall keep my own probity unstained, keep honor at
least, whatever else goes by the board. One must be

logical. My quiet unassuming practice of religion and my constant love which once derided time and change —and, in fact, the entire code of ideals by which I have lived so comfortably for all of thirty-six years,— appear to have been founded everywhere upon delusion and half-knowledge. Yet Helmas, I find, was truly wise. I also shall keep up my dignity by not letting even fate and chance upset me with their playfulness, and I shall continue to do what was expected of me yesterday. For the code by which I have lived contents me, or, rather, I am subdued to it. So I must go on living by it while living lasts."

"Yet if this romantic code of yours be based upon nothing—"

"If I have wholly invented it, without the weaving into its fabric of one strand of fact,—why, then, all the more reason for me to be proud of and to cherish what is peculiarly mine. Do my dreams fail me? That is no reason why I should fail my dreams,—which indeed, Collyn, have erred solely in contriving a more satisfactory world than Heaven seems able to construct."

"And does all this, too, mean something?"

"A pest! it seems to mean at least my destruction, since it is an article of my code that a gentleman may not in any circumstances break his word. For the rest, I find that abstract questions of right and wrong are too deep for me, too wholly based upon delusion and half-knowledge, so I shall meddle with them no more. Good and evil must settle their own vaporous battles, with which I am no longer concerned."

"To fling down your cards in a rage profits nobody."

"But do I indeed rage? Do I speak bitterly? Well, for thirty-six years I have taken sides, and for thirty-six years I have been the most zealous of churchmen, only to find at the last that not one of my irregularities has been charged off. I can assure you, Collyn, that it is quite vexing to have the business credit of one's religion thus shaken by the news that so much piety has ended with more debts than assets."

The small predatory beast still waited warily: and never for an instant did her unwinking tilted yellow eyes leave looking at Florian.

"So many of you, master, I have served! your father, and your grandfather, and all the others that for a brief while were here. And in the end—excepting only shrewd old Gui de Puysange, who came to much worse,—in the end you all come to nothing."

"Ah, Collyn, if the life of a Puysange be of no account,—although that is an unprecedented contention, let me tell you—then so much the more reason for me to shape what remains of that life to my own liking."

Florian thought for a while. Florian shrugged. That was the deuce of listening to yourself when you were talking. Florian, who had come hither to purchase aid from the Collyn, had logically convinced himself, through this sad trick of heeding his own words, that Puysange must stand or fall unaided. Yes, vexing as it was, that which he had spoken with so much earnestness was really true.

"All these years," said Florian, rather sadly, "you have lain here at my disposal, prepared to serve me in my need, with no small power. And I, unlike the others of my race, have bought of you nothing. What I have wanted I have taken, asking no odds of anyone, whether here or below. It is true I have made to Heaven some civil tenders, in the shape of good works and church-windows, just as I have been at pains to supply you with blessed wine and wafers. It seemed well, in logic, to preserve a friendly relation with both sides. For the rest, whatever I felt my life to lack I have myself fetched into it, even holiness and beauty, even"—Florian smiled,—"even `Melior and Hoprig. It is perhaps for this self-sufficiency that I am punished in a world wherein people are expected to live and to act in herds because of their common distrust of the future and of one another. I do not complain; and I remain self-sufficient."

"In fact, with me to aid you, master, you need lack for nothing."

That was precisely what Florian had been thinking when he came hither. But Florian had since then been listening to that most insidious of counsellors, himself. He was utterly convinced; and one must be logical.

So Florian replied languidly: "My dear creature! but I do not require your aid. Instead, I am come to declare you free from your long bondage to the house of my fathers. Yes, you are free, with no claim upon me, alone of all my race, since now that I renounce good I shall put away evil also. For I am Puysange: I dare to look into my own heart, and I can find there no least admiration for Heaven or for Heaven's adversaries. It may be I am fey: I speak under correction, since that is not a condition with which I have had any experience. But it seems to me that gods and devils are poor creatures when compared to man. They live with knowledge. But man finds heart to live without any knowledge or surety anywhere, and yet not to go mad. And I wonder now could any god endure the testing which all men endure?"

At this sort of talking the Collyn purred.

"Master, you shall evade that testing, for you shall have unbounded knowledge. Ah, but what secrets and what powers I will give you, my proud little master, for a compact and a price."

"No, Collyn: I have not any doubt the powers you offer are very pleasant, very amusing to exercise, and all that; but I have had quite enough of compacts."

"I will give you the master-word of darkness, that single word which death speaks to life, and which none answers. I will give you the power of the crucified serpent, and the spell which draws the sun and the moon to bathe in a silver tub and do your will. There is wealth in that spell, the wealth which purchases kingdoms. And I will give you, who have smiled so long, the power to laugh. I will do more, my proud little master: for I will give you the bravery to weep—"

But Florian answered: "You cannot give me anything worthy of comparison with that which I once had, and now have lost. I had my dreams of beauty and of holiness. I had the noblest dreams imaginable. These dreams I have embodied as no other man has ever done before me: these dreams I have made vital things, and I have introduced them into my living, full measure. No, you can give me nothing worthy of comparison with what I have lost. And you are free. In all these years the one service I have asked of you, who have been so long the mainstay and the destroyer of Puysange, is now at the last to reveal to me the shortest way to my patron saint."

"From these saints you will get a quick and ugly shrift: from me long years of ease and wisdom, master, —of utter wisdom, and of no more restless doubting about anything."

Then on a sudden Florian felt that this small fawning creature was loathsome: and, just as suddenly, Florian was weary of all things that are and of all that was ever to happen anywhere. But Florian said only:

"No, Collyn: I reputiate your wicked aid; and I set you free, not really hating evil or good either. But I honestly prefer to owe allegiance to nobody except myself. Because of that preference I shall go undefended to yet another high place in quest of my embodied dreams,—for I journey now toward the high place of holiness, with a somewhat different intent."

"You march toward death and toward utter destruction, my proud little master, when even now my power might save you. There is no other power that would befriend you now, for you march up against Heaven."

"Yes, yes! that is regrettable of course, it tends to establish a bad precedent. But it is my ill luck to be both a gentleman and a poet,—a poet who, I can assure you," Florian said, hastily, "has never written any verses. That, at least, nobody can charge me with. Now to a gentleman destruction is preferable to dishonor: and to a married poet, Collyn, there are worse things than death."

LORIAN left Bellegarde at dawn. For once, he did not travel in his favorite bottle-green and silver. Good taste suggested that a plain black suit, with his best Mechlin ruffles, was the appropriate wear in which to court destruction. Thus clad, he girded on Flamberge, and he set out as merrily as might be, afoot: no horse could come into Upper Morven, where once had stood the grove of Virbius.

Florian journeyed first to Amneran, and went to a very retired cottage built of oak and plaster upon a stone foundation. Here was his last hope of aid, and of succor which he might accept without any detriment to the pride of Puysange, for this was the ill-spoken-of home of his half-sister, Marie-Claire Cazaio. She was alone at her spinning when he came into the room. He took her hand. He kissed it.

"You told me once, dear Marie-Claire, a long while since, that in the end I would come to you in an old garden where dead leaves were falling, and would kiss your hand, and tell you I had loved you all my life. I wonder, Marie-Claire, if you remember that?"

"I have forgotten," she said, "nothing."

"You were wrong as to the garden and as to the dead leaves. But in all else you were right. This is the end, Marie-Claire. And in the end I fulfill your prophecy."

She looked at him, for no brief while, with those

182

small darkened eyes which seemed to see beyond him. "Yes, you are speaking the truth. I had thought that when this happened it would matter. And it does not matter."

"Only one thing has mattered in all our lives, Marie-Claire. I was at Storisende last week. I remembered you and our youth."

"And were you"—she smiled faintly,—"and were you properly remorseful?"

"No. I have regretted many of my doings. But I can find nowhere in me any of the highly requisite repentance for those of my actions which people would describe as criminal. I suppose it is because we of Puysange are so respectful of the notions of others that we do not commit crimes rashly. We enter into no illegal turpitude until rather careful reflection has assured us of its expediency. I, in any event, have sometimes been virtuous with unthinking levity, and with depressing upshots: but my vices, which my judgment had to endorse before prudence would venture on them, have resulted well enough. So I can regret no irregularities, and certainly not the happiness of our far-off youth."

Again Marie-Claire was in no hurry to reply. When she spoke, it was without any apparent conviction either one way or the other. "Our happiness involved, they say, considerable misdoing."

This stirred him to mild indignation. "And is love between brother and sister a misdoing? Come, Marie-Claire, but let us be logical! All scientists will tell you that endogamy is natural to mankind as long as men stay uncorrupted by over-civilization. The weight of history goes wholly one way. The Pharaohs and the Ptolemies afford, I believe, precedents that are tolerably ancient. Strabo is explicit as to the old Irish, Herodotus as to the Persians. In heaven also Osiris and Zeus and I know not how many other supreme gods have, in cherishing extreme affection for their sisters, set the example followed upon earth by the Kings of Siam and Phœnicia, and by the Incas of Peru—"

She shook that small dark head. "But, none the less—"

"—An example followed by the Sinhalese, the Romans of the old Republic, the Tyrians, the Gaunches of the Canary Islands—"

"Let us say no more about it—"

"—An example, in short, of the best standing in all quarters of the globe. In the Rig-Veda you will find Yami defending with unanswerable eloquence the union of brother and sister. In Holy Writ we see Heaven's highest blessings accorded to the fruit of Abraham's affection for his sister Sarah, nor need I allude to the marriage of Azrun with her two brothers, Abel and Cain. And in the Ynglinga Saga—"

She laid her hand upon his mouth. "Yes, yes, you have your precedents: and in your eyes, I know, that is the main thing, because of your dread of being unconventional and offending the neighbors. We were not wicked, then, whatever our less well-read father thought: we were merely"—and here she smiled,— "we were merely logical in our youth. In any event, we wasted our youth."

"Yes," Florian admitted, "for I was then logical, but not sufficiently logical. I could, as easily at that time as later, have cured our father of his habit of meddling with my affairs. But I turned unthinkingly away from the contented decades of technical criminality which we might have shared. For I was in those days enamored of the beauty that I in childhood had, howsoever briefly, seen: even while my body rioted, my thoughts remained bewilderedly aware of a beguiling and intoxicating brightness which stayed unwon to; and I could care whole-heartedly about nothing else."

"I know," she answered. "You were a dear boy. And it does not matter, now, that you went away from

me, and played at being a man about whom I knew
nothing and cared nothing. For old times' sake my
sending followed you to Brunbelois, and even there for
old times' sake I warned you. But you would not
heed—"

"I cared for nothing then save the beauty of Melior.
And now her beauty," he said, with a wry smile, "is
gone. And that also does not matter. For months her
beauty has been the one thing about her I never think
of."

"She is flesh and blood," said Marie-Claire, as if
that explained everything. "It is a combination which
does not long detain Puysange. What is this peril that
you go to encounter to-day?"

"I go into Upper Morven to keep my word as
frankly and as utterly as I gave it; and thereby to be
embroiled, I am afraid, in open conflict with my patron saint."

"That is bad. You must keep your word of course,
because favoritism to anybody is wrong. But these
saints do not understand this; they build all upon
Heaven's favoritism: and these holy persons are stronger than we, precisely because they are immune to
such clear seeing as we are cursed with."

"But your powers of sending and perverting and
blighting and so on," he said,—"are none of these to
be enlisted in my favor?"

"Not against Hoprig," she replied, "for the elect
have that invincible unreason and stupidity against
which alone our powers are feeble. No, my dearest, I
cannot aid you. For these saints are stronger than we
are: and in the end, whatever grounds they may afford
us for contempt or for laughing at them, they conquer
us."

It was in some sort a relief to find there was no
hope anywhere. Florian spoke more animatedly.

"No, Marie-Claire. Even at the last let us adhere to

logic! These saints do not conquer; they destroy us, that is all. The ruthless power of holiness is strong enough for that, but it is not strong enough to hold me, not for one instant, in subjection."

"Ah, and must you still be playing, dear boy that was, at being a most tremendous fellow?" she said, still smiling very tenderly. "Heaven will destroy you, then: and this is the hour of your return, the hour which I once prophesied, the hour which comes—so unportentously!—to end our living. So let us not waste that hour in quibbles."

"You are so practical," he lamented, "and with all that is lovable you combine such a dearth of admirable sentiments. In brief, you are Puysange."

She said pensively: "You were not lonely in my little time of happiness. You would not ever have been lonely with me."

"Have you divined that also, Marie-Claire? Yes, it has been lonely. I have had many friends and wives and mistresses. Perhaps I have had everything which life is able to give—"

He had paused. He sat there looking moodily at two queer drawings done in red and black upon the plaster of the wall: one represented a serpent swallowing rods, the other a serpent crucified. Beneath these drawings was a dark shining stone, and in its gleaming he saw figures move.

Then Florian turned toward the one person with whom he had ever been familiar, and he said:

"But since I left you, O my dearest, I have lived quite alone, with no comprehension of anyone, and with so much distrust of everybody! And now it is too late."

She considered this: she spread out her hands, smiling without mirth. "Yes, it is too late, even with me. Nothing is left, where all was yours once, Florian. I seem a husk. I do not either love or hate you any longer. Only,"—again that dark blind staring puzzled over him,—"only, it is not you who wait here in this fine black suit."

That made him too smile, and shrug a little. "It is what remains of me, my dear,—all that remains anywhere to-day. Such is the end of every person's youth and passion. I sometimes think that we reside in an ill-managed place. For look, Marie-Claire!" He waved toward the window, made up of very small panes of leaded glass, through which you saw the first vaporous green of the low fruit trees and much sunshine. "Look, Marie-Claire! spring is returning now, on every side. That seems so tactless."

But Marie-Claire replied, with more tolerance: "That is Their notion of humor. I suppose it amuses the poor dears, so let us not complain."

Then they fell to talking of other matters, and they spoke of shared small happenings in that spring of eighteen years ago, talking quite at random as one trifle reminded them of another. The son of Marie-Claire, young Achille Cazaio, was away from home in the way of business: for at seventeen he had just set up as a brigand, and he was at this time only a hopeful apprentice in the trade through which he was to prosper and to win success and some fame. So these two were undisturbed; and Florian that day saw nothing of the stripling bandit, whom gossip declared remarkably to resemble his half-uncle.

And Florian stayed for some while in this neat sparsely furnished room. He was content. At the bottom of his mind had always been the knowledge that by and by he would return to Marie-Claire. Such events as had happened since he left her, and the things that people had said and thought and done because of him, and in particular the responsibilities with which he had been entrusted,—his dukedom, his wives, his order of the Holy Ghost, a whole château to do with whatever he pleased,—were the materials of a joke which he was to share with his sister some day, when the boy that had left her came back after having hoodwinked so many persons into regarding him as mature. Marie-Claire alone knew that this fourth Duke of Puysange was still the boy who had loved her; and her blind gazing seemed always to penetrate the disguise.

Well! he had come back to her, to find that both of them were changed. The fact was sad, because it seemed to him that boy and girl had been rather wonderful. But it did not matter. Probably nothing mattered. Meanwhile he was again with Marie-Claire. It was sufficient to be home again, for the little while which remained before his destruction by that pigheaded and meddlesome Hoprig. And Florian was content. . . .

Toward midday, after they had dined together, Florian parted with his sister for the last time. He found it rather appalling that neither she nor he was moved by this leave-taking. Then he reflected:

"But we are dead persons, dead a great while ago. This is the calm of death."

He saw that this was true, and got from it the comfort which he always derived from logic.

Nevertheless, he went back very softly, and he peered through the door he had left not quite closed. Marie-Claire now knelt before the dark polished stone in whose gleaming moved figures.

"Lalle, Bachera, Magotte, Baphia—" she had begun.

Florian shrugged as, this time, he really went away from the house of oak and plaster. He knew whom she invoked. But that did not matter either. And, in fact, for Marie-Claire to pass from him to that other was profoundly logical.

XXV

The Gander That Sang

LORIAN followed the brook. Florian went hillward, walking upon what seemed a long-ruined roadway. As he went upstream, the brook was to his left hand: to his right was the hillside thick with trees. Florian, whose familiarity with rural affairs was limited, was perforce content to recognize among these trees the maples, the oaks, the pines and the chestnuts.

"Only, I should by every precedent, now that I go to inevitable destruction, be observing everything with unnatural vividness," he reflected: "and to face everywhere so many familiar looking but to me anonymous trees and bushes makes my impression of the scenery quite unbecomingly vague."

Midges danced vexatiously about his face, and now and again he slapped at them without gaining the least good. So much of the ruined roadway had collapsed into the brook, in disorderly jumbles of stones and clay and splintered slate, that what remained was very awkward to walk on: your right foot was always so much higher up the hill than your left. All was peculiarly still this afternoon: it startled you, when, as happened once or twice, a grasshopper sprang out of your way, rising from between your feet with vicious unexpected whirrings. That did not seem wholly natural, in April.

Florian came at last to a log hut beside three trees. Here then was the hermitage of Holy Hoprig, wherein

Florian was to encounter the unpredictable. Florian regarded this hut with disfavor. He had never thought to be destroyed in such an unimpressive looking building.

He shrugged, he loosened Flamberge in the scabbard, he went forward, and he pushed open the door. "Now if only," he reflected, "I had the height and the imposing appearance of Raoul!" Florian made the most of every inch; and entered with the bearing becoming to a Duke of Puysange.

The hut was unoccupied, save that in one corner was a cage painted brown; and inside this sat, upon a red silk cushion, a large gander.

"Do not disturb me," said this bird, at once, "for I have had quite enough to upset me already."

Florian for an instant stayed silent and somewhat confused. For this evidently was not the Saint's hermitage, and a talking gander seemed not wholly natural. Then Florian recollected that Upper Morven had always been the home of sorcery. So Florian replied, with great civility, that he had not meant to intrude, but merely happened to be passing. And Florian then talked with this gander, who told of the quite disgusting scene he had witnessed when a woman, riding upon a magic staff, had come into the hut, and had there been delivered of a child.

"Children are not usually acquired so," said the gander, "for as a rule, a stork brings them, and that is a much nicer method."

"But where," said Florian, "is now this honorarium?"

"I do not know what that means," the bird replied, "but I do know that if it means anything objectionable it has almost certainly been in here to-day to annoy me."

And the bird told of how a dove had come and had carried off in its beak the ring which the woman had given to this dove. He told how presently had come a fine looking man with a shining about his head, not flying but luxuriously riding through the air upon a gold cloud, with cherubs' heads floating about him; and how the woman and the child had gone away upon this same cloud, surrounded by, the gander thought, extremely fretful looking cherubs.

"The whole affair has upset me very much," said the gander, "for I was composing, and I can never bear to be interrupted."

And the gander sang to Florian of the proper way in which children should be born and should live thereafter. About the glory of love and the felicities of marriage, about patriotism and success in business and about the high assurances of religion, the gander sang, and about optimism and philanthropy and about the steady advancing of every kind of social improvement. And of man that is the child and heir of God, and of the splendor of man's works, and of the magnanimity of human nature, and of the wonder of man's living upon earth, the gander sang also, just as this gander had once sung to Florian's far-off progenitor, old Kerin of Nointel, in the dry well of Ogde. For the song of this gander is immortal, and it leaves untroubled, at one time or another time, the common-sense of no man who has lived upon earth.

Now Florian shook every curl in his peruke.

"Parbleu, but let us be logical about this!" said Florian. "Your art is very pleasing; but it embellishes a lazar-house with pastels. For human living is not at all like the song you have made concerning it."

"So much the worse for human living," the undying gander answered. "It does not bother me here in my cage. Besides, the purpose and the effect of my singing, like that of all great singing, is to fill my fellows with a sentiment of their importance as moral beings and of the greatness of their destinies. So I do not mimic. I create."

Florian looked at the gander for some while, and Florian sighed. This creature too had in it nothing of the realist, Florian reflected, and this gander preferred, precisely as Florian did, to live by his own private code: but, to the other side, the æsthetic theories of this insane bird coincided rather oddly with St. Hoprig's theories. . . . And the hermitage of that—in some way—ambiguous Hoprig was still to seek.

Florian left the imprisoned gander singing very gloriously in the last outpost of romance: and Florian went now across Upper Morven, that place of abominable fame. These uplands were thickly overgrown with a queer vine that had large oval leaves, the green of which was mottled with red, somewhat like the skin of snakes. Here also grew strawberry vines. As he walked, this undergrowth was continually catching in the buckles of Florian's shoes. Everywhere were inexplicable soft noises, and about his face danced a small cloud of midges.

There was no other sign of life except that, once, five large black and white birds rose from the ground immediately before him, seeming to rise from between his feet as the grasshoppers had done. This did not frighten Florian, exactly, but the suddenness of it, in this lonely place, gave him a shock not wholly delightful. . . . These birds, he saw, had been feeding there upon the berries of a small bush, upon purple berries which were about the size of a wren's egg, and whose outer sides had been pecked away by the birds, leaving the seeds exposed. All this was natural enough until you reflected that in these latitudes no bush produced berries as early as April. . . .

Now toward twilight Florian came to clumps of big and vividly yellow toad-stools, which seemed fat and poisonous and very evil. He passed among these, breaking many of them with his feet, and reflecting that the tiny screams which appeared to be uttered by these broken, loathsomely soft things must be the cry of some other kind of queer bird hidden somewhere near at hand. And he presently saw the appearance of a man coming toward him, and about the head of this man was a shining, as Florian perceived from afar, and was so assured that here at last was St. Hoprig.

And Florian went forward intrepidly, once he had loosened Flamberge in the scabbard. But this was not Hoprig. It was, instead, an incredibly old man in faded blue, who carried upon his arm an open basket filled with small roots. At his heel came a blue and white dog. The old man looked once at Florian, with peculiarly bright eyes, like the eyes of those who had watched the Feast of the Wheel, and he passed without speaking. But the dog paused, and without making any noise, sniffed about Florian's legs once or twice, as if this inspection were a matter of duty, and then the beast followed after this old man who had about his head a shining. It was odd, but the dog made no noise when he sniffed thus close to you; and neither the man in blue nor the blue and white dog made any least noise as they passed through the thick and tangled vines underfoot; nor did their passing at all move these vines which caught at the buckles of Florian's shoes so that he was continually tripping. These things rendered it difficult to believe that the man and the dog could be wholly natural. . . .

And still those pertinacious midges danced before Florian's eyes: and he was tired of slapping at them without ever driving them away. Upper Morven did not appear a merry place, upon this the last day of April, as Florian toiled through an ever-thickening twilight, in search of Holy Hoprig's hermitage, wherein was now the child that Florian had need of.

XXVI
Husband and Wife

OWARD evening Florian came into the Saint's hermitage. Inside, it proved a most comfortable hermitage, having walls builded of logs with the interstices filled with plaster. It seemed rather luxuriously furnished, to Florian's glance, which took exact note of nothing more specific than the skull upon the lectern and the three silver-gilt candelabra. These twelve candles, as you came in from the twilight, made the room quite cosy. Florian did not, however, look at the room's equipment with the interest he reserved for his wife.

Melior sat there, alone except for the newborn child in her lap. At the sound of Florian's entrance she had drawn the child closer, raising her blue mantle about it in an involuntary movement of protection: and as she faced him thus, Florian could see, without any especial interest, that with motherhood all her lost beauty had returned. It seemed inexplicable, but Melior was, if anything, more lovely than she had ever been: it was probably one of Hoprig's miracles: and Florian found time to wonder why he should be, so unquestionably and so actively, irritated by the sight of a person in every feature so pleasing.

Neither spoke for a while.

"I thought that you would be here before long: and all I have to say is that I wonder how you can look me in the face," observed Melior, at last. "Still, that you should be so bent upon your own destruction that you have followed us even here, does, I confess, astonish me. Why, Florian, have you no sense at all!"

"My dearest, you underestimate the power of paternal affection." Florian came to her, and gently uncovered the child's face. The baby, having supped, was asleep. Florian looked at it for a moment and for yet another moment. He shrugged. "No: I am aware of none of the appropriate emotions. The creature merely seems to me unfinished. Its head, in particular, has been affixed most unsatisfactorily; and I lament the general appearance of having been recently boiled. No, I sacrifice little."

Melior now put the sleeping child into the cradle yonder, a cradle which Florian supposed that Hoprig must have created extempore and miraculously when a cradle was needed. It hardly seemed the most natural appurtenance of an anchorite's retreat.

Then Melior turned; and she regarded Florian with her maddening air of dealing very patiently with an irrational person.

"Do you actually think, Florian, that, now, you can harm the little pet? Florian, that is one fault you have, though I am far from saying it is the only one. Still, as I so often think, no one of us is perfect: and perpetual fault-finding never gets you anywhere, does it? Even so, Florian, there is no denying you do not like to take a common-sense view of the most self-evident facts when the facts are not quite what you want them to be, and that much I feel I ought to tell you frankly. Otherwise, Florian, you would comprehend at once that I have only to cry out to St. Hoprig, who is back yonder chopping the wood to cook our supper, after those cherubs were positively rude about being asked to do it, and then he will blast you with a miracle."

She had gone back to her outlandish mediæval clothing. He recognized, now, the dreadful gown she was wearing the morning he first came to her upon the mountain top,—that glaring, shiny, twinkling affair, which reminded you of an Opéra dancer's costume in some spectacular ballet. For a Duchess of Puysange to be thus preposterously attired was unbecoming, and was in quite abominable taste.

"First, madame," said Florian, with a vexed, rather tired sigh, "let us explain matters. I have loved you since my boyhood, Melior, with a love which no woman, I think, can understand. For I loved you worshipfully, without hope, without any actual desire: and I loved you, by ill-luck, with a whole-heartedness which has prevented my ever loving anything else. . . . It is droll that a little color and glitter and a few plump curves, seen once and very briefly, should be able to make all other things not quite worth troubling about. But the farce is old. They used to call us nympholepts; and they fabled that the beauty which robbed us of all normal human joys was divine. . . . Well, I have no desire to discuss the nature of divinity, madame, nor to bore you with any further talking about what no woman understands. It suffices that I loved you in this pre-eminently ridiculous fashion; and that a way was offered me by which I might very incredibly win to you."

To which Melior replied: "You mean about your bargaining with Janicot, I suppose, and I am sure I never heard of such nonsense, in my life. Why, Florian, to think that the moment I let you out of my sight, even if it was a little while before I first actually saw you, because that does not in the least alter the principle of the thing,—quite apart from its happening the same morning, anyhow,—that you should be mixing yourself up with such people! It is positively incredible! But, as for your supposing that I am going to let you and your Janicots lay one finger on my precious lamb—!"

"Madame," he replied, "let us be logical! I can conceive of no possible reason why you should especially value this child. It may be no more repulsive looking than other babies: that is a point upon which I cannot pretend to speak with authority. But it is certainly not in itself an attractive animal. And your acquaintance with it, dating only from this morning, is far too brief to have permitted the forming of any personal attachment. For the rest, this bargain with Monsieur Janicot is an affair in which I have given my word. I can say no more. It is in your power, of course, to summon my patron saint, who, from what I know of him, will probably attempt to coerce me into rank dishonesty; and in that case the issue remains doubtful. The most probable outcome—need I say?—in view of his boasted proficiency in blasting, cursing and smiting, seems my annihilation. Would you, madame, who are of royal blood and are born of a race that is more than human, —would you have me, on that account, hold back in an affair in which my honor is involved?"

"Why, Florian, since you are asking my advice, I think it is not quite nice to speak of the power of a saint as being at all doubtful. We both know perfectly well that he would resent any impudence from you with a palsy or an advanced case of leprosy or perhaps a thunderbolt, and make things most unpleasant for everybody. And besides, it is just as well to avoid the subject of doubtfulness, because after talking with your other wives, I confess, Florian, that I have the very gravest doubts as to what you are planning to have become of me."

"You will vanish, madame, after the usual custom of your race. I am sure I do not know whither the Léshy usually vanish."

"I decline to vanish. Now that I am a Christian, Florian, I should think that even you would know I must decline to take any part, not to speak of all argument being bad for my milk, in any such silly and irreligious proceedings—"

To which he answered patiently, "But I have given my word, madame."

And still this obstinate woman clung to her pretence that he was behaving irrationally. She said, with an effect of being almost sorry for him:

"My poor Florian! now but let us be perfectly friendly about this. I am disposed to bear no malice, because, as I so often think, what is the odds? In the long run, I mean—"

"Madame, it is my misfortune never quite to know what you mean."

"Why, I mean that we all make mistakes, and that it is to be expected, and the least said about it, the soonest mended. Besides, as I was telling you, I do not know of course who it was that first set women upon a pedestal, and even if I did, I would be willing to overlook his mistakes too—"

"But you have not been telling me about this overimaginative, unmarried person! You were talking, madame, as I understood you, about malice and vanishing and milk."

"—Still, I certainly would not thank him, because I have had to pay for that mistake, even more heavily than women do now. Ah, Florian, as I so often think, it is always the woman who pays! For, you conceive, in my first life, back at Brunbelois, I mean, in those perfectly awful days of chivalry, I used to be worshipped, or at least that was what it came to in practice, as a symbol of heavenly excellence—"

Florian said, with an attempt at gallantry, "I can well imagine—"

"Oh, it was without any actually personal application, you understand: it was just that all ladies were regarded in that light. It was considered that in making women Heaven had revealed the full extent of Heaven's powers. So they made us sit upon uncomfortable thrones at their tournaments—"

"But," Florian protested, "these honorable and extremely picturesque customs—"

"My dear, that is all very well! but they used to last for a week sometimes. And there we would have to sit, from six to seven hours a day, with canopies but no cushions, and with no toilet conveniences, and with nothing whatever to do except to watch them sticking and poking and chopping one another in order to show how they respected us,—though I could never understand just how that came in, because my back hurt me too much, apart from my other troubles—"

"But as a symbol—" This horrible woman seemed resolved to leave him no one last shred of his dream.

"It was not the symbolism I objected to, Florian, but the endless inconvenience. The tournaments were only a part of it; and of course even after them you could get liniment, and you soon learned not to drink anything with your breakfast. But they walked off with your sleeves and handkerchiefs, with or without your leave: and when you go to put on your gloves, let me tell you, it is most annoying to find that the other one is several miles away in somebody's helmet—"

"Now," Florian said, yet more and more shocked, "you illogically apply prosaic standards to the entirely poetic attitude of chivalry—"

"Oh, as for their poetry, telling what marvelous creatures they thought us, they were all over the place with it. That was trying enough in the daytime; but, when it came to being waked up long before dawn, and prevented from getting a wink of beauty-sleep at night, by their aubades and serenas about how wonderful you were, I do assure you, it was really very tiresome—"

"I can see that." Logic compelled the admission, howsoever repulsive it was to find a woman blundering into logic. "But, still, madame—"

"Yes, you can see that, Florian, now, because you now comprehend you have been as foolishly exaggerative as any of them. Florian, you are a romantic: and from the first that has been the trouble, because it was that which made you fall in love with your notion of Melior. That was just what you did, Florian, without stopping to think how serious marriage is very often, or without having as much as talked with me—"

"Parbleu, but certainly it was without having heard you talk—"

"And as far as it went, it was quite nice of you, Florian, for you to appear even to have imperilled your soul —which, to be sure, must have been in a rather dangerous way already,—through your desire to have me for your wife. Nobody thinks of denying that was a very pretty compliment, but, if you ask me, it was a mistake—"

This seemed to Florian such a masterpiece in the art of understatement that he said almost sullenly,—

"We needs must love the highest—"

"Nonsense, Florian, I am far from being the highest. And so, let me tell you, is any other woman. After a month or two of sleeping with and mooning around me,—who, you must do me the justice to admit, never laughed at you once, though I do not deny that I was tempted, for, Florian, my dear, it seems only fair to tell you that at times you are simply—! But then, it is not as if other men were very different—"

"Let us," said Florian,—who was reflecting that he had never really detested anybody before he met this woman,—"let us turn to more profitable topics than masculine romanticism—"

"So you made the appalling discovery that I did not belong upon a pedestal. That was inevitable, though I must say it was not as if I had endeavored to hide it from you. And you resented it fiercely. That too, I suppose, was only you romantic men all over, though it was just as foolish as the mooning. And from what I can gather, you appear to have been equally rash and —if you do not mind my saying so, dear,—equally inconsiderate, in your treatment of your other wives. Though, to be sure, whatever you could see in those women, even at the first—!"

"I am a Puysange. We are ardent—"

"In any event, it is not as if anything could be done about them now. So, really, Florian, taking one consideration with another, I do not see why, now that we have talked it over amicably, and you have more or less explained yourself,—and, I am willing to believe, are quite properly sorry,—we should not get on tolerably well. And about men I say nothing, because one does want to be kind, but I doubt if any woman anywhere really hopes for more than that when she marries."

Melior had stopped talking. Not that fact alone had roused Florian to chill amazement. He said,—

"You plan, madame—?"

"Why, first of all, I plan for both of us to appeal, in a suitably religious and polite manner, to your patron saint. That is the plain duty of a Christian. For if this Janicot has any real claim upon the little darling, you surely must see how much nicer it would be, in every way, for Hoprig to be working miracles against him instead of smiting you with something unpleasant. And, besides, I do not see how he can have any real claim—"

Florian resolutely thrust aside the suspicion that this obstinate and shiny and gross-minded woman was now planning, among other enormities, to return to living with him. He said only:

"I am astounded. I am grieved. You would have me

meanly crawl out of my bargain by invoking the high powers of Heaven to help me in a swindle, very much as one hears of dishonest persons repudiating fair debts through the chicanery of a death-bed repentance. Pardieu, madame! since you suggest such infamies, and since you will not hear reason, I can but leave you, to defy this Hoprig to his ugly nose, and to perish, if necessary, upon his woodpile with untarnished faith."

He turned sadly from this woman who appeared to have no sense of logic or honor, not even any elementary notion of fair-dealing. And as Florian turned, he saw the door open, and through the doorway came first an armful of faggots and, behind it, the flushed but still benevolent face of Hoprig.

XXVII
The Forethought of Hoprig

———▶◀——▶◀◀——▶◀———

OME now," said St. Hoprig, as he laid down the wood, "but here is that abominable ward of mine! and upon the point of defying me too!" Whereon he shook hands cordially with Florian.

"Ah, but, monsieur," said Florian, "be logical! We meet as enemies."

"Frequently," said the Saint, "that is the speediest way of reaching a thorough understanding. I suppose that you have come about your foolish bargain with Janicot."

"Upon my word," replied Florian, "but all my business affairs appear to be well known to everybody upon Upper Morven!"

The Saint had turned to Melior, with a wise nod. "So, you perceive, madame, our precautions were justified. Now, my dear son, do not worry any more about your contract with the powers of evil, but off with your things, and have some supper with us. For I have excellent news for you. You were to sacrifice to Janicot the first child that you and Madame Melior might have, and she was then to vanish. Your bargain is void, or, rather, the terms have not yet been fulfilled."

Florian looked forlornly at his wife, then toward the cradle, and he said,—

"I fail to perceive the omission, Monsieur Hoprig."

"Luckily for human society, my son, a great many persons are similarly obtuse."

"Ah," said Florian, "but let us have no daring coruscations of wit where plain talking is needed."

"I must tell you, then," the Saint continued, "that when my suspicions were aroused at Brunbelois, I communicated with higher powers, and the Recording Angel obliged me with a fair copy of your first interview with Janicot. He objected to giving it: but I stood up for my rights as a saint, and in the end, after some little unpleasantness, he did give it. One really has to be firm with these angels, I find, in order to get the least bit of service. After that, at all events, the way to foil your wicked scheme was clear enough: in fact, it was the one possible way to prevent, without open scandal, your begetting of a child upon your wife for deplorable purposes. I advised the Princess to follow this way, and to make sure before marrying you that you should win to her embraces a bit too late to be the father of her child."

"That seems to be unprecedented advice," said Florian, sternly, "to have come from a saint of the Calendar."

He tried, at least, to speak sternly: but a dreadful thought had smitten him, and Florian knew that he, who had wondered what people meant when they talked about fear, had done with wondering.

"It was for your own good and eternal salvation," observed Melior, "though, to be sure, all men are like that, and, as I often think, the more you do for them, the less they seem to appreciate your trouble—"

Florian said only, "May I inquire, madame, without appearing unduly intrusive, who was your collaborator in arranging this infant's début?"

"Why, but of course she received all the necessary assistance," replied St. Hoprig, "from me. I never grudge the efforts necessary to a good action of this sort: and all night long, my son, I labored cheerfully for your salvation. For it was my plain duty as your celestial patron to save you, at any cost, from falling into grave sin: and, besides, it was a matter hardly to be entrusted to any other gentleman without considerable possibilities of scandal."

Florian looked from one to the other. "So it was to prevent scandal that my wife and my patron saint have put together their heads: and beauty and holiness—they also!—must combine to avoid offending against the notions of the neighbors. You will permit the remark that here is ambiguous logic."

"Ah, but my dear," replied Melior, "can you with logic deny that we did it for your own good? So often, when affairs look wrong, if you will just regard the spirit of the thing—"

"Madame," said Florian, without unkindliness, "let us not argue about that. I am sure you were persuaded as to the spirit of the thing, when no doubt Monsieur Hoprig went into it at full length—"

Yet Florian spoke perturbedly, for in his heart remained despair and terror. To find that he had been hoodwinked was not a discovery to upset a person used to the ways of the world and of more wives than he had ever married: to be hoodwinked was the métier of husbands. Moreover, reflection had already suggested that the Saint had followed the honorable old tradition of various nations who deputed exactly the task which Hoprig had spared Florian to their most holy persons.

Florian took snuff. With his chin well up, he inhaled luxuriously. . . .

Yes, Florian reflected there were priests everywhere, the Brahmans of Malabar, the Piaches of the Arawaks, the Dedes of Lycia, the Chodsas of the Dersim uplands, and the Ankuts of the Esquimaux,—to all these priests was formally relegated the performing of this task when a woman was about to marry. Every part of the world wherein mankind remained unspoiled by civilization, reflected Florian, afforded an exact and honorable precedent: and he could advance no ground for complaint. For one was logical. Certain physical reservations were made much of, to be sure, in Holy Writ and in the sermons preached in convents to auditories of schoolgirls. And this theory perhaps did no great harm. But, after all, there was a grain of folly in this theory that to-day's letters still in the post contained of necessity more virtuous matter than did yesterday's letters, whose seals had been broken. No, let us be logical about this theory. . . .

He closed his snuff-box. The lid bore the portrait of poor Philippe. He regretted Philippe, who had been destroyed with no real gain to anybody. Florian slipped the box into his waistcoat pocket. . . .

Hoprig's painstaking forethought, then, gave a philosopher no ground for wonder or dissatisfaction. But, none the less, in the heart of Florian was despair and terror. The terms of his bargain had not been fulfilled; and the one course open to a gentleman who held by his word was to go on living with his disenchanted princess for, at the very least—he estimated, appalled,— another full year. . . .

Florian extended his right hand, dusting the fingers one against the other. He liked those long white fingers. But this was simply dreadful: and he would have to speak now, he would have to say something. They were both waiting. Negligently he straightened the Mechlin ruffles at his throat. . . .

Then with a riotous surge of joy, he recollected that the current conventions of society afforded him a colorable pretext to provoke the Saint into annihilating him. As against continuing to live within earshot of Melior's insufferable jabbering,—as against a year of hourly frettings under a gross-minded idiot's blasphemies against the bright and flawless shrine of beauty which he inhabited,—the everywhere betrayed romantic had still the refuge of bodily destruction in this world and damnation in the next. And all because of a graceful social convention! all because of one of those fine notions which,—precisely as he had always contended,—made human living among the amenities of civilization so much more comely and more satisfying than was the existence of such savages as lived ignobly with no guide except common-sense. The Piaches and the Brahmans and the Ankuts were all savages and their obscene notions were wholly abominable. . . .

"Madame," said Florian, with his best dignity, "whatever the contrast between the purity of your intentions and of your conduct, I shall cling to the old simple faith of my ancestors. I am a Puysange. I do not care for airdrawn abstractions, I do not palter with such dangerous subtleties you suggest, I prefer to act with the forthright simplicity which becomes a gentleman, and I avenge my wounded honor."

Whereupon, with due respect for the possible incandescence of a halo, Florian struck Hoprig on the jaw.

"Now, holy Michael aid me!" cried the Saint, and he closed upon Florian, straightforwardly, without any miracle-working.

And as Hoprig spoke, there was a great peal of thunder. The crash, with its long shuddering reverberations was utterably appalling, but Hoprig was not appalled. Instead, he had drawn away from Florian, and Hoprig was now smiling deprecatingly.

"Dear me!" the Saint observed, "but I am always forgetting. And now, I suppose, they will be vexed again."

XXVIII

Highly Ambiguous

ND then as the last shaken note of thunder died away, and as Melior fell to comforting the awakened baby, a tall warrior entered. He wore the most resplendent of ancient corselets, and embossed greaves protected his legs, but no helmet hid his flaxen curls. He now laid down an eight-sided shield, emblazoned argent with a cross gules, and he rustled his wings rather indignantly.

"Really, Hoprig," said the new-comer, "this is carrying matters entirely too far; and you must not summon the princes of Heaven from their affairs to take part in your fisticuffs."

"What more can you expect, good Michael, of misguided efforts to make saints of my people?"

This was a voice which was not unknown to Florian. And he saw that Janicot too had come,—not in that unreserved condition in which Florian had last seen him, but discreetly clothed, and showing in everything as the neat burgess of Florian's first encounter. And it was evident that this Janicot was not a stranger to St. Michael, either, when the Archangel answered:

"It is well enough for you to grin, but with us the matter is no joke. This Hoprig has been duly canonized. When he invokes any of us we are under formal obligations to minister unto him, for he is entitled to all the perquisites of a saint: and he puts them to most inappropriate uses. For I must tell you—"

"Come, Monseigneur St. Michael," observed Hoprig, waving toward Melior's back, where she was comforting the mewing baby without the least attention to anything else,—"come, let us remember that a lady is present."

"And for that matter, upon how many nights since you began going about earth— But I shall say no more upon a topic so painful. It is sufficient to state that the entire affair is most unsettling, and has displeased those high in authority. The Church has canonized you, and we have of course to stand by the Church, with which our relations have for some while been, in the main, quite friendly. I do not deny that if anything could have been done about you, just quietly— But we find the Church has provided no method whatever for removing saints from the Calendar—"

"You might remove him from Earth, however," Janicot suggested, helpfully. "A thunderbolt is not expensive."

"It has been considered. But the effect, we believe, would not upon the whole be salutary. It would discourage the pious in their efforts toward sanctity to observe that bolt coming from, of all quarters, heaven. Besides, as a saint, he must, directly after being killed, ascend to eternal glory. You ought to understand that we would be the last persons actually to hurry him."

"I think I see," said Janicot. "You are bound to stand by the Church as faithfully as I do, if not through quite the same motives. Now, I hold no brief for this saint. He has swindled me,—cleverly enough, but with that lack of common honesty which as a rule lends ambiguity to pious actions,—out of Madame Melior's child. I name only the mother, because, as I understand—?"

He had turned to Florian, and Janicot's raised eyebrows were sententious.

Florian answered them, "Yes, Monsieur Janicot; it

appears that I have acquired an increase of grace through works of supererogation."

"Ah! and I had thought you were ardent! The child, in any event, is a detail about which there is no hurry. I am not fond of children myself—"

And Florian marvelled. "Then, why—?"

"It is merely that my servants have a use for them. Yes, my servants make them quite useful, by adding the juice of water parsnip and soot and cinquefoil and some other ingredients. And I endeavor to supply my servants' needs. However!"—and Janicot waved the matter aside,—"when I am beaten I acknowledge it. The disenchanted princess remains yours: and I shall have no claim upon you until"—here Janicot smiled again,—"until the great love between your wife and you has approached a somewhat more authentic fruition."

"Monsieur Janicot," replied Florian, "you set the noble example of confessing when one is beaten. I was very careful when we made the compact which secured me this flawlessly beautiful lady as my wife. I am no longer careful. I cannot live with her for another year, not for a month, not for a half-hour! As you perceive, at the bare thought I grow hysterical. I tell you I cannot face the thought that this is the woman whom I have worshipped so long! I am a broken man, and I repent of every crime I committed in order to get her. Therefore let us make a second compact, my dear Monsieur Janicot, a compact by which she will be taken away from me! And you may name your own terms."

"Ah, but you are all alike!" sighed Janicot. "You palter and haggle about the securing of your desires: but once you have your desires, no price appears too high to rid you of them. I cannot understand my people, and my failure quite to comprehend them troubles me: yet I could have told you, Florian, the first day we met, that it would come to this. But you were that droll creature the romantic, the man who cherishes superhuman ideals. And I really cannot put up with ideals—" Janicot ceased from talking half as if in meditation. He now glanced from one to another of the company with a sort of friendly petulance. "However, why is everybody looking so solemn? I like to have happy faces about me."

"It is well enough for you to philosophize and grin," Michael returned, in lordly indignation. "But grinning settles few religious difficulties, and philosophy muddles them worse than ever. Yet, if you ask why I look solemn, it is because this saint here has become a scandal on Earth, a nuisance in heaven and an impossibility in hell. And after all our conferences we can find nowhere in the universe any suitable place for him."

"Yet the affair is really very simple," replied Janicot. "Let Hoprig and Melior, and their child too, return to Brunbelois and to the old time before he was a saint. Let them return to the high place and to the old time that is overpast now everywhere except at Brunbelois. Thus Earth will be rid of your scandal-breeding saint, and Hoprig of his halo and Florian of his threatened hysteria. And this Melior and this Hoprig will no longer be real persons, but will once more blend into an ancient legend of exceeding beauty and holiness. And nobody anywhere will be dissatisfied. This I suggest because I like to have happy faces about me, and happy faces everywhere, even in heaven."

Michael said: "You are subtle. That is not our strong point, of course. Still, I really do wonder why, after so many conferences, we never thought of such a wholly obvious solution as to antedate him at Brunbelois."

And Michael looked at Hoprig.

Hoprig smiled, benevolently as always, but not in the least repentantly, and Hoprig said: "Why, after all, I have seen quite as much of this modern world as interests a saint in the prime of life; this halo certainly is, in ways we need not go into, sometimes an inconvenience; and there is no real pleasure in being ministered unto by unwilling angels. So I incline, as always, to leave the upshot to the lady."

Now Melior arose from beside the cradle, wherein the child was now once more asleep. And Melior looked at Florian, without saying anything: but she was smiling rather sadly; and Florian knew that nowhere in this world, at any time, had there been any person more lovely than was his disenchanted princess.

And Florian said: "A pest! but, in the name of earth and sky and sea, in the name of Heaven and all the fiends, let this be done! For the moment you are again a legend, madame, I shall recapture the dear misery of my love for you and for that perfect beauty which should be seen and not heard."

"Indeed," she replied, "I daresay that is the truth. So, for all our sakes, Hoprig and I will go back to the time before I married you: and then, on account of the baby, I suppose I will have to marry Hoprig, who at least takes women as he finds them."

"You speak, I assume, metaphorically," observed the Saint, "but, in any case, I believe you exhibit good sense. So let us be going."

Then Florian said farewell to Melior and to Hoprig also. Florian had put aside his dapper look: he had quite lost his usual air of tolerating a mixture of vexation and mirth: and for that moment he did not show in anything as a jaunty little person of the very highest fashion.

"Now that you two," said Florian, "become again a legend and a symbol, I can believe in and love and worship you once more. It is in vain, it is with pitiable folly, that any man aspires to be bringing beauty and holiness into his daily living. These things are excellent for dilettanti to admire from afar. But they are not attainable, in any quantity that suffices. We needs believe in beauty: and there needs always flourish the notion that beauty exists in human living, so long as memory transfigures what is past, and optimism what is to come. And sometimes one finds beauty even in the hour which is passing, here and there, at wide intervals: but it is mixed—as inextricably as is mixed your speaking, bright-colored enemy of all romance,—with what is silly and commonplace and trivial."

"It seems so very vexatious," Melior stated, as if from depths of long deliberation, "when you can distinctly remember having brought your hat, to be quite unable— Yes, go on talking, Florian. It is on the peg by the door, and how ever could one possibly have missed it, and we are all listening."

"And I would like to believe," continued Florian, "that there is holiness in human living; but I at least have always found this also mixed with, I do not say hypocrisy, but with some ambiguity. . . . Mankind have their good points, but—to my knowledge,—no firm claim of any sort on admiration. I have been familiar with no person without finding that intimacy made some liking inevitable and any real respect preposterous. I deduce that in no virtue, and in no viciousness, does man excel: his endowments, either way, are inadequate. So holiness and beauty must remain to me just notions very pleasant to think about, and quite harmless to aim at if you like, if only because such aiming makes no noticeable difference anywhere. But they remain also unattained by mortal living. I do not know why this should be the law. I merely know that I overrode the law which says that only mediocrity may thrive in any place; and that I have been punished, with derision and with too clear seeing."

"Yes, but," said Janicot, "but you are punishing everybody else with verbosity—"

"I also can perceive no reason, my son," declared

St. Hoprig, "for talking highflown bombast and attempting to drag an apologue from the snarls of a most annoying affair. It should be sufficient to reflect that your romantic hankerings have upset heaven, and have given rise—I gather from the sneers of this brown fiend,—to unfavorable comment even in hell. And there is simply no telling into what state my temple of Llaw Gyffes may have got during the months you have held me in this frivolous modern world."

"Your temple of Llaw Gyffes!" said Florian, sadly. "But can it be, monsieur, that, after having been a saint of the Calendar, now that you return to heathen Brunbelois and the old time——?"

"My son, in any time," Hoprig replied, "and in any place, my talents are such as qualify me only for the best-thought-of church. My nature craves stability and the support of tradition and of really nice people. New faiths sometimes allure unthinking hot-heads like that poor dear Horrig, but not ever me: for I find that any religion, when once it is endowed and made respectable, works out in its effect upon human living pretty much like any other religion. Meanwhile, of course, one naturally prefers to retain a solid position in society. So that really it does seem foolish to quarrel, in any time or place, with the best-thought-of faith. . . . No, Florian, creeds shift and alter in everything except in promising salvation through church-work: but the prelate remains immortal. And I will tell you another thing, Florian, that you should remember when we are gone: and it is that all men and all women are human beings, and that nothing can be done about it." And Hoprig at this point regarded Florian for some while with a sort of pity. "In any case," the Saint continued, "do you look out for another celestial patron, and for a second father in the spirit, now that sunset approaches, and this is the last cloud going west."

Then Melior took up the still sleeping child, without

saying anything, but smiling very lovelily at Florian: and she and Hoprig entered into a golden cloud, and these two went away from Florian forever. They went now, he supposed, southeasterly, toward the high place in Acaire. He did not know. He only knew they went as a blurred shining: for Florian was recollecting a child's desire to be not in all unworthy of these bright, dear beings; and Florian somewhat wistfully recalled that brave aspiring, and that glad ignorance, which nothing now could ever reawaken any more.

XXIX

The Wonder Words

"BUT now," said Florian, "what now is to become of me, who have no longer any standards of beauty and holiness?" And he looked expectantly from Janicot to the Archangel, and back again, to see when they would begin their battling for possession of the Duke of Puysange. Both of them seemed, as yet, unflatteringly unbellicose.

And Michael seemed, also, a bit puzzled. "I have not any instructions about you. I did not come hither in the way of official duty, but only at the impudent summons of that fellow— It is really a very great comfort to reflect that, now he has gone back to the old time before he was canonized, he is no longer a saint! Still, as for you, your ways have been atrocious, and it is hardly doubtful that your end should be the same."

Florian at that had out the magic sword Flamberge. "Then, Monseigneur St. Michael, logic prompts one to make the best of this: and I entreat that you do me the honor of crossing blades with me, so that I may perish not ignobly."

"Come," Michael said, "so this shrimp challenges an archangel! That is really a fine gesture."

"Yes, there is spirit in this romantic," Janicot declared. "It seems to take the place of his intelligence. I cannot see it matters what becomes of the creature, but, after all, old friends will welcome any excuse to chat together. See, here is excellent wine in the Saint's cupboard, and over a cup of it let us amicably decide what we should do with this little Florian."

"It is well thought of," Michael estimated, "for I have been working all day upon the new worlds behind Fomalhaut, with the air full of comet dust. Yes, that rapscallion Hoprig fetched me a long way, and I am thirsty."

So these two sat down at the table to settle the fate of Florian. Janicot poured for Florian also: and Florian took the proffered cup, and a chair too, which he modestly placed against the log-and-plaster wall at some distance from his judges.

Florian's judges made an odd pair. For resplendent Michael showed in everything as divine, and in his face was the untroubled magnanimity of a great prince of Heaven. But Janicot had the appearance of a working man, all a sober and practical brown, which would show no stains after the performance of any necessary labor, and his face was shrewd.

"First," said Janicot, "let us drink. That is the proper beginning of any dispute, for it makes each think his adversary a splendid fellow, it promotes confidence and candor alike."

"Nobody should lack confidence and candor when it comes to dealing with sin," replied Michael: and with one heroic draught he emptied his cup.

Florian sipped his more tentatively: for this seemed uncommonly queer wine.

"Sin," Janicot said now, as if in meditation, "is a fine and impressive monosyllable."

"Sin," Michael said, with sternness, "is that which is forbidden by the word of God."

"But, to be sure!" Florian put in. "Sin is a very grave matter: and to expiate it requires stained glass and candles and, worst of all, repentance."

"Ah, but a word," said Janicot, "has no inherent meaning, it has merely the significance a mutual agree-

ment arbitrarily attaches to that especial sound. Let me
refill your cup, which I perceive to be empty: and,
Monsieur the Duke, do you stop talking to your
judges. That much—to resume,—is true of all words.
And the word of your god has been so variously pro-
nounced, my good Michael, it has been so diversely interpreted, that, really, men begin to wonder—"

"I did not sit down," cried Michael, "to hear blasphemies, but to settle the doom of this sinner. Nor will
I chop logic with you. I am a blunt soldier, and you
are subtle. Yes, the world knows you are subtle, but
how far has your subtlety got you? Why, it has got you
as far as from heaven to hell."

Florian vastly admired that just and pious sum-
ming-up as he leaned back in his chair, and looked toward Janicot. Florian was feeling strangely complacent, though, for Hoprig's wine was extraordinarily potent tipple to have come from the cupboard of a saint.

"Ah, friend," returned Janicot, smiling, "and do you
really put actual faith in that sensational modern story
that I was an angel who rebelled against your Jahveh?"

"It was before my time, of course," Michael
conceded. "I only know that my Lord created me with
orders to conquer you, who call yourself the Prince of
this world. So I did this, though, to give the devil his
due, it was no easy task. But that is far-off stuff: a soldier bears no malice when the fighting is over: and I
drink to you."

"Your health, bright adversary! Yet what if I were
not conquered, but merely patient? Why should not I,
who have outlived so many gods, remain as patient
under the passing of this tribal god come out of Israel
as I stayed once under Baal and Marduk? Both of
these have had their adorers and tall temples hereabouts: and Mithra and Zeus and Osiris and I know not
how many thousands of other beautiful and holy dei-

ties have had their dole of worship and neglect and oblivion. Now I have never been omnipotent, I am not worshipped in any shining temple even to-day; but always I have been served."

Florian, through half-closed eyelids,—for he felt a trifle drowsy after that extraordinary wine,—was admiring the curious proud look which had come into the brown face of Janicot. Florian began complacently to allow this fiend had his redeeming points. This Janicot was quite distinguished looking.

"For I," said Janicot, "am the Prince of this world, not to be ousted: and I have in my time, good Michael, had need to practise patience. You think with awed reverence of your Jahveh: and that in your station is commendable. Yet you should remember, too, that to me, who saw but yesterday your Jahveh's start in life as a local storm-god upon Sinai, he is just the latest of many thousands of adversaries whom I have seen triumph and pass while I stayed patient under all temporary annoyances. For in heaven they keep changing dynasties, and every transient ruler of heaven is bent upon making laws for my little kingdom. . . . Oh, I blame nobody! The desire is natural in omnipotence: and many of these laws I have admired, as academic exercises. The trouble seemed to be that they were drawn up in heaven, where there is nothing quite like the nature of my people—"

"A very sinful people!" said Michael.

"There, as in so many points, bright adversary, our opinions differ. You perceive only that they are not what, in accordance with your master's theories, they ought to be. I am more practical: I accept them as they are, and I make no complaint. That which you call their lust and wantonness, I know to be fertility—" And Janicot spread out both hands. "But it is an old tale. God after god has set rules to bridle and to change the nature of my people. Meanwhile I do not

meddle with their natures, I urge them to live in con-
cord with their natures, and to make the most of my
kingdom. To be content and to keep me well supplied
with subjects, is all that any reasonable prince would
require. And, as for sin, I have admitted it is a fine
word. But the wages of sin—in any event, very often,"
said Janicot, and with a smile he illuminated the par-
enthesis,—"is life."

"To all this," said Michael, extending his empty
cup, "the answer is simple. You are evil, and you lie."

"Before your days, before there were men like those
of to-day," said Janicot, indulgently, as he poured
sombre wine, "and when the dwarf peoples served me
in secret places, even they had other official gods.
When your Jahveh is forgotten, men will yet serve me,
if but in secrecy. Creeds pass, my friend, just as that
little Hoprig said. And it is true, too, that the prelate
remains always, as my technical opponent. But the
lingham and the yoni do not pass, they do not change,
they keep their strong control of all that lives: and
these serve me alone."

"If my Lord passes," Michael answered, very nobly
and very simply, "I pass with Him. We that love Him
could then desire no other fate. Meanwhile I have faith
in Him, and in His power and in His wisdom, and my
faith contents me."

"Faith!" Janicot said, rather wistfully. "Ah, there we
encounter another fine word, a wonder word: and I
admit that your anodyne is potent. But it is not to my
taste. However, this wine here is emphatically to my
taste. So let us drink!"

"It is a good wine. But it begets a treacherous soft-
ness of heart and an unsuitable, a quite unHebraic tendency to let bygones be bygones. I mean, unsuitable
for one in my service. For, after all, old adversary,
without intending any disrespect, of course, we were
originally for martial law and military strictness, for

smiting hip and thigh when the least thing went wrong: and in spite of our recent coming over to these new Christian doctrines— And, by the way, that reminds me of this sinner here. We seem to keep wandering from the point."

They had looked toward Florian, who discreetly remained lying back in his chair, watching them between nearly closed lids.

"Indeed, we have so utterly neglected him that he has gone to sleep. So let us drink, and be at ease," said Janicot, "now that we are relieved of his eavesdropping. . . . This Florian annoys me, rather. For he makes something too much of logic: so he rebels against your creed of faith and of set laws to be obeyed, asking, 'Why?' Did you never hear the creature crying out, 'Let us be logical!' in, of all places, this universe? And he rebels against my creed, which he believes a mere affair of the lingham and the yoni, saying, 'This is not enough.' Such men as he continue to dream, my friend, and I confess such men are dangerous: for they obstinately aspire toward a perfectibility that does not exist, they will be content with nothing else; and when your master and I do not satisfy the desire which is in their dreams, they draw their appalling logical conclusions. To that humiliation, such as it is, I answer, 'Drink!' For the Oracle of Bacbuc also— that oracle which the little curé of Meudon was not alone in misunderstanding,—that oracle speaks the true wonder word."

Michael had listened, with one elbow on the table, and with one hand propping his chin. Michael had listened with a queer mingling, in his frank face, of admiration and distrust.

The Archangel now slightly raised his head, just free of his hand, and he asked rather scornfully,—

"But what have we to do with their dreams?"

"A great deal. Men go enslaved by this dream of

beauty: but never yet have they sought to embody it, whether in their wives or in their equally droll works of art, without imperfect results, without results that were maddening to the dreamer. Men are resolved to know that which they may whole-heartedly worship. No, they are not bent upon emulating what they worship: it is, rather, that holiness also is a dream which allures mankind resistlessly. But thus far,—by your leave, good Michael,—they have found nothing to worship which bears logical inspection much better than does Hoprig. The dangerous part of all this is that men, none the less, still go on dreaming."

"They might be worse employed." Michael himself refilled his cup. "For I could tell you—"

"Pray spare my blushes! Yes, they obstinately go on dreaming. Your master is strong, as yet, and I too am strong, but neither of us is strong enough to control men's dreams. Now, the dreaming of men—mark you, I do not say of humankind, for women are rational creatures,—has an aspiring which is ruthless. It goes beyond decency, it aspires to more of perfectibility than any god has yet been able to provide or even to live up to. So this quite insane aspiring first sets up beautiful and holy gods in heaven, then in the dock; and, judging all by human logic, decrees this god not to be good enough. Thus their logic has dealt with Baal and Toupan and Tvastri; thus it will deal—" Janicot very courteously waved a brown and workmanlike hand. "But let us not dwell upon reflections that you may perhaps find unpleasant. In the mean while, me too this human dreaming thrusts aside, and even makes jokes about me, as not good enough."

It was plain that Michael distrusted Janicot in all and yet in some sort admired him most unwillingly. Michael asked, with a reserved smiling,—

"What follows, O subtle one?"

"It follows that all gods imaginable by men must always fall away into defeat and exile, because of men's implacable dreaming about more than men can imagine. It follows, too, that I go rather quietly about my kingdom, on account of my poor people's insane and toplofty dreaming." Here Janicot sighed. "Yes; it is humiliating: but I also have my anodyne, I have my master word. And it is, 'Drink.' "

"Of course it would be," Michael replied, with the most dignified of hiccoughs, "since drunkenness is a particularly low form of sin."

"The drinking I advocate is not merely of the grape. No, it is from the cup of space that I would have all drink, accepting all that is, in one fearless draught. Some day, it may be, my people here will attain to my doctrine: and even these fretful little men will see that life and death, and the nature of their dreams, and of their bodies also, are but ingredients in a cup from which the wise drink fearlessly."

Janicot had risen now. He came toward Florian, and stood there, looking down. And Florian discreetly continued his mimicry of untroubled slumber.

"Meanwhile he does not drink, he merely dreams, this little Florian. He dreams of beauty and of holiness fetched back by him to an earth which everywhere fell short of his wishes, fetched down by him intrepidly from that imagined high place where men attain to their insane desires. He dreams of aspiring and joy and color and suffering and unreason, and of those quaint taboos which you and he call sin, as being separate things, not seeing how all blends in one vast cup. Nor does he see, as yet, that this blending is very beautiful when properly regarded, and very holy when approached without human self-conceit. What would you have, good Michael? He and his like remain, as yet, just fretted children a little rashly hungry for excitement."

Michael stood now beside Janicot. Michael also was looking at Florian, not unkindly.

"Yes," Michael said. "Yes, that is true. He is yet a child."

Then the two faces which bent over Florian were somehow blended into one face, and Florian knew that these two beings had melted into one person, and that this person was prodding him gently. . . .

XXX

The Errant Child

IS father, after all these years, was
still wearing the blue stockings with
gold clocks. Florian noted that first,
because his father's foot was gently
prodding Florian into wakefulness,
as Florian's father sat there under
the little tree from the East. Beyond
the Duke's smiling countenance, beyond the face which
was at once the face of Michael and of Janicot, Florian
could now see a criss-crossery of stripped boughs, each
one of which was tipped with a small bud of green.

"Come, lazybones, but you will get your death of
cold, sleeping here on the bare ground, at harvest-
time."

"At harvest-time— I have been dreaming—"

Florian sat erect, rubbing at his eyes with a hand
whose smallness he instantly noted with wonder. The
ground, too, seemed surprisingly close to him, the
grass blades looked bigger than was natural. . . . He
could feel sinking away from him such childish notions
about God and wickedness, and about being a grown
man, as the little boy—who was he, as he now recollected,—had blended in his callow dreaming: and Florian sat there blinking innocent and puzzled eyes. . . .
He was safe back again, he reflected, in the seven-
teenth century: Louis Quatorze was King once more:
and all the virtues were again modish. And this really
must be harvest-time, for the sleek country of Poic-

tesme appeared inexpressibly asleep, wrapped in a mellowing haze.

Florian said, "It was a very queer dream, monsieur my father—"

"A pleasant dream, however, I hope, my son. No other sort of dream is worth inducing by sleeping under what, they used to tell me, is a charmed tree, and by using for your pillow a book that at least is charming."

And the Duke pointed to the book by Monsieur Perrault of the Academy, in which Florian had that very morning read with approving interest about the abominable Bluebeard and about the Cat with Boots and about the Sleeping Beauty and about Cendrillon and about a variety of other delightful persons.

But Florian just now was not for fairy tales; rather did all his thoughts still cling to that queer dream. And the child said, frowning:

"It was pleasant enough, but it was puzzling. For there were beautiful ladies that nobody could stand living with, and a saint that was an out-and-out fraud, and"—Florian slightly hesitated,—"and a wicked man, as bad almost as Komorre the Cursed, that did everything he wanted to, without ever being exactly punished, or satisfied either—"

"Behold now," Monsieur de Puysange lamented, "how appalling are the advances of this modern pessimism! My own child, at ten, advises me that beauty and holiness are delusions, and that not even in untrammeled wickedness is to be found contentment."

"No: that was not the moral of my dream. That is what bothers me, monsieur my father. There was not any moral: and nothing seemed to be leading up to anything else in particular. I seemed to live a long while, monsieur my father, I had got to be thirty-six and over, without finding any logic and reasonableness anywhere—"

"Doubtless, at that advanced age, your faculties were blunted, and you had become senile—"

"—And the people that wanted things did not want them any longer once they had got them. They seemed rather to dislike them—"

"From your pronominal disorder," the Duke stated, "I can deduce fancies which are not a novelty here in Poictesme. Such was the crying, in a somewhat more poetic and grammatical version, of our reputed begetters, men say,—of Dom Manuel and of Jurgen also, —in the old days before there was ever a Puysange."

"Yes, but that was so long ago! when people were hardly civilised. And what with all the changes that have been since then—! Well, but it really seems to me, monsieur my father, that—just taking it logically, —now that we have almost reached the eighteenth century, and all the nations have signed that treaty at Ryswick to prevent there ever being any more wars, and people are riding about peaceably in sedan chairs, and are living in America, and even some of the peasants have glass windows in their houses—"

"Undoubtedly," said the Duke, "we live in an age of invention and of such material luxury as the world has never known. All wonders of science have been made our servants. War, yesterday our normal arbiter, has now become irrational, even to the most unreflective, since one army simply annihilates the other with these modern cannons that shoot for hundreds of feet. To cross the trackless Atlantic is now but the affair of a month or two in our swift sailing ships. And we trap and slaughter even the huge whale to the end that we, ignoring the sun's whims, may lend to nights of feverish dissipation the brilliancy of afternoon, with our oil-lamps. We have perhaps exhausted the secrets of material nature. And in intellectual matters too we have progressed. Yet all progress, I would have you note, is directed by wise persons who discreetly observe the great law of living—"

"And what is that law, monsieur my father?"

"Thou shalt not offend," the Duke replied, "against the notions of thy neighbor. Now to the honoring of this law the wise person will bring more of earnestness than he will bring to the weighing of any discrepancies between facts and well-thought-of notions as to these facts. So, at most, he will laugh, he will perhaps cast an oblique jest with studied carelessness: and he will then pass on, upon the one way that is safe—for him, —without ever really considering the gaucherie of regarding life too seriously. And his less daring fellow will follow him by and by, upon the road which they were going to take in any event. That is progress."

"Thou shalt not offend against the notions of thy neighbor!" Florian repeated. "Yes, I remember. That was part of my dream, too." He was silent for an instant, glancing westward beyond the gardens of his home. The thronged trees of Acaire, as Florian now saw them just beyond that low red wall, seemed to have golden powder scattered over them, a powder which they stayed too motionless to shake off. "But— in my dream, you know,—that had been learned by living wickedly. And you have always taught Little Brother and me to be very good and religious—"

"My son, my son! and have I reared an errant child, an actual atheist, who doubts that in the next world also we have—a Neighbor?"

"Do you mean the good God, monsieur my father?"

"Eh," said the Duke, "I would distinguish, I would avoid anthropomorphology, I would speak here with exactness. I mean that in this world we must live always in subjection to notions which a moment's thought shows always to be irrational; and that nothing anywhere attests the designer of this world, howsoever high His place or whatever His proper title, to be

swayed at all by what we describe as justice and
logic."

"I can see that," said Florian: "though I have been
thinking about another sort of high place—"

But the Duke was still speaking: and now, to Florian's ear, his father's tone was somewhat of a piece
with this sun-steeped and tranquil and ineffably lazy
October afternoon, which seemed to show the world as
over-satisfied with the done year's achievements.

"So life, my son, must always display, to him who
rashly elects to think about it, just the incoherency and
the inconclusiveness of a child's dreammaking. No
doubt, this is to be explained by our obtuseness: I design, in any event, no impiety, for to be impious is un-
wise. I merely mean that I assume Someone also to be
our neighbor, in His high place, and that I think His
notions also should be treated with respect."

"I see," said Florian. But all that was youthful in
him seemed to stir in dim dissent from unambitious
aims.

"I mean, in short, that the wise person will conform
—with, it may be, a permissible shrug,—to each and
every notion that is affected by those neighbors whose
strength is greater than his. I would also suggest that,
if only for the sake of his own comfort, the wise person will cultivate a belief that these notions, howsoever
incomprehensible, may none the less be intelligent and
well-meaning."

"I see," the boy said, yet again. He spoke abstractedly, for he was now thinking of brown Janicot and of
resplendent Monseigneur St. Michael, in that queer
dream. His father appeared in some sort to agree with
both of them.

And as the Duke continued, speaking slowly, and
with something of the languor of this surrounding au-
tumnal world,—which seemed to strive toward no
larger upshots than the ripening of grains and fruits,

—it occurred to Florian, for the first time in Florian's life, that this always smiling father of his was, under so many graces, an uneasy and baffled person.

The Duke said: "To submit is the great lesson. I too was once a dreamer: and in dreams there are lessons. But to submit, without dreaming any more, is the great lesson; to submit, without either understanding or repining, and without demanding of life too much of beauty or of holiness, and without shirking the fact that this universe is under no least bond ever to grant us, upon either side of the grave, our desires. To do that, my son, does not satisfy and probably will not ever satisfy a Puysange. But to do that is wisdom."

The boy for some while considered this. He considered, too, the enigmatic, just half-serious face of his father, that face which was at once the face of Michael and of Janicot. To accept things as they were, in this world which was now going to sleep as if the providing of food-stuffs and the fodder for people's cattle were enough; and to have faith without reasoning over-logically about it: all these grown persons seemed enleagued to proffer Florian this stupid and unaspiring advice.

But Florian, at ten, had learned to humor the notions of his elders. So he said affably, if not quite without visible doubtfulness,—

"I see. . . ."

An Epilogue

Not Unconnected with a Moral

"Le monde par vos soins ne se changera pas;
Et quand on est du monde, il faut bien que l'on rend
Quelques dehors civils que l'usage demande."

An Epilogue

Not Unconnected with a Moral

T is gratifying to relate that, in a world wherein most moral lessons go to waste, young Florian duly honored the teaching of his dream. Therefore, as the boy grew toward maturity, he reduplicated in action all the crimes he had committed in fancy, and was appropriately grateful for his foreknowledge that all would turn out well. But, when he had reached the thirty-sixth year of his living and the fourth chapter of this history, he then, at the conclusion of his talking with Marie-Claire Cazaio, decorously crossed himself, and he shrugged.

"Let sleeping ideals lie," said Florian: "for over-high and over-earnest desires are inadvisable."

Thereafter he rode, not into Acaire, but toward the Duardenez. He forded this river uneventfully; and four days later, at Storisende, was married, *en cinquièmes noces,* to Mademoiselle Louise de Nérac.

It is likewise pleasant to know that this couple lived together in an amity sufficient to result in the begetting of three daughters, and to permit, when the fourth Duke of Puysange most piously and edifyingly quitted this life, in the November of 1736, the survival of his

233

widow. . . . The moral of all which seems to be that no word of this book, after the fourth chapter, need anybody regard with any least seriousness, unless you chance to be one of those discomfortable folk who contend that a fact is something which actually, but only, happens. A truth—so these will tell you,—does not merely "happen," because truth is unfortuitous and immortal. And this rather sweeping statement ought to be denied—outright—by no pious person who believes that immortals go about our world always invisibly.

EXPLICIT